SEASONS OF REVENGE

SEASONS OF REVENGE

WILLIAM PAUL

SEVERN HOUSE PUBLISHERS

This first world edition published in 1985 by
SEVERN HOUSE PUBLISHERS LTD of
4 Brook Street, London W1Y 1AA

Copyright © William Paul, 1985

British Library Cataloguing in Publication Data
Paul, William
    Seasons of revenge
I. Title
823'.914[F]   PR6066.A883/

ISBN 0 7278 1172 X

Typeset by Nene Phototypesetters Ltd, Northampton
Printed and bound by Anchor Brendon Ltd,
Tiptree, Essex, England

Part One

SPRING

THE train passing over the bridge and through Kingsbank Station set the spirit bottles which crowded the shelves behind the bar of the Station Inn rattling gently. Jim Anderson, leaning on his elbows against the bar, stared morosely at the pattern of concentric circles the vibration was causing on the surface of his beer and watched them fade away to nothing. He tried not to look up at the old pendulum clock above the door but he couldn't stop himself. It was just after nine and the ponderous ticking that echoed the sharper sound of dominoes on plastic-topped tables carried the time relentlessly forward. He looked away and gripped his beer glass more firmly to stop his hand trembling.

The public bar of the Station Inn was always busy on a Friday night. The lounge was full of married couples and the pool room on the other side catered for the young folk of the village, but the public bar was for the serious drinkers. The old brewery mirror with flaking gold lettering behind the bar made the place look quite big but it was actually very small and cramped, like somebody's front room. An electric fire was mounted on the wooden panel blocking off the old fireplace. There were two framed pictures side by side above the narrow mantelpiece. One was of the village's brass band in 1902 with all the names listed below in neat columns. The trumpet player second left in the third row was Anderson's great uncle. The other picture was an ink drawing of a desolate, bombed-out landscape with a pipe-smoking soldier finding a bottle of whisky in a pile of wreckage. The caption read: The First Sign of Civilisation. The pub walls were painted a cheerless brown. Cigarette smoke clung to the low ceiling like lumps of dirty cotton wool.

Everybody in the bar knew everybody else. Anderson was the youngest man there. Pete Guthrie was an ex-miner with black speckled coal dust engrained in his skin. He sat studying the dominoes cupped in the palm of his hand, his overcoat buttoned up to the neck, his walking stick lying across his lap. Under his chair lay his old mongrel dog, the grey hairs round its muzzle making it look as if it had been drinking milk. At the other side of the table was Donald Williamson, a withered old farm worker who could not go thirty seconds without coughing and spluttering. He had a habit of rubbing the back of his hand across his nose, making it red raw. Anderson watched disinterestedly as Williamson selected a domino from his handful and stretched out a thin arm to place it on the table. Guthrie looked at it, thought for a moment, then rapped the edge of the table twice with one of his dominoes. Williamson tried to smile as he placed his last one on the table to claim victory but it was lost in a bout of harsh coughing. He lit himself another cigarette and sucked at it thankfully.

There were two other pairs playing dominoes. The tapping on the tables at times was like a message being sent in Morse code. Willie Campbell, another retired miner, was hunched over as if he was eating a bowl of soup. His partner was Bob Tranter, a huge bear of a man who had worked on the railways all his life. Willie Duffus was almost eighty but still worked in his little chemist's shop. He was playing with Gordon Barclay, a man with a crescent of hair ringing his bald head who had never held down a steady job in his life. They usually played in silence, stopping only to order more drink or roll their own cigarettes or pass round the Player's full strength. The loose strands of tobacco were always being left on their lips and they had to spit them delicately on to the floor.

They had all been old men when Anderson was born. They had remained old as he grew up. They were old men when he left the village, and they were old men when he returned. It was all reassuringly familiar to Anderson, the kind of familiarity that he liked to have around him. Another familiar sight was the village idiot, Daft Davie, shuffling round the tables collecting the empty glasses and forever tripping over the hole worn in the linoleum in front of the fireplace. Davie was a fifty-year-old with a mental age of six. Another old man.

Anderson knew them all, and they knew him. That was why he had moved back to Kingsbank. They knew about him being wounded in Northern Ireland and they were proud of him in a grudging sort of way. But they didn't know the whole story. Nobody but Anderson knew the whole story, and he would never tell it.

He reached down to massage his right knee. There was no pain but rubbing his knee had become a nervous mannerism. He no longer noticed that he was doing it.

Daft Davie came over beside him at the bar and put down two empty glasses. Anderson remembered how, as a child, he had been one of the worst for annoying Davie; always screaming insults at him; sneaking up to kick his backside so that he would dance like some lunatic puppet, his gangling limbs thrashing wildly about so that they looked in danger of flying loose; getting him to bray like a donkey and go down on his hands and knees to give rides to the children. Davie never got angry. He was as meek as a lamb. His only pleasure came from pleasing others.

As Anderson grew older the game ceased to be funny, but there were always other kids ready to take on the role of chief tormentor. A strong bond formed between Anderson and Daft Davie. Anderson would chase off the tormentors whenever he could. It was a small service that hardly made up for all the times he had been the tormentor.

Davie lived with his widowed mother. She was a very old woman who walked about the village in her carpet slippers, using the roads as pavements and ignoring the traffic which had to make way for her. There was a brother, quite normal, who was married and lived in London. But when the mother died nobody knew or wanted to think about what would happen to her poor youngest son.

'How are you Davie?' Anderson said. 'Want a drink?'

Davie nodded enthusiastically. His jug ears, pudding-bowl

haircut and huge mouthful of teeth that his lips could barely cover marked him unmistakably. He was capable of speaking but he had such a bad stammer that he rarely bothered to try. Anderson called Bill Gardiner over and pointed to Davie. Bill was the owner of the Station Inn, known to everyone as Digger. He poured out a bottle of tonic water. Davie wasn't allowed alcohol.

'I'll take another pint as well, Digger. And give me a double nip to go with it,' Anderson said. He wanted to be drunk by midnight and there wasn't much time left.

Digger was a heavily built man who always wore a tight tartan waistcoat and expanding metal armbands to hold back his shirt cuffs. He had bought the pub four years before and had moved into the flat above it with his wife who was serving in the lounge. At first he had refused to let Davie into the bar but the locals had boycotted the place, doing their drinking in the Crown up the road, and forced him to relent. Digger set up the pint and used a small pewter measure to fill a whisky tumbler.

Anderson and Daft Davie knocked their glasses together. Davie giggled, spraying saliva, when some of his tonic water slopped over the edge. Anderson snatched another quick glance at the clock. He would have to go soon, he told himself. He wanted to be alone at midnight.

When the stranger entered, Anderson saw him in the big mirror behind the bar. It was an unusual event for a stranger to be in the pub unless he was brought in by one of the locals. The domino players peered at him curiously. Davie stared directly at him, mouth open.

He was a small, worried-looking man with thinning hair and startlingly fair eyebrows. He was wearing a camel coat and leather gloves which he removed carefully, finger by finger. He looked round casually and smiled uncertainly at Davie who was gaping at him inquisitively. Davie took his cue and did his party trick of waggling his huge ears as he snorted with laughter. The stranger looked on amazed until Digger flicked Davie with a towel to get him to stop.

The stranger stayed about ten minutes, drank one bottle of lager, then replaced his gloves and left. As the door swung shut behind him, Pete Guthrie lifted his walking stick and pointed at the clock with the rubber tip. 'He must be getting the last train to Edinburgh,' he said confidently and the other domino players nodded in agreement before going on with their games. The mongrel dog looked up as Guthrie accidentally knocked it as he replaced his stick on the floor. After a few moments, it laid its head back on its paws when it realised it was not yet time to go home.

Digger bent over to wash some glasses in the sink underneath the bar. He spoke loudly so that everyone could hear him. 'That bloke was looking over the Fraser house earlier today. Mrs Beaton told me. She keeps the keys.'

'Oh aye,' said Anderson. The Fraser cottage was next to his house. It had lain empty for six months since Tommy Fraser and his wife had inherited a lot of money from a rich aunt and bought themselves a big house in Dunfermline. The place was subsiding at the back and they couldn't sell it so they were trying to rent it out.

'Mrs Beaton said he was an Irishman and that he seemed taken with the house. I wonder what he's been doing until now?'

'Well then, Jim,' said Pete Guthrie, puffing out his ruddy cheeks with their network of broken veins. 'How do you fancy an Irishman for a neighbour?'

Anderson massaged his knee and felt a great sense of weakness creeping over his whole body. A persistent ache established itself on one side of his forehead. The memory of one particular Irishman with cold, grey eyes and bloodless lips made his insides tighten painfully; the only man who knew his secret. What a cruel coincidence that an anonymous Irishman should inspire that memory only a few hours before Anderson intended to begin the self-imposed annual ritual to purge it from his mind for another year. Midnight meant that it was seven years since Bill Lowrie's death. Nothing had changed in that time. Anderson had learnt to live with his secret, that was all. He lived with it because it would not go away.

Pete Guthrie was poking him in the leg with his walking stick. 'Maybe he'll have a go at your other knee, Jim,' he chuckled.

'It's all in the past,' Anderson said quietly. 'I bear no grudges.'

9

He did, of course. But he knew he could never do anything about it. He had been proved to be a coward and there was no escaping that fact. He would never be free from the guilt and shame that he carried inside his mind. In seven years there had been no respite for him. He could look forward to none in the next seven.

The bottles behind the bar began to shake as a train drew into the station. It would soon be midnight. He had time for one more drink, he decided. Just one more drink then he would go home.

The fresh, cold outside air was a welcome change from the smokey atmosphere of the pub when Anderson emerged, ducking under the low lintel of the doorway. On the other side of the road he saw old Jock Shaw stooped over the padlock on the gate at the bottom of the station steps, fiddling with the key. Above him, on the embankment, the bulk of the old station house blotted out the moon. Jock Shaw finally managed to lock the gate and hurried across the road, blowing into his cupped hands. He was wearing his regulation British Rail overcoat with the collar pulled up round his neck. His cap sat on toothbrush-straight grey hair sweeping up from his forehead. Grey stubble peppered his large chin. Anderson remembered him at his parents' funeral; the only time he had ever seen him properly shaven.

'That's the first time for three months I've had a passenger get on the late Edinburgh train,' Jock Shaw said as he stepped into the hazy pool of light spilling round the corners of the curtains drawn across the window of the bar. A clock in the shape of a pint of Guinness had fallen on to its side on the ledge.

'He was looking over the Frasers' house,' said Anderson for want of something better to say.

'He was looking all over my bloody station as well,' Jock Shaw said. 'He must have spent hours marching up and down the platforms. I thought he was some kind of inspector or something but no: "Just looking," he told me. Pretty queer, eh?'

'Pretty queer,' Anderson agreed, aware of the tension in his stomach.

'I always get a few coming on the late train from Edinburgh and Kirkcaldy, but hardly ever anyone going the other way at this time of night. You going in for a drink, Jim?'

Anderson said he was going home and watched Jock Shaw disappear down the step leading to the public bar. Then he walked off down the road, limping slightly because of his knee. He was light-headed but far from drunk. He had an unopened bottle of whisky at home. That might do the trick.

Jim Anderson still managed to keep himself fit. He drank too much and too often but he burned most of it off in lunchtime sessions at the sports centre along the road from the factory in Glenrothes where he worked as a supervisor. At the age of thirty-eight his six-foot frame was lean and muscular. Only the heavy flecks of grey in his dark hair betrayed his age.

As a child, he had been tall and skinny. School blazers never had sleeves long enough to contain his arms. In old pictures he looked ridiculous, and he had been hopelessly uncoordinated. Kicking a ball took a good few minutes of mental concentration and when he ran, his legs flicked out sideways in an awkward manner that even brought a smile to the granite face of the gym teacher. He couldn't make up for it in the classroom like some of the other misfits. He hated being cooped up and he hated having to read all the boring books they gave him. His parents tried to encourage him to be more like his brother Michael who was always top of his class, but he preferred to daydream about joining the army. His bedroom walls were plastered with posters and pages cut from magazines showing every aspect of military life. He dreamed of the excitement and the danger and he lay in bed at nights sweating at the very thought of it.

Then, at the age of fifteen, he suddenly filled out physically. It was as if he had been inflated by a huge puff of air. In what seemed like a matter of weeks, hard muscles began to bulge on his skinny arms and thighs. Boys who had ignored him previously began to make friends and, of course, there were lots of girls drawn to the swan transformed from the ugly duckling. He discovered sex and was a bastard to them all.

His new-found physical prowess and presence established

11

him on the games field. When he swung his foot at a ball it invariably connected and flew exactly where it was intended to go. He could run fast and far. He had speed and stamina in excess of every other boy in the school. He became captain of the football and basketball teams and school sports champion.

His parents wanted him to follow his older brother to university. He stayed on at school a year longer than necessary to keep them happy but he could not stick it any longer than that. On his last day at school he had the young biology teacher in a stationery cupboard next door to the staffroom. They could hear the other teachers chatting and drinking coffee as they made silent, passionate love over a stack of new jotters. Then he signed up for the paratroopers.

He served in Belize, and Hong Kong, and West Germany and he loved every minute of it, but Northern Ireland was even better. That was where the real danger was: danger that made the hairs stand out on the back of your neck and that made your heart thump furiously. He did two tours, one in the bandit country around Crossmaglen and the other in the streets of Belfast.

It was in Belfast in the early seventies that he shot the only man he had ever killed. It happened on the same day the news arrived that his parents had died in a car crash. A sniper on the first floor of a terraced house had opened fire on the patrol just before they had started a systematic search of the whole street. A bullet tore into the lower leg of the squaddie beside Anderson, pitching him on to his face on the pavement. The other soldiers scattered and dived for cover but Anderson had his rifle at his shoulder within a split second. The sniper's indistinct silhouette disappeared as he felt the gentle push of the rifle butt after releasing two quick shots.

They had surrounded the house, evacuated the street, and waited for two hours before it became obvious that the sniper must either have been hit or somehow escaped. Anderson and five others rushed the stairs and battered open the door to the bedroom.

A young boy, no more than eighteen, was sitting propped up against the wall beneath the window. His head was lolling forward and his hair looked greasy and wet. A motionless finger

12

was curled round the trigger of the rifle lying on the floor beside him. He was plainly dead.

The soldiers entered behind a bristling procession of gun barrels. A sergeant squatted down to put his hand under the boy's chin and lift his head up. They all saw that where his nose had been there was a pulpy red mass and on either side of it the eyes squinted crazily inwards as if desperately trying to see what had bored its way into his face. On the wall beside the door they found splinters of skull from the back of his head.

Anderson's platoon commander asked to see him back at the base. Anderson thought it would be to congratulate him but it was actually to tell him the news of the crash.

The army flew Anderson home so that he could attend the funeral. Michael flew back from Canada and they stayed at their Aunt Morag's. There was a good turnout from the village at the crematorium on a day when wind and rain lashed at the full-length windows overlooking the garden of remembrance as the minister said his piece. After the service he stood at the door with his brother and shook hands with everyone as they left. Then it was back to Kingsbank for tea and sandwiches at Morag's and personal expressions of sympathy from relatives and friends. Michael had flown back to Canada within the week and he hadn't seen him since.

Anderson had always taken the most dangerous jobs the army could offer. After his parents' funeral he seemed to care even less about his own safety. He began to dream about dying in battle. Dying with his boots on, saving the regiment by holding a position against overwhelming odds, sentencing himself to certain death to give the others a chance to live, dying in a hail of gunfire with his own gun blazing to the last, taking as many as he could with him.

It seemed natural to apply to join the army's élite, the Special Air Service. Even though the paras sneered at them they knew they were the best. It was on SAS selection that Anderson first met Bill Lowrie. Both of them were loners but they immediately struck up a friendship. Lowrie was from a small Yorkshire village and they shared the same outlook on life. They became inseparable, bivouacing together on operations in the Welsh mountains and rooming together at the Hereford camp headquarters. They ate together, drank together, and picked up women together. They got through a lot of women, sharing quite a few. Lowrie was always saying he was falling in love but it never lasted. They were too young to be tied down.

They were posted back to Belfast on undercover work controlling a network of informers, known as Paddies. It was not as exciting as they had anticipated – though it had its moments. Anderson missed the overt violence of the street riots and the petrol bombs but he still did his job well. He did it well until the fatal night when the storyline he had worked out for his life began to go badly wrong.

Anderson's house was only a couple of hundred yards from the Station Inn. He passed under the bridge that carried the railway and into the cold moonlight on the other side. He stumbled on the rough surface of the pavement in the shadow of the low garden walls. He walked along the row of single storey cottages with long, narrow front gardens until he reached his own. Next door was the Fraser house, identical apart from the colour of the windows and the big sycamore tree with branches that overhung his own garden and rattled against his bedroom window in high winds. The Frasers' garden was hopelessly overgrown. A For Sale sign was strapped to the gatepost.

Anderson walked up the gravel path to the door of his cottage, cutting across the lawn and tripping over the six-inch high border fence guarding the encircling flower beds. It was late March and the early flowers were patches of grey in the darkness.

Once inside the house, he immediately went to the kitchen and got the bottle of whisky. It was still wrapped in the tissue paper from the off-licence. He poured himself a generous amount and swallowed a mouthful big enough to make his eyes water. He felt like a small boy waiting to enter the headmaster's study for punishment. He poured himself another large whisky.

He went upstairs to his bedroom and sat on the bed. The old house creaked gently under his weight, just as he remembered it doing when he was a child. He kicked off his shoes and lay back. The ceiling was rotating slowly above him. When he tried to drink he spilled whisky over his face and it ran on to the covers.

The phone began to ring downstairs in the hallway. He tried to ignore it at first but irrational thoughts suddenly spurred him into action. Perhaps Bill was trying to reach him. He jumped up, close to panic, fearful that the phone would stop ringing and he would be left completely alone. He rushed down the stairs, bouncing off the walls, sliding on the carpet. He grabbed the receiver.

'Who is it?' he shouted urgently.

'It's me, Kathy. What's the matter?' said a familiar female voice.

Anderson relaxed. His breathing slowed automatically. He was glad it was Kathy. He had put her out of his mind and that was another reason he had tried to drink himself into insensibility. He had thought she wasn't available to help him through Saturday.

'What's the matter?' she repeated.

'Nothing. I've been at the Station.' He was in control again, sobering up fast. He could almost smell Kathy over the phone. He wanted her with him but he had not dared to hope. He did not deserve her. A man like Bill Lowrie deserved a woman like Kathy. Anderson was a poor substitute.

'I want to come round now,' she whispered urgently.

'What about George?'

'He's snowbound in Shetland. He can't get away until tomorrow morning at the earliest. It looks as if we have at least one bonus night, lover.'

'I'm waiting.'

Anderson put down the phone and went to lift the latch on the front door. Then he went through the kitchen and pulled back the curtain, rubbing a clear space on the condensation on the window. Kathy's house, the old manse at the top of the hill, was in total darkness. He stared at the tree-lined path she would follow to his house but it was impossible to see anything. At the front he could hear the folk from the pub making their way home.

He was excited by the prospect of sleeping with Kathy. Her body was a wonderful store of competing pleasures. They had

15

said their goodbyes the previous night and he had regretted losing her at the very time he needed her most. She was the one person who could make him forget completely. Bill would have understood. He would have done the same, given the chance. There would be plenty of time to remember.

Upstairs in the bedroom, Anderson took off his clothes and climbed into bed. The curtains were open and the elongated shadows of the sycamore branches waved to and fro above his head. He lay and waited for Kathy and heard the dull sound of the bell in the church tower slowly striking the hour of twelve.

Kathy Manders was twenty-two years old, a fraction over five feet tall, well endowed up front and nicely rounded at the rear. She had shoulder-length blonde hair shaped closely round a face noticeable for its high, almost oriental looking cheekbones, wide mouth, and large green eyes shaded by remarkably long lashes. She came from the south of England and spoke with a perfect public school accent with the merest hint of a lisp. That was something Anderson found incredibly sexy. He thought the vaguely slurred quality of her voice made her sound as if she was permanently on the verge of orgasm.

She and her husband, George, had come to live in Kingsbank about a year before. He was more than twenty years older than her; she seemed to go for older men. They had not been married long when they arrived in the village and many people had, at first, taken him for her father. He was short and portly with the corrugated forehead of a long serving sea captain. In fact he was a toolpusher on the North Sea oil rigs, making big money and preferring the peace and quiet of rural life to the bright lights of the city. They had bought the old manse, a big draughty barn of a place that needed a lot doing to it, and turned it into a comfortable home. George was a likeable, easy-going sort of a bloke but he seemed more proud of his house than he was of his young wife. He had been married twice before, and twice divorced.

Anderson had first slept with Kathy at the New Year party they had thrown in the manse three months previously. There

16

had always been a chemistry between them. Often she would sit with George in the lounge of the Station and he would watch her through the doorway behind the bar. Regularly she would glance up at him and a teasing little smile would play about the corners of her lips. He knew it was only a matter of time.

At the party he had contrived to be alone with her in the kitchen where the roaring Raeburn stove drowned out the loud music. He willed her to make the first move and did not have to wait long. A snatched kiss, a fumbling grope, and then she was leading him upstairs past the huge arched, blue and red stained glass window to a bedroom where they made frantic love with the party in full swing below them.

Since then they had got together as often as they could: two weeks on, two weeks off, according to George's shift pattern. Then there was the occasional early evening session when she could think of an excuse to get away from him for a few hours when he was at home.

Kathy had a voracious appetite for sex and Anderson was often hard pushed to satisfy her. She was young and eager and he needed all the benefit of his experience. In a matter of weeks, Kathy was saying she was in love with him. She wanted to leave George and come to live with him. He was the best thing that had ever happened to her and she was so lucky to find him. She had married too young and missed so much. George couldn't make her feel the way Anderson could. She wanted to be with him all the time.

Anderson was in love with her, too, but he refused to admit it to himself. She was something different from all the one-night stands his sex life had mostly consisted of. But he was afraid to commit himself. He longed to tell her how he felt but he was afraid that if he did it would somehow be an invitation to disaster. He had no right to claim Kathy as his own. He had no right to anything on this Earth. He had forfeited everything seven years before.

He persuaded her to wait. Let's see how we feel in a few months time, he said. Let's just keep it a secret for now. The whole village knew about the affair, of course. Anderson knew that as soon as he had left the Station that night they would begin to talk about him. Kathy always used the path across the

17

common when she came to his house. Nobody could see her and yet everybody knew.

Anderson seldom went to the old manse. She said she preferred to meet him in his house because the manse was already part of her past. He preferred it too. It meant that it was all left up to her. If, one night, she failed to appear it would be no more than he deserved.

He heard the front door click shut and footsteps cross the lobby and begin to climb the stairs. Kathy came silently into the bedroom and he saw a brief flashing smile through the shadows covering her face. She was wearing a short fur coat and tight-fitting jeans with thick knee-length leg warmers. Neither of them spoke. There was no need for words.

Anderson watched in growing anticipation as she undressed and her body was unveiled in front of him. He folded back the bedclothes and she got in beside him, naked except for the thin gold chain she always wore on her ankle. Her skin was cold against his but it warmed rapidly under his hands. Their mouths fastened together and their tongues pushed urgently against each other. Kathy made it clear that she had little interest in the preliminaries. Anderson rolled on top of her and felt her legs spread open beneath him and squeeze into his sides. She was ready for him right away and breathed out a long sigh of welcome as he sank slowly into her. Immediately she began to push upwards insistently, one hand gripping his hair, the other kneading at his thigh. He let his body weight restrain her until the hair-pulling became painful, then he began to ride powerfully over her. Each stroke of the rhythm brought a tiny grunt from her. As he rode faster the sounds merged into a constant stream of gasps and she was biting at the hairs on his chest, both her hands were pulling in the small of his back, her feet were locked behind his knees. She reached a climax first and he came seconds after her. Briefly, the tension in their bodies held them like pieces of overstretched elastic, then they relaxed and tumbled apart to lie together in a soft, warm bundle. Around them the house creaked like a sailing ship rocking gently on a calm sea. How long had it taken, Anderson wondered? A few more minutes gone from his life. A few more minutes closer to his death.

18

Kathy's head lay on his chest. He could feel her hot breath. The perfume of her hair was strong in his nostrils. When she spoke it was very softly and with her lips moving against his skin.

'I love you,' she said.

She waited for a reply and he wanted to answer her; he wanted to shout it out loud so that the whole world could hear. But he said nothing. A gust of wind made the sycamore branches tap on the window. Today of all days he could say nothing.

Kathy turned over on to her back and reached out to get herself a cigarette. She sucked the smoke deep into her lungs and blew it out in a long, steady stream. Anderson watched her face. It was a beautiful face. He watched the rise and fall of the sheets gathered round her breasts. He stroked her hair and she tilted her head so that her cheek touched the back of his hand. He didn't deserve a woman like Kathy.

'Can I have a fag?' he asked.

'But you don't smoke,' she said, reaching for the packet.

'I used to. I feel like one now.'

She lit a cigarette from her own one and handed it to him. He sat up to smoke it. A cloud blotted out the moon for a moment. The bedroom darkened and then grew lighter again.

'That funny friend of yours gave me a real scare today,' Kathy said.

Anderson stared out of the window. He was relieved Kathy had decided to make small talk. He liked to lie in bed and chat, just like any other loving couple.

'Who? Daft Davie?'

'Who else? He was poking about our garden this afternoon. When I shouted at him all he did was stand there and waggle his ears like an idiot.'

'Davie is harmless. He's always being chased out of other people's gardens.'

'I've caught him in ours a couple of times. Once I found him looking in the living-room window.'

'He's like a wee boy. He's just curious.'

'Well it's not right, him looking in windows. He'll get into trouble doing things like that. You ought to tell him.'

'If I tell him to keep away from the old manse he'll be up there the next day to see what he's missing. He's like that.'

Kathy grimaced. 'He gives me the creeps. That horrible face leering at me. Who knows what is going through his head?'

'Who knows indeed,' Anderson said.

They lapsed into silence. Anderson rubbed his knee. Kathy turned on her side and cuddled up against his arm. He leaned over her to stub out his cigarette in the ashtray. She held up her mouth to be kissed, moaning slightly as their lips parted.

'I should go back,' she whispered, looking up at him from under her long eyelashes. 'He could phone at any time.'

'Don't go,' he said quickly, too quickly. Then more slowly: 'I want you here with me.'

She nestled closer against his body, her head under his chin, a leg astride his hip. Anderson pulled the sheets up round them.

'I'll have to go soon,' she murmured, already half asleep.

'Soon,' he said, squeezing her tightly against him. Tiredness swept over him suddenly. He couldn't keep his eyes open. With Kathy beside him he knew it would be all right to sleep. He did not try to fight it.

The darkness was all around him and in the darkness there was the heat. There was something next to him; something as cold as ice while the heat was suffocating and intense. He felt as if flames were flickering over his body. There was no escape from the heat. It was running like a liquid in through his unseeing eyes, up his nose, into his mouth and ears. It was eating him up, consuming him. He gulped in some almost solid air. The heat was in his lungs, in his stomach, in his head. It was coursing through his blood, pumping in a scalding torrent into his heart.

And there, with the heat, was something else. Something, or somebody, lying invisible in the darkness. A memory stirred in the back of his mind. The darkness was receding and blinding white light was spilling around him to replace it. He screwed up his eyes against the bright light but he could see a face, a familiar face, only a few inches from his own. The grey eyes in the face stared at him accusingly. They were wide open, ignoring the light. Anderson tried to jerk his head away but the face followed him. It was always just a few inches away. He tried to push it away with his hands but it was stiff and unyielding. He began to panic. He opened his mouth to scream but no sound came out. Instead, the screaming was inside his head.

'It's all right darling. It's all right.'

Kathy was on her knees in the bed beside him. She had his head pressed firmly into her breasts and was kissing his hair continuously.

'It was only a dream,' she kept repeating, her voice almost breaking with emotion. 'Only a dream.'

Anderson clung like a baby to the warmth and softness of her bosom. She was hugging him tightly, rocking back and forward, humming a tune he did not recognise. The effect was like a gentle hand softly brushing his forehead, wiping away all the pain, all the bad memories. Then she was pushing him down on to his back, crouching on all fours over him, her beautiful face lit up by a smile, her heavy breasts swinging free.

'I know exactly what you need,' she breathed into his ear.

She began to kiss his shoulder, then his chest, then his stomach. Her fingers ran lightly up the inside of his leg. He arched his back instinctively to try to get closer to her, feeling the excitement swell all around him. Her moist lips sent messages spinning upwards into the pleasure-giving regions of his brain. Nothing mattered except what Kathy was doing to him. The whole world outside had ceased to exist. There was nobody, nothing but the two of them in his room, in this bed.

She straddled his body and settled herself down on him with a tiny shake of her hips. She was kneeling, her hands resting on the taut muscles of her thighs. Her head was thrown back and her hair was damp and sticking to her neck and cheeks. Her lips were moistened by a darting tongue. Her face glowed. Anderson reached out and took a full breast in each hand. He brushed the nipples with his thumbs so that they rose hard and erect. She whimpered like a puppy at his touch and began to sway from side to side. The shadows of the sycamore branches flashed across her glistening back like the strokes of a silent whip. She moved up and down, lifting her entire body from the knees and sinking back again. Her breath began to come in

21

short, sharp gasps interspersed with little yelps of ecstasy. Anderson kept his eyes open watching her, enjoying her obvious pleasure. He matched his movements to hers as they became rougher and more irregular. Her fingernails scored his stomach where she had to hold on to balance herself.

When it was over she collapsed on to him, her hair falling into his mouth. She waited until he had grown small inside her then she rolled off to lie at his side.

'Was it a very bad dream?' she asked after a while.

He had forgotten the dream. She had made him forget it. Now she reminded him again. He shook his head.

'Do you want to tell me about it?'

He didn't say anything. He could never tell anybody the real story. Not the real story.

'It's to do with what happened to you in Ireland, isn't it?'

She knew only what everybody else knew about his time in Ireland. That he had been captured and kneecapped and pensioned out of the forces because of his injury. Did she suspect there was more to it than that? He wished it was darker so that he could hide from her.

'My poor darling,' she said, almost sobbing. 'Let me help you.'

She pulled him close in against herself and began to hum the soothing, unknown tune. He closed his eyes. Soon she would have to leave him alone but a few more hours would have been safely passed. The hour of his death would be a few hours nearer.

Kathy woke him just before seven. She leant over the bed to kiss him on the mouth and handed him a mug of coffee. She had showered and washed her hair and was wearing his black silk dressing gown, the one with a colourful Chinese dragon on the back. She sat on the edge of the bed to use the hair-dryer. The black silk fell away to reveal a smooth, white leg. Anderson remembered the events of the night and sighed gratefully, stretching his muscles and wiping the sleep from his eyes. He hoped she wouldn't ask about the dream again.

'You'll be all right, won't you?' she asked, concern in her voice.

'Of course, I'm fine,' he said, smiling to reassure her.

'If the plane can't get off today I'll be back like a shot.'

'I'll keep my fingers crossed.'

She finished with the hair-dryer and leaned over to kiss him again. She smelled fresh and clean.

'One of these days I won't have to leave like this,' she said, forcing him to look at her by holding his chin.

He nodded. 'One of these days,' he echoed.

He watched her dress. Then they kissed again and she was gone, down the stairs and out the door. He was alone. Outside it was a bright day and a strong wind was buffeting the house. Birds were singing noisily. He remembered what he had to do.

Now that he had let Kathy go, he wanted her back immediately. If she did return, he would tell her how much he loved her. He would marry her and they would both live happily ever after. He looked at his watch and set a deadline of two hours. If she was coming, she would be back then. The decision on what would happen was out of his hands.

He lay and waited, listening for the door or the phone. The mug of coffee quickly grew cold on the bedside table. The birds chattered on endlessly. He heard people passing by in the street. A train rumbled into the station. He propped his watch up in the sheets so that he could watch the second hand sweeping round. If he listened very carefully he could just hear it ticking.

Time marched on. The deadline he had set got closer and closer. Sweat gathered in the palms of his hands. He was constantly rubbing at his knee. He imagined that if he concentrated hard he would be able to stop the watch, but time kept marching on, seeming to gain speed as he willed it to slow down. The deadline was suddenly in the past. The decision had been taken for him.

Anderson got out of bed and did his regular morning exercise routine; thirty press-ups, thirty sit-ups, thirty isometric hand clasps of ten seconds duration, and two minutes of running on the spot. He noticed at the end that he was breathing harder than normal. Too much drink, he told himself.

He put on the dressing gown and went to take a shower. The sharp needlepoints of water really got his circulation going. He dried himself carefully and dusted on some talcum powder. Then, as he always did, he examined the six-inch surgical scar running through the centre of his right knee. The knee-cap below was artificial. He could pinch it between his fingers and feel the rounded edges and move it around. The vertical scar was a pasty white colour. They had said it would fade with time, but it never had.

He got dressed and collected the milk from the doorstep. He had a plate of cornflakes and fried himself some sausages and egg. Kathy had tidied away the whisky bottle he had left in the kitchen but he found it in a cupboard when he was looking for the tomato sauce. He took it through to the living room so that he would know where it was. He would probably need it tonight.

The living room was large and sparsely furnished, mainly with old stuff Anderson had picked up at auctions and in second-hand shops. There was a small oak roll-top desk in the corner beside the window which looked out over the back garden. In front of it was a high wing red leather chair, all cracked and torn. He moved the chair out of the way and unlocked the desk. Inside he kept things like insurance policies and mortgage statements, neatly filed in a row of narrow pigeon holes. There was a central section with two drawers. He pulled open the lower one and took out a buff envelope containing a flat blue cardboard box. He removed the lid and looked at the round, silver disc inside. He lifted it out, holding it by the crimson and blue riband it was attached to. He studied the Queen's head on one side and turned it to read the engraved words on the other side: For Distinguished Conduct In The Field. The Distinguished Conduct Medal. Proof that he was a hero. He laughed, shaking his head. There was no amusement in the sound. Then he replaced the medal on its soft pad in the box. He put the lid on the box, the box in the envelope and the envelope in the drawer.

He opened the upper drawer with trembling fingers. Inside was a single photograph. It was old and faded, and a crease ran diagonally across one corner where it had been folded at one time. The colour photograph was of two men wearing army camouflage combat uniform. They were standing in front of

24

what appeared to be a high hedge and each had an arm round the other's shoulders. The dappling effect of the light coming through the hedge gave the picture a curious contrast of shades. Some parts of it were very dark, almost black, while other parts were brilliantly illuminated. The brightest point of the whole picture was the face of the man on the left. It shone as if picked out by an individual spotlight. The other man by comparison was lost in shadow.

The man on the left was Bill Lowrie, pictured as he was several months before his death, his arm round his best friend, Jim Anderson. The face was like that of a little boy; chubby cheeks, inquisitive eyes under bushy eyebrows. It was the face Anderson saw in his dreams. A face that would never grow any older.

Anderson slowly replaced the photograph. As he closed the drawer he thought of Lowrie's coffin being lowered into his grave. He remembered his mother shaking him by the hand and thanking him for being her son's friend. Tears stung his eyes but he did not allow himself to cry. It was too easy to cry.

Anderson rolled down the top of the desk and locked it. He walked out into the lobby and took his anorak from the coatstand. The wind outside caught him as he left the house and almost knocked him against the wall. He went to the garage and upended the door. His Vauxhall Viva was newly washed. He always put it through the car wash after finishing work on a Friday night. The light blue paintwork sparkled in the early morning sun as he drove out into the road. The rust at the bottom of the driver's door and spreading along one wing was like a rash on the shiny metal. He drove past the Co-op. Mrs Rippon and Mrs McLeish were standing talking at the entrance. They waved to him as he went past. He nodded back. He turned at the junction and took the road up past the cemetery and then the steep hill out of the valley, having to change down into second gear half way up.

It took him about ten minutes to reach the place he wanted. He drove along a little-used road on the crest of the lime hills. It was full of tight hairpin bends and the mangled bodies of dead rabbits and crows. This was the kind of place courting couples

25

went after dark. He had brought Kathy here one night to an old quarry. That was not where he was going now.

He turned off at an almost invisible gap in a section of young trees. The car bounced over a rough forestry road for a few hundred yards, emerging from the tunnel of trees on to a grassy platform where the land fell away sharply in front of him. He switched off the engine and settled back in his seat.

Anderson looked down on the patchwork fields in the wide Howe of Fife, a valley gouged by the glaciers millions of years before. To the west were the Lomond Hills and to the north, under an approaching canopy of dark grey clouds, he thought he could just make out Dundee. Half a dozen villages were scattered over the valley floor, neatly outlined against the surrounding countryside. He could see Kingsbank with the church tower poking up and the railway embankment going in one side and out the other, like thread through the eye of a needle.

He let his mind wander, uncontrolled. It was time to honour the memory of his dead friend, Bill Lowrie. This was to be the annual day of penance when he acknowledged the guilt he kept firmly bottled up for the rest of the year. The penance took the form of recalling events seven years ago in Northern Ireland exactly as they had happened, giving himself no opportunity to say: No, that is not how it happened. He would run the events through his head like the reels of an old film. It was the least he could do for an old friend and it was the safety valve that allowed him to carry on normally at other times. It allowed him to go to work, to sleep with Kathy, and to drink at the Station. It was what had kept him alive.

The wind blew strongly, nudging at the car. There was a hint of rain in the air. Anderson wrapped his anorak more tightly around himself and unconsciously rubbed at his knee. He began to remember.

The safe house in South Belfast was a seedy Victorian mansion of peeling paint and warped window frames. A transient population of Queen's University students occupied the upper floors. The basement with its barred windows and low ceilings

26

was more like a wartime bunker, hence the name the under-cover squads gave to it. It was in a quiet backwater full of similar mansions that held either students or church-going pensioners. The security services had a rule that safe houses should not be used by squads for more than three nights in a row. Anderson and Bill Lowrie were on their third night and were due a fortnight's leave from the next day.

There was another rule that no alcohol should be consumed on the premises. It was a sensible rule that was seldom broken because of the need to be ready for instant deployment, but that night they had allowed themselves a couple of cans and a bottle of cheap wine. It was boring, sitting all night with nothing to do but watch the television, and the prospect of their leave had made their throats more than usually dry. They were not drunk, far from it, and if nothing had happened they would probably have gone out for more later on. Maybe even risked going upstairs to one of the wild parties the students were forever holding at the weekends, especially on Friday nights.

The call came through when Lowrie was in the kitchen trying to put together a decent evening meal from what packets there were there. Anderson answered it and by the time he had the receiver to his ear, Lowrie was at his shoulder. They listened together to the background hum of the scrambling equipment on the line, already regretting the few drinks they had taken.

'Red sky at night . . .' a cultured voice said casually.

'Is a soldier's delight,' Anderson replied quickly completing the codewords as he felt the hairs on the back of his neck prickle with the thrill of anticipation. They had been chasing their own tails for weeks but the law of averages dictated that this call would be something solid.

It was the duty MI5 office boy shuffling his secret papers at Stormont Castle and relaying a message that had come in for them from a Paddy. The Paddy was a good one and was worth taking note of. Twice in the previous few months he had come up with the goods; once on a big arms cache of fifty rifles and thousands of rounds, and later on the location of a most-wanted who had been lifted from the streets without a shot being fired and was now safely behind bars.

The Paddy's motive was, of course, money. He had been paid well for the information he had provided. Well enough to keep him coming back from the top ranks of the Belfast Brigade, to which he seemed to have ready access, with more of the same for more of the same. He did it despite the obvious danger he was placing himself in among his own people. Greed could be a powerful motive, but maybe it was something other than that. After all, the army would never make millionaires of Anderson and Lowrie but that didn't put them off.

The message was a simple one: a request for an immediate meeting at a pre-arranged site. Every Paddy claimed the information they had was desperately urgent but this one's past record meant they believed him when he said it.

Anderson told the MI5 man exactly where they were going and had him repeat it. That message would be passed on to their superior, Major Henderson, in due course. Lowrie took some money out of their float hidden, miser-style, beneath the sideboard.

'Two hundred should be enough to start the conversation,' he said, handing a bundle of notes to Anderson. They were tattered and dirty as if mice had been eating away at them. Paddies preferred dirty money. It would not be clever for them to be seen flaunting crisp new fivers all over the place. Anderson took off one shoe, laid the notes flat along the sole, and put it back on again.

It took them only a matter of minutes to get ready to go out. They talked in short bursts, speculating on what the Paddy might be about to offer them. At the same time they were acutely aware of the rise in their blood pressures and heart rates. They inspected each other's clothing to see that their guns were not showing and that they looked as ordinary as possible. Lowrie was all in denim, his hair straggling into his eyes. Anderson was much smarter, in brown trousers and tweed jacket, like a country farmer. With Lowrie's baby face making him look like a teenager they could almost have been mistaken for father and son.

They checked outside from all three front facing windows before they left the safe house. The front door had steel shutters behind it that were always closed when the place was occupied,

28

allegedly making it capable of withstanding any attack for long enough to have the cavalry called in to the rescue. The bunker had never been tested in that manner, but it seemed to most of the undercover squads that a simple homemade petrol bomb between the bars and through the windows, which had no steel shutters, would be more effective than a rocket against the reinforced door. Window shutters had been officially requested but nothing had ever happened about them.

Their car sat in the driveway beside a pile of litter that the wind always built up against the corner of the house and the overgrown hedge separating the gardens. The undercover cars were constantly changed around and were designed to look like old bangers that would be owned by relatively young men-about-town in Belfast. That way nobody gave a second glance to two men cruising the streets. The one they had this week was a battered dark blue Escort with a rusty bumper and a number plate tied on with string. It had a sun visor with the names Brian and Melanie written over the driver's and passenger's seat respectively. There was even a pair of furry dice hanging from the rear-view mirror. The boot was caked with dirt and somebody had traced on it with their finger: IRA all the way.

Lowrie got in behind the steering wheel and unlocked the door to let Anderson in beside him. The engine started first time.

'If you're sitting comfortably, Melanie, darling,' Lowrie said, slipping the car into gear. 'Then we'll begin.'

Anderson tried to smile but the tension was building up inside him and his reaction was more like a snarl. The butt of his pistol was pressing painfully into his kidney but he made no attempt to relieve it, rather he was grateful for the irrational sense of security the pain gave him.

Lowrie moved the car out of the run-in and bounced over the pavement on to the road. Behind drawn curtains, in the early evening half-darkness, respectable families barely touched by the Troubles were living their lives quietly. Dustbins stood like sentries at every gate along the street and Anderson almost expected them to snap to attention and salute as they drove past.

They followed the set route out of the city – braking sharply only once when a mongrel ran across in front of them – and turned on to the motorway at the first opportunity, speeding up as they headed west to their meeting place.

It was a mild night, almost warm. There was a transparent veil of cloud over a full moon. Anderson lit two cigarettes with the dashboard lighter and handed one to Lowrie. They travelled in silence, staring through their own reflections which seemed to hover just outside the windscreen.

After forty minutes of steady driving they turned off the motorway to the north and headed into wooded countryside. Another fifteen minutes and they turned off on to an unmade road lined by tall trees. The car lurched drunkenly over deep pot-holes and the tyres crunched their way through loose gravel. Lowrie suddenly switched off the engine and the car coasted to a halt only a few yards from the edge of Lough Neagh. They sat for a moment looking out over the water. Then they checked their watches and their guns. Anderson lit another two cigarettes. Lowrie turned off the headlights and the darkness crowded in around them.

The shimmering black and silver water in front of them stretched to the horizon. A dark shape in the near distance could have been a boat or an island. There was a crimson glow in the bottom half of the sky. Red sky at night is a soldier's delight, Anderson thought. From where they sat the trees obscured the moon. Strips of cloud were pink on the underside and grey above. They looked like pieces of cardboard pasted up as background scenery with the water as the stage. There was not a breath of wind. The only noticeable sound was the ticking of the engine as it cooled.

Anderson wound down his window and flicked the half-smoked cigarette out. It traced an orange arc through the darkness and disappeared. He opened the door and stepped out. The warm air stroked itself against his body like a friendly cat. Lowrie got out of the car as well and they both walked over to the edge of the trees and emptied their bladders. Then they turned to go to the edge of the water where tiny waves were lapping over the miniature beach of rounded pebbles. Invisible flies gathered over their heads. When they moved it was like walking into a screen of delicate cobwebs that parted to let you through.

The redness of the sky was fading fast, as if it was draining down and out of one corner. Stars were beginning to appear, one by one, then in handfuls. Anderson looked up and was able to see the moon. He tried to find its face just as his mother had taught him as a child. Yes, there was the nose and the chin and the eyes. The face of the man in the moon.

An owl hooted nearby and there was the rustling of branches as a pair of wings beat a way through the trees. There was a splash as a fish jumped for flies and landed back in the water. Anderson looked at his watch. The Paddy still had five minutes.

The voice suddenly crashed into the stillness of the evening. 'Don't move soldier boys. Or you're dead.'

Anderson and Lowrie froze, their minds racing. It was an ambush. They were trapped, silhouetted against the sky. Black figures were emerging from the trees. There were at least four of them. One went over to the car, opened the driver's door and switched on the headlights. The figures became invisible behind the glaring lights. Footsteps crunched on the gravel. Perhaps there were more than four of them.

Anderson wondered if he should go for his gun. Should he dive to one side and fire from the ground? Would he be quick enough? Lowrie was whispering something but he could not make it out. He dared not turn his head. The slightest movement might be enough to kill them both. The sweat was beading on his forehead and running over his cheeks. There was a terrible itch on the side of his nose but he could not scratch it. They should have been more careful.

'Get down. Spreadeagled. Face down.' The voice was cold and merciless.

Anderson did not move. Saliva gathered in his mouth. He was afraid to swallow. There was a tug at his sleeve. It was Lowrie, pulling him down. They had no choice. They had to do as they were instructed. They both got down on their knees and lay forward on their faces. Anderson could taste the dirt and stones. Footsteps came slowly towards them. He felt his gun being taken away. There was a great weight between his shoulder blades and someone was thrusting something against his mouth and nose. It smelled bitter. He tried to move his head

31

but it was held firmly. His arms were pinned to his side. He tried to hold his breath but he could not do it for long. He had to breathe. Everything started to blur. He struggled against it but the swirling grey mass in his mind steadily grew blacker and blacker. It was like falling asleep. In the morning he would wake up and it would be just another day.

Anderson swam slowly back to consciousness. His head ached and it was difficult to breathe because of the tightness across his chest. The bitter taste of the chloroform was in his mouth. He could not remember opening his eyes but suddenly he was able to see.

He was naked, tied securely to a wooden chair on a straw-covered concrete floor. Coarse rope bit deeply into his wrists, ankles and chest. The only part of his body he could move was his head. He could see Lowrie, lashed to a chair beside him, also naked, his head drooping senselessly. There was a hurricane lamp burning near his feet, giving off a circle of sickly yellow light. It smelled heavily of paraffin.

Anderson realised how cold it was. His breath billowed outwards like cigarette smoke. Individual hairs stood out all over his body. There was a freezing draught. The lamp's flame flickered. He guessed they were in some kind of barn. An irregular metallic thumping could have been a door banging in the wind. He could hear the wind howling, scrabbling like a wild animal in the darkness all round him. His heart was beating very fast and he was scared, very scared.

He heard a noise behind him. Shuffling footsteps. His eyes were making no impression on the gloom beyond the central pool of light. He flexed his fingers. The rope was unyielding. He tried to breathe deeply to calm himself, but he could only manage shallow gasps. He tried to look behind him. The rope cut into his flesh. The chair legs scraped on the ground. The wind rose and died away, screamed and whispered. He braced himself for the pain and jerked the chair a few more inches round.

There was that noise again. There was definitely somebody walking towards him. His skin crawled with fear. A hand touched his shoulder, lying there. His body shivered. His teeth chattered. He jerked the chair a few more inches. It scraped loudly. A piece of straw had become caught between his toes. It itched maddeningly.

The hand moved from his shoulder, leaving a warm spot. Its owner came round and squatted in front of Anderson. He was wearing a denim shirt and jeans and cradling a pistol in his hands. Anderson could see only the top of his head, a mass of tight black curls. One foot was outside the circle of light, lost in the darkness. Anderson looked sideways at Lowrie. He was still unconscious. The contents of Anderson's stomach began to climb up into his throat.

The man looked up. There was several days' growth of black beard round his chin as if it had been painted on. His eyes were deep-set, shining pinpoints. His lips were perfectly modelled, almost like a woman's. So were his hands. Anderson noticed the fingernails had no dirt under them. There was a small wedge-shaped blemish high on his left cheek. When he spoke, his voice was calm and measured, like an experienced schoolteacher talking to an unruly pupil.

'You've woken up then, have you?' he said.

Anderson cringed away from him. The lamp flickered, sending shadows scuttling across his face, transforming it into that of a hideous devil. The flame steadied itself. The shadows settled.

'You see, I have this problem,' he went on. 'We only want one of you alive and I have to decide which one it's to be.'

Anderson stared at the gun, now held loosely in the man's interlocked hands. It was an American-made Smith and Wesson, thirty-eight calibre, with a varnished wooden butt. A very effective weapon.

'You've woken up first so perhaps you would like to choose. Will I kill your friend here?' He nodded to Lowrie. 'He won't feel anything. He'll just never wake up.'

The man paused. He was waiting for an answer. The metallic thumps from outside fell into step with the beating of Anderson's heart and the hard pulse of blood in his neck. He suddenly felt very hot.

'No?' The man sounded disappointed. 'Then maybe you'd prefer me to shoot you? Is that to be the way of it?'

33

He waited again. Anderson moistened his dry lips with his tongue. He swallowed to keep the sickness down.

'No? I'll tell you what, then. We'll play a little game, shall we now. I know the very thing.'

He stood up. The light reached up to just below his neck. He took a copper-coloured bullet from the breast pocket of his shirt put it in the palm of his hand and showed it to Anderson.

'I have two of these,' the voice said in the darkness. 'Just the two.'

He opened the chamber of the gun. It was empty. He inserted the bullet and flicked the gun shut. He rolled his hand against the side to spin the chamber. It clicked rapidly and loudly, stopping at random.

'Now. Which one of you will begin our little game?' Anderson heard the words flying at him, disappearing past his head. What was happening was unreal. The straw between his toes felt like a red hot piece of metal. He looked down at it. It was only a piece of straw.

'Your friend, I think,' said the man thoughtfully. 'I will begin with him.'

He walked over and stood in front of Lowrie. Anderson followed his movement, cruelly fascinated. He was shivering again.

'The rules of this game are very simple. It won't take you long to learn.'

The man bent down and pressed the barrel of the gun against the back of Lowrie's hand. He squeezed the trigger. The hammer drew back and snapped shut. The wind howled mournfully in the silence which followed.

'Hands,' said the man.

He shifted slightly and Anderson saw him place the barrel against Lowrie's knee. The hammer jumped back and closed harmlessly.

'Knees,' he said.

He stood up and the darkness fell over his face like a veil. He reached out a hand and lifted Lowrie's unconscious head from his chest. Anderson thought of the sergeant tilting back the head of the boy he had killed in Belfast. The gun came up and was laid against Lowrie's forehead. Anderson watched

34

the hammer rise with agonising slowness. Then it snapped loudly.

'And Boomps-a-Daisy,' said the man amusedly.

He came over and stood in front of Anderson.

'Three chances left and now it is your turn to play the game.'

The man crouched down and his face came very close to Anderson's. There was a hint of a smile on the feminine lips. The image burned itself into his mind like a branding iron. He felt the cold steel of the gun on the back of his hand. He closed his eyes tightly and gritted his teeth, grinding them hard. There was a loud click.

'Hands.'

Anderson panicked. He spoke in a torrent of words.

'I'll tell you anything you want to know. Names. Anything.'

The man tapped the gun barrel against his chin. The smile spread across his face.

'I know you will,' he said quietly. 'Either you or your friend. I do not doubt it. But I only need one of you to tell me.'

'I'll tell you. I'll tell you,' Anderson screamed.

'I gave you your chance earlier. You decided we should play the game. You can't back out now. I won't let you.'

He pressed the gun against Anderson's knee and squeezed the trigger. The sound of the explosion was deafening. Anderson felt as if he had been hit by a sledgehammer in the leg. The bullet passed clean through and ricocheted off the wall of the barn, whining like the wind.

The man was standing up again. Anderson's knee throbbed. Damaged nerve ends clashed and sent waves of pain surging through him, weakening him.

'The game isn't over yet.'

Anderson could hardly hear the voice for the ringing in his ears. He watched as the gun was reloaded in front of him. His knee was almost numb. Faintness washed over him. Everything went completely black for a few seconds but then he was able to see again.

'One more bullet. The game isn't over yet.'

The voice sounded so reasonable. There was still another bullet. How could the game be over until the last bullet was gone? Anderson turned his head so that he could see the game being played. The gun was against Lowrie's hand. The trigger was pulled. Nothing.

'Hands,' said the man.

The gun was against Lowrie's knee. Please go off this time, Anderson said silently to himself. Please. This time. Lowrie moaned. He was coming round. There was a loud click. The wind sighed softly.

'Knees.'

Lowrie's head was tipped back. He shook it and it fell away from the man's hold. The man grabbed a fistful of hair and pulled the head back. The gun was against his forehead. Lowrie's eyes were opening. The hammer of the gun was moving back as the eyes opened. Please. This time. Anderson prayed. He screwed his eyes tightly shut and prayed that the gun would go off.

The sound of the explosion of the shot echoed round the barn and died away.

'Boomps-a-Daisy,' the man said when it was quiet.

Anderson was grateful to be alive. He forced himself to look across at Lowrie. The chair had fallen back. His eyes were open and staring upwards in surprise. A small black hole was above them. Blood trickled from the corner of his mouth and his nose. Anderson looked away. Thank you God, he thought.

The man was behind him. Chloroform fumes were in his nostrils. They stung his eyes. A pad was over his nose and mouth.

'You and I will be having a talk soon. Think about what you'll be telling me,' the man said.

Anderson did not struggle. At least he was still alive. He let himself slip under.

He had opened his eyes and it was still dark. Coloured lights appeared and faded in what would have been his field of vision. His body was stiff and uncomfortable but he couldn't move. He seemed to be jammed tightly between two surfaces. The one behind him was hard and smooth. The one in front was pliable, like cold plastic, following the rise and fall of his rib cage as he breathed. There was no sound but the rasping of his breath.

36

The air around him was warm. It made him sleepy. His mind was dulled. There was a persistent ache in his knee. He tried to relax the muscles but they were held fast, coiled like flattened springs. He could just feel his fingers and he could make them tap softly on his leg. He was naked. There was rope round his chest and waist binding his arms to his side and holding him against the plastic sheet or whatever it was in front of him.

He suddenly remembered what had happened and the coloured lights before his sightless eyes began to streak and soar like a silent fireworks display. He remembered the black and silver water and the taste of the dirt and the feel of the metal circle of the gun barrel on his hand and knee. And he remembered Lowrie on the tipped back chair, staring upwards in surprise.

He had wished him dead. He had wished his best friend dead so that he could live. There had been little or no hesitation on his part. A few seconds had destroyed a lifetime's resolve. His heroic dreams of sacrifice and bravery had been pure fantasy. He had been proved a coward. He had let his best friend die and he was grateful because of it.

But how long did he have to live? What did they now intend to do with him? He knew the names of two other Paddies. Perhaps he could bargain his way out. He was ashamed of the way his mind was working. This was not how he had imagined it at all. He should be defying them, spitting in their faces, laughing at their threats, ignoring the potential pain. But a very strong instinct had taken control of him; the instinct of self-preservation. He would do anything to stay alive. His so-called death-wish had been a sham. He had come close enough to death to taste it. The brutal choice had been put to him with no way out, no shades of grey, no escape. Be a dead hero or a live coward. He had made his choice.

Anderson was lying on his side. His neck twisted. He found that he was able to move it just enough to gain some temporary relief. His cheek brushed against something. He drew back. There was something a few inches from his face. He could sense its solid presence in the blackness. A deep sense of foreboding seized him. The rushing of his blood pounded in his ears and he tingled all over with helpless fear. Cautiously, he moved his

37

cheek back. He touched a soft point. It pressed into his skin. He snatched himself away. He had to open his mouth to breathe more easily. Sweat ran into his eyes. He wanted to back away but there was nowhere to go.

He lay for minutes, or it may have been hours, until he had calmed down. He was acutely aware of the rough plastic sheeting clinging to him the length of his body. He forced unwelcome thoughts out of his mind. He told himself it could not possibly be true. It could not be. It could not be. The heat was stifling him. He thought he had passed out for a time. Pains all over him were gathering in a crescendo inside his brain. He listened intently. There was nothing to hear but his own breathing and his heart ticking like a clock.

He did not want to. He tried to stop himself but could not. His face moved slowly forward of its own accord. The soft point nudged his cheek, ice cold. He had to go on. He had to be certain. He slid his cheek down. It fell away from the point, sliding on to another smoother surface. This surface seemed to stick to his cheek. He felt it follow the motion. He kept moving his head as if he was trying to look over his shoulder. His cheek was stuck. Then, abruptly, it was free. The cold substance sprang back to its former position.

A sick realisation gripped Anderson like a vice. He jerked his head back, cracked it on the wall behind him and automatically pulled it forward again pushing his lips against the cold rubbery lips of his dead friend in a macabre kiss. Their teeth knocked together. Irrationally, Anderson thought he was about to be bitten. He hit his head off the wall again as he broke the contact. He screamed as loudly as he could. Then he gulped in air and screamed again. He thrashed around trying to loosen the ropes but they would not budge. He screamed until his voice was little more than a hoarse whisper. Then all he could do was lie still, his head pressed firmly against the wall, staring into the darkness which seemed to heave and swell and swirl around him. And he began to wonder if he was not the one that had been killed. If it was not he who had died and come to this Hell. Perhaps he was to remain here for eternity, cheek to cheek with a corpse. That was to be his fate for betraying his friend and being afraid to die. How very appropriate, he thought.

Time had no meaning. Anderson was not aware if he was unconscious or awake. He could only lie and watch the dead body in front of him although he could not see anything. Sometimes he would find their faces were touching and he would snatch himself away. Sometimes he would think he could hear a different noise and his skin would crawl with fear. Strange images floated in and out of his mind. Bill Lowrie's face would suddenly spring towards him out of the darkness, teeth bared, going for his throat. There was nothing he could do except wait for the flesh to be torn apart and the warm blood to gush out. But it didn't happen. Then he could see himself and Lowrie standing together. They were playing a game. They patted the palms of their hands together. 'Hands,' they sang. They patted their own knees. 'Knees,' they sang. They turned and bumped their backsides together. 'Boomps-a-Daisy,' they sang. Then they were rolling on the ground, rolling over and over. They were rolling down a steep hill, faster and faster, locked together as one. At the bottom they came to a stop. Anderson was lying on top of his friend. Lowrie was looking up at him as he began to get up. Lowrie did not move. There was a small round hole exactly in the centre of his forehead. They played the game again and again. It always ended the same way.

Anderson began to talk to himself, babbling nonsensically, pretending he was speaking to a whole procession of figures conjured up out of his past; his mother, his father, his brother, old schoolfriends. His throat became sore and swollen. His tongue grew to fill his whole mouth. Hunger pangs gripped him as tightly as the ropes and then they would pass, leaving him feeling drained and weak, as if his entire body was nothing more than an empty shell. And all the time Lowrie lay beside him, watching him, reminding him.

Sometimes he would laugh in a kind of strange, gargling chuckle, amused at his predicament. White shadows loomed round him. They were like cartoon characters. White shadows with black holes for eyes. And if he listened very carefully he could hear them whispering together. He could just hear the whispers but he could not make out the words. Their whispers formed themselves into a single note that resonated deeply like the peal of some gigantic bell, like the humming of a million bees. And the rhythmic sound echoed through his head while the unceasing coloured lights adapted to its monotonous melody and danced in time.

He measured the time by the beating of his heart. Seventy beats to the minute had been his normal pulse rate. He counted seventy beats. That was one minute. Another seventy. Two minutes. Another seventy. Three minutes. But then, suddenly, he could no longer hear his heart and he thought he was dead. He strained to hear but there was nothing; absolutely nothing. The darkness howled in terrifying silence. Then it began again. The regular thump, thump, thump of his heart. He sighed contentedly. He was still alive.

There was a new sound. A scraping. And voices. Real voices. A current of cool air, delightfully cool, wrapped itself round his body. Anderson saw the insides of his eyelids become a light pink colour. White light, blinding white light, smashed into his senses as he tried to open his eyes. He screwed them firmly shut and opened them slowly, very slowly, letting the light in gently.

'Jesus Christ. Will you look at this.'

It was an Engligh voice. Cockney or West Country. Definitely not Irish. Fear ran out of him like dirty water from a sink. He was safe at last. He was not going to die after all.

He could open his eyes just enough to make out the outline of the face in front of him. The features grew more obvious as he stared at them, as if they were being drawn in with a heavy pencil at that very moment. He saw the mouth with the teeth bared in a half smile, and a stream of dried blood running from the nose and splitting in two to follow the line of the top lip like some comical moustache, and the milky grey eyes wide open despite the flood of light. And he could see his own face reflected in the dull black pupils and his own shadow on the deathly white skin.

Then they were lifting him up. Lowrie continued to look at him even when his head fell slightly to one side. Soldiers surrounded them. The familiar camouflage uniforms were everywhere. A knife was cutting the ropes. Blood forced its way back through constricted veins pumping life to every limb. Strong arms held Anderson as Lowrie was cut free and lowered away from him. They covered his face with a flak jacket.

40

'You're all right now. You're all right. You're safe.'

A thousand different pains swarmed over him. A blanket was put over his shoulders. Anderson closed his eyes and sought the welcome relief of the darkness.

It had lasted less than forty-eight hours from the time they had reported leaving the Belfast command centre. When the first check call failed to come in, a yellow cross was put on the file. When the time for the second call had passed, it was replaced with a red cross. After no third call, a patrol was sent out to inspect the rendezvous point at Lough Neagh. They found a wrist watch half buried in the soft ground on the edge of the water. In Belfast it was identified as belonging to Lowrie. It confirmed that they had been kidnapped. The kidnappers would have made for the border immediately with their captives and with the head start they had would be long over it by now. All border crossing points were alerted. A few helicopters were sent clattering over the countryside, but the conventional wisdom was that they could do little but wait for the bodies to turn up.

In fact, the kidnappers had travelled less than twenty miles to a partly-disused group of farm buildings just outside Dungannon. There was nothing out of the ordinary to draw the army's attention to the place. There were thousands like it all over the six counties. To search them all would take years.

But a sharp-eyed lieutenant, who did not even know about the kidnapping at the time, noticed that the road up to the steading looked unnaturally smooth. He would have expected it to be much more rutted and uneven. It looked as if it had been raked over, perhaps to hide tyre-tracks or something like that. He reported his suspicions and the information quickly percolated through the system and was linked with the disappearance of the two undercover officers. An entire company was detailed to surround the place and check it out. When they finally moved in there was evidence of a hasty departure. A small gas cooking stove had been left burning under a pan of baked beans, but the occupants had melted away. In the barn hundreds of straw bales, their sides covered in black mould, had been hurriedly piled against one wall. The barn door thumped in the wind as the soldiers moved them and found Lowrie and Anderson jammed into a stone chamber that was designed for channelling cattle muck away from the stalls. Anderson was alive. Lowrie had been killed by a single bullet into the brain.

'You're lucky to be alive,' Major Henderson told Anderson as he sat beside his hospital bed telling the story. The major, who had a moustache straight off the Kitchener Your Country Needs You posters, had come to hear Anderson's version of events. Anderson told him about being tied to the chair and Lowrie being shot. He did not tell him about the game or that he had wished Lowrie dead to save his own skin.

'They must have put you in that hole to soften you up. You were lucky we managed to get back to you before they did,' the major said, frowning. 'You didn't tell them anything?'

Anderson shook his head wearily, wishing the major would leave him alone.

'And Lowrie? You were together all the time before he was shot?'

'Yes. He told them nothing.'

'You're sure?'

'I'm sure.'

Anderson saw himself and Lowrie, lashed together, tumbling over and over. The white shadows with black holes for eyes fluttered around him. He shivered.

'Well, I'll leave you now. You look tired.'

Major Henderson stood up and they shook hands. He had already decided to recommend both men for awards. A posthumous Mentioned in Despatches for Lowrie and a Distinguished Conduct Medal for Anderson. The only difference between them being that Lowrie was dead. Medals for his boys showed a fine spirit. It reflected well on him.

The police and the army had both questioned Anderson. He had told them the same story, leaving out the bit about the deadly game and the fact that he would have told them everything if only they had given him the chance. If they had asked him there and then he would have handed over every

42

scrap of information he knew. But they had thought it would be tougher than that to break an SAS man. They had thought they would need to work on him some more so they had buried him alive, attached to a corpse, in an attempt to make him crack. They had not realised he had been unable to resist them from the moment they had him face down in the dirt at their mercy. They had broken him all right. They had shattered him into little pieces. He tried to tell himself that it had made no difference that he had willed the gun to go off when it was pressed firmly against Lowrie's forehead. He could have yelled no a million times and it would still have killed him. He had not had any influence on the final outcome. No, he had not influenced the outcome but he had wanted it to be that way. That was what was wrong.

The blind was half closed on the window of his room. Parallel lines of light ran across the floor and on to the blankets of the bed. An attractive nurse in a crisp white uniform came in periodically to take his temperature and his blood pressure. Our Hero, she called him. She had dark red hair piled high on top of her head, with two loose strands dangling on either side in front of her ears, and a cloud of freckles over the bridge of her nose. She was unfailingly pleasant but he refused to respond. He tried not to look at her, afraid that she might guess at his secret.

They brought him a book of mug-shots and he found who he was looking for in the first few pages. The pictures, a full-face and a profile, were in black and white and were almost uncannily similar to Anderson's memory of the soft-spoken man in the uncertain light of the paraffin lamp. The nick out of his cheek looked like a fly settling there. His name was Brian Heaney, a most-wanted high flyer in the provisionals. The Secret Service man who had brought the book raised his eyebrows when Anderson pointed him out. They had thought he was in the south.

'Christ. He's a real bastard. You're lucky to be alive.'

Anderson nodded. So people keep telling me, he thought, watching the man write down the name in a notebook. Then he had to go over his story again, remembering what had to be left out. The Secret Service man wrote slowly in longhand, asking him to repeat everything at least twice so that he could get it down accurately. It took more than an hour.

There were complications with his knee that kept Anderson in the hospital for a month. Mary, the nurse with the red hair won his confidence. He was able to look directly at her, even smile at her. She kept calling him Our Hero. She could not tell what was going on inside his head. She really thought he was a hero.

It became obvious that the knee was not going to heal properly. Major Henderson arrived to break the bad news that he was to be invalided out of the army. There would be a lump sum in compensation and a good pension, of course. By the way, he added, your medal will come through the post.

When the time came for Anderson to leave the hospital Mary escorted him to the door where a military ambulance was waiting to take him to the airport for a scheduled civilian flight to Edinburgh. She helped him into the back of the ambulance and then, without warning, kissed him gently on the lips. Instinctively he jerked his head away.

'I don't do that for all my patients,' she said, blushing in embarrassment.

Anderson's heart was racing. The touch of her lips had recalled the horrific moment in the barn. She was looking at him curiously. He had to do something to rescue the situation. He leaned forward, put his hand round the back of her neck, and pulled her mouth on to his and held it there. When he let her go she was blushing with pleasure.

'Goodbye Mary,' he said.

'Goodbye, my hero,' she replied.

Anderson smiled. She still thought he was a hero.

The army were as good as their word. The compensation was generous, as was the pension. Anderson stayed with his Aunt Morag in Kingsbank until the chance came up to buy his parents' old home. The army's old boy network also got him a good job as a supervisor in a Glenrothes electronics factory run by an ex-paratrooper who was a personal friend of Major Henderson.

Anderson forced himself to go and visit Bill Lowrie's mother at a village north of Leeds. She was a small lady of fifty, prematurely aged, with bones in her face that looked as if they would burst through the paper-thin grey skin at any moment. She took him to her son's grave with its simple headstone. He stood there and imagined the coffin being lowered into the ground and had a brief, absurd image of Lowrie lying at the bottom of the grave on an upturned chair, staring up at him in surprise. The image unsettled him. He felt the grip of Lowrie's mother on his arm and he looked down into the liquid pools of her eyes. Silently, she was asking herself why her son had died and this stranger had lived. Where was the justice in it? Where was the reason in it? They were questions Anderson could not answer for her but the obvious depth of her sorrow affected him greatly. When he had wished for Lowrie's death he had wished this on his mother. He was responsible for how she felt today. Suddenly he found himself blinded by his own tears. He was no longer able to read the name on the gravestone.

There was sleet in the wind battering Anderson's car. Tiny flakes of snow stuck to the passenger side and skidded horizontally over the windscreen. He reached out and wiped the condensation from the inside of the glass and it was like wiping away tears. The familiar sight of the Howe of Fife spread out below him, darkening perceptibly before his eyes as the storm clouds rolled together to seal off the sky. The church tower at Kingsbank stood tall like a gravestone above the houses of the village clustered around it. He emerged from the trance he had fallen into and shivered in the cold.

The annual ritual was over. He had unleashed the shame and the guilt that lurked inside him and allowed them to roam freely for a few hours. Now he was confident that he would be able to control them for another year. They would not go away. They would always be there, just below the surface, but they would not get the better of him.

Anderson switched on the engine and revved it up. He opened his door so that he could see to reverse. The heater poured cold air around his legs. Gradually it became warm.

It was just before three in the afternoon. He was another few

45

hours closer to the moment of his death, he thought, as he drove down the hill towards Kingsbank. He had lived seven years beyond the time of Bill Lowrie's death. Seven years was not a long time. The car he was in was older than that. It had been on the road when Lowrie was alive. Perhaps the engine had been running when the bullet entered Lowrie's brain.

Anderson had a morbid fascination with the passage of time. For the last seven years he had seen himself being pulled inevitably towards his death, a death that lay in wait for him, a death that he would not need to seek out; it would come to him. He had tried to stop the pull. He frequently drank himself insensible. That worked until he sobered up. He lived in the house where he had been conceived in an attempt to slow things down, a futile attempt to retreat as far away from his life as he could get. Still he was dragged relentlessly forward.

He had never seriously contemplated suicide. He did not have the courage for that.

He thought of Kathy for the first time since leaving the house that morning. He was conscious that since she had come into his life the pull on him had seemed stronger. The momentum was building every time he was with her, every time she touched him, with every word she spoke. He could not tell her he loved her for fear of tempting fate; the same fate that had decreed that Bill Lowrie should die rather than Jim Anderson. But he could love her secretly. He was good at keeping a secret. And she was the first person to make him feel really alive since his discovery that he was not the man he believed himself to be. To him, Kathy was a sweet-tasting poison. Sooner or later he would die because of her. She was too good to last.

He turned into his driveway and parked the car in the garage. He limped to the front door of the house, momentarily optimistic that Kathy would be waiting there for him. The house was empty. Only the whisky bottle was waiting.

Anderson closed the curtains in the living room and took the old photograph out of the desk. He propped it up on the mantelpiece and sat back in his armchair to look at it. He poured himself a drink and felt the liquid burn its way down

46

into his stomach. He held the glass in his lap and the late afternoon sunlight creeping in through the chinks in the curtains sparkled on the carved crystal. The house creaked around him and shuddered as a train thundered over the bridge, not stopping at the station.

Part Two

SUMMER

The grey-haired man with the very pale eyebrows did not rate a second glance from his fellow pedestrians as he walked among them along the central path bisecting the parkland known as The Meadows on his way from his flat on the south side of Edinburgh to his office at Waverley Station in the city centre. Carrying a briefcase and wearing his usual camel coat and leather gloves he blended in perfectly with the rush hour crowds. At five o'clock that night he would join them for the return journey.

Bob Stone always walked with his head down, studiously ignoring everyone around him. He looked up only when he had to avoid a collision with people who insisted on stopping to gossip in the middle of the path, or to check the traffic before crossing one of the busy main roads. It took him twenty-five minutes to reach Waverley if he walked at a steady speed, and he could easily have followed the route blindfolded having done it so many times. It was a case of going up Middle Meadow Walk, at first between the big open expanses of grass, and then into a built-up area with the university on one side and the hospital on the other. The pathway ended at Forrest Road which led down past the statue of Greyfriars Bobby and on to George IV Bridge, across the Royal Mile at the traffic lights outside the Sheriff Court and down some steep steps to Market Street and the station entrance on Waverley Bridge. It was a pleasant walk to work in the summer, not so pleasant once the winter set in. Stone knew that the coming winter was not something he had to worry about.

It was just as well he did not have to pay close attention to where he was walking because Stone's mind was occupied by thoughts of another place. Since his first visit to Kingsbank Station in Fife more than a month previously he had been carrying a mental picture of it round inside his head that was capable of superimposing itself on any surroundings. When he looked up, the people in front of him seemed to be moving along the platforms. When he looked from side to side before crossing a road, it was as if he was looking up and down the railway tracks leading into and out of the station. Buildings he passed took on the shape and form of the station buildings he had examined so thoroughly. Kingsbank Station seemed to have grown to such a massive size it was impossible for him to escape from its boundaries. Everywhere he turned it confronted him, dominating his life.

He had been to the station several times, mostly travelling there by train but sometimes driving over in his own car. Once he had gone on a round trip to Dundee from Edinburgh, not getting off at Kingsbank but being content to see the station during the two brief stops there, one on the way north, and one on the way back again. The whole place was tailor-made for the job, right down to the house for rent less than a hundred yards away.

His cousin John had been impressed by his description and had given him the authority and the funds to go ahead. The heady feeling of setting the operation in motion had inspired one of those periodic rushes of self-confidence that made Stone do things that were totally out of character. On this occasion he had strolled into the pub at the foot of the station steps as if he did not have a care in the world. All the locals had stared at him suspiciously. It had been a foolish thing to do and his brittle self-confidence had disintegrated to the extent that he was physically sick in the toilet of the train taking him home.

At times Stone was staggered by the enormity of what he was involved in. He would stare at himself in mirrors and find it hard to believe that the person he saw there was actually him. He would sometimes almost succeed in convincing himself that everything that had happened was part of some weird hallucination he was undergoing, but then there were the constant reminders that it was all real. There were the phone calls from his cousin and that morning, before he left for work, the postman had delivered the registration documents for the Piper Cherokee aircraft he had bought at the weekend. Events were beginning to gain their own momentum. Soon it would be the last time he walked this route to work.

Boston was waking up. Traffic began to clog the roads; people appeared on the sidewalks; shopkeepers removed the overnight boarding from their windows; a fruit seller set up his stall and laid out his wares; a newspaper seller screamed unintelligible headlines. Shafts of sunlight poked through the early morning mist. The city was coming alive, a vast living machine of crashing and jarring gear wheels struggling together to produce another day for its inhabitants.

In an apartment near the harbour Brian Heaney lay in bed not yet fully awake. He was aware of the four-inch space between the bottom of the faded white roller blind and the window sill. It burned with the intensity of a neon tube, growing ever brighter as the dark grey air of the night retreated into the furthest corners of the bedroom. The new morning gradually imposed itself on the room like a snake casting its old skin and emerging anew.

How long had he been here now? Three years it was. And four years before that in New York, persuading ignorant Americans to part with their dollars for the sake of the cause. Second and third generation Americans who had never set foot in Ireland but who professed their love for the mother country as the soldier does for the pin-up picture above his bed. They loved Ireland from afar with no intention of returning, except perhaps for a holiday to see how peasants lived. At a fund-raising dinner once he had made an emotional plea for everyone of Irish descent to go back, to resettle in the old country. They had applauded him to the echo and then gone home to their comfortable apartments and brownstones to tell each other how wonderful it would be, if only they could.

In seven years he had managed to buy a lot of guns and ship them over. Two years ago he had finally managed to get hold of three Russian-made surface-to-air missiles. They had cost him a fortune but had been worth it. He personally supervised their storage in a consignment of car spares destined for Belfast, watching them being taken apart and distributed in small packages in the freight container. And he was arrested when the container was seized at the docks. The FBI had been tipped off. Only his contacts in the police and city council saved him. His sources had promised to supply another three missiles but they had never materialised. The informant had been identified and had lost when he played the game, but the missiles were bad news. That had been his greatest disappointment but it was now somebody else's problem because six months ago Big John Colquhoun had asked Heaney if he would be willing to take on a job, one that would have the Brits spitting blood. He didn't have to ask twice. America was about to be part of his past.

Big John was the only one of the three members of the provisional high command he still knew personally. The other two were just names to him. He had been out of the mainstream too long. Was it really seven years since he had been at the top of the army's wanted list and things had got too hot for him in Ireland? Seven years since it had been suggested that it would be safer if he took over the American gun-running operation for a while? He had been good at it. That was why he had stayed. He had realised how important the job was and overcome his distaste for the Americans themselves and taken their money and their guns. Now there was to be another important job for him. He had spent the last few months putting together his last shipment of arms. Not as many as he would have liked, but a fair amount. When it sailed with the tide tonight, he would be with it.

Heaney sat up in bed, shoving a pillow in behind the small of his back. Outside a ship's horn wailed. The room was filling with oppressive heat despite the constant whine of the air-conditioning system. It was May and a warm summer was forecast. He was not sorry he would not be spending it in Boston. Seven years was a long time. He was glad to be going home.

He threw the thin cotton sheet off the bed. A black woman

51

was lying face down beside him. He drew his hand along her spine, leaving a trail like a finger mark on a frozen window pane. He spread his fingers wide over one buttock and gently dug in his perfectly manicured nails. He saw the ebony flesh change to a lighter shade of chocolate brown. The woman grunted and lifted her head to look at him. The multi-coloured beads threaded through her hair clicked together like wind-blown chimes. Pink eyes and brilliant white teeth contrasted sharply with her black face. Heaney squeezed more tightly. She moaned, rising on her elbows and began laboriously to turn over on to her back. He let his hand lie loosely on her body as she moved round until it came to rest between her legs.

'Come on baby,' he said. 'I want to say my goodbyes to America.'

Brian Heaney was ashamed of his hands. They were small and delicate, out of proportion with the rest of his body. At school the other boys teased him about his hands. They were like a little girl's, they said. He let them get filthy. He scratched the backs of his hands against walls. He wanted them to be rough and manly. He curled them into tiny fists; he laid them palm against palm and finger against finger and prayed that they would change.

Sister Teresa made him stand in front of the class. The children sniggered as she told him to hold out his hands. He looked down, letting his thick dark curls fall over his eyes so that he could not see.

'Your hands are filthy, Brian, are they not?'

She was holding his hands in hers. Her hands were strong and masculine with long, powerful fingers and tough skin. His were small and fragile, nestling in her grip like those of a little baby. He looked up. He was almost as tall as her, yet his hands were so small.

'Yes, Sister,' he said.

'And there is dirt under your fingernails.'

She looked round the classroom seeking other owners of dirty hands. Brian Heaney felt a small pain like a pinprick stab his stomach. It passed and then came back again. He wanted to hold his stomach but Sister Teresa was clutching his hands.

'Brian, do you know what happens if you do not clean the dirt from under your nails at least once a day?'

The pain nagged at him. 'No, Sister,' he said, breathing deeply.

'Devils take root and grow there.' Sister Teresa was a good story-teller. The children fell completely silent. 'And they burrow into your flesh and ride along through your blood and they can reach any part of a boy's body they choose and there, by trampling with their sharp hooves, they can cause the most terrible pain. They stamp and kick and lash their pointed tails and flames from their nostrils burn up your skin from the inside . . .'

Brian Heaney could feel the devils inside him. He stared at the black tips of his fingernails as the pain grew steadily worse. It throbbed to the rhythm of their pounding feet. The heat from it spread down into his legs and up into his chest. He imagined the flames burning him up inside, flames that came from picture book devils with black leathery skin and yellow teeth and eyes.

'So boys should always clean under their fingernails to keep the devils away,' Sister Teresa was saying. She finished with a half smile on her face, pleased that the class seemed to be taking her warning seriously. 'You will keep them clean in future, won't you, Brian?'

He snatched his hands away from her grasp and the movement made him stagger against the blackboard. He held his stomach tightly where the pain was as if it might burst through at any moment, a legion of tiny devils would be scattered across the classroom floor. He was on his knees. Sister Teresa was standing over him, looking down. The devils danced furiously inside him. He fell on his side drawing his knees up to his waist, squeezing himself into a tight ball, trying to crush the pain inside him.

They took him to hospital and removed his appendix. The devils were gone when he finally woke up. Sister Teresa and some of the other nuns came to visit him. He showed them how clean his fingernails were. He scrubbed them as often as he could. They smiled in approval.

Brian Heaney was born and brought up in Londonderry. He was the youngest of five, two boys and three girls. He shared a bedroom with his brother who was ten years older than him and who used to bully him mercilessly. When he was twelve his brother left home to get married and he had the room to himself. The first night he slept there alone he imagined himself to be the only person left alive in the whole world.

His parents were very religious. Plaster saints occupied corners in every room. Solemn-faced priests and smiling nuns were always being invited to the house for meals. Candles were constantly burning. His mother, a small woman always tightly wrapped in a grey woollen shawl, used to kneel beside him at night as he said his prayers. He would pray out loud automatically, all the time watching her with her eyes screwed firmly shut and her lips jerking rapidly. He saw real fear of God on her face and was frightened himself.

He joined the IRA when he was fifteen. Everybody he knew did, going through a simple initiation ceremony and swearing an oath over the republican flag. He had been involved in a few riots, had thrown a few stones, nothing serious. His involvement had only been half-hearted. He was terrified of being caught and having to explain to his parents. He hovered in the background, jealous of the brave ones who went right up to the army lines and flung their stones. He wished he had the courage and made up a story about him hurling a petrol bomb that had set fire to a soldier. He told the story to Father Reilly at his next confession, expecting a heavy penance. The priest behind the small wooden-barred window in the confession box did not hesitate after hearing the confession. 'God will forgive you, my son,' he said immediately. There was no penance to be done.

His father died a few weeks before he was due to leave school. His mother's praying became even more frantic after that. He could almost watch lines appear on her face, like an eggshell cracking in slow motion. She died herself within six months. Two of his sisters had married and left home. He remained there with his eldest sister, Noreen. All his friends thought Noreen was the most attractive sister and nobody could understand why she didn't get herself a man. One night, filled with unaccustomed drink, he asked her. She had to be careful, she confided in him, because she was secretly engaged to a British soldier. He was shocked. He had suspected nothing. He shouted at her, calling her a fool and worse. It was wrong. He did not doubt for a moment that it was wrong for his sister to be going out with a British soldier. She seemed surprised at his reaction. She had thought her brother was not particularly interested in nationalist politics. He had never shown any real signs before.

Brian Heaney brooded over what his sister had told him for a few weeks and then he decided to let the fact be known. The same night two men kicked down the front door of the house and dragged Noreen out of her bed. He heard it all from where he lay in his own bed. She was screaming as they cut off her long black hair and the screams went on and on.

From his bedroom window he watched as they carried her over to a children's play area opposite and tied her to a climbing frame there. She was naked and they were pouring stuff over her head. He saw a knife and his heart leapt but it was only used to cut open a pillow so that they could cover her in feathers. In the morning, when it was light, she was still tied there, hanging by her wrists, patches of white scalp showing through her ragged hair. Green Tate and Lyle syrup tins lay round about her like spent cartridge cases. The feathers sticking to her skin stirred in the light breeze and some drifted away every so often like the white flowers blown from a dandelion clock.

A sullen crowd of people gathered to look at her. Nobody said anything. They just looked. Brian Heaney watched over their heads, crouching at the window so that he could not be seen. He was just able to hear Noreen sobbing. Only once did she look, and then it seemed to him that she was staring straight at him. He ducked below the window and when he looked out again her head was down.

Eventually an army patrol arrived. The crowd watched silently as they cut her free. One soldier put a blanket round her shoulders and helped her into the back of an armoured Land-Rover. Brian Heaney wondered if it was her boyfriend. The patrol took her away. He left the house and went to stay with friends to avoid any police questioning. He never went back. He never saw Noreen again.

The IRA took care of him. They fed him and clothed him and gave him a regular wage. He planted his first bomb when he was sixteen, killed his first policeman two years later. He remembered the look of terror on the policeman's face as the motor bike drew up alongside his car and he realised a pistol barrel was pressed against the glass of the window; the same look Heaney had seen on his mother's face when she knelt beside him praying. At nights, after a job, he liked to lie alone and recall the words of the old priest: 'God will forgive you, my son.'

He was moved around a lot, between Londonderry and Belfast mainly. He quickly acquired a reputation and found himself giving orders rather than taking them. He supervised riots, organised the building of barricades, the hijacking of cars and lorries, and the distribution of petrol bombs. One night in Belfast he was hit in the face by a doctored rubber bullet. It gouged a chunk of skin out of his cheek and left him permanently scarred. Afterwards people no longer seemed to notice his hands, they noticed his scar.

He was arrested by both police and army several times. He was given a good going over but they were never able to get anything on him. He moved south during internment and became more involved in the political side of things but he did not like to become too detached from what he liked to call his front-line troops. His name began to carry a lot of weight. He was identified in Sunday papers as a leading terrorist. The pressure grew. The Brits had him as a marked man.

He set himself up as an interrogator of suspected informants, crossing and recrossing the border, always on the move. He devised a game to play with them; a variation on Russian Roulette. It was taken from a child's game his mother had taught him as a boy, a stupid pointless game he endowed with vicious meaning. The game was called Hands – point the gun at their hand – Knees – point the gun at their knees – Boomps-a-Daisy – point the gun at their foreheads. A game of chance. No cheating allowed. Let them brush up against death as close as possible. It always produced that look of absolute terror on their faces that reminded him so much of his mother at her prayers.

The look of fear in the eyes of the last one he had done, a captured undercover soldier, had been so similar to how he remembered his mother it had thrown him completely. The reflected candlelight on the closed eyelids of his mother, the writhing lips; they were uncannily reproduced on the man's face. He let him live to see if it would be the same a second time but that was a mistake because the Brits had discovered the farm and were closing in. They had only had time to throw some straw bales over the hole before escaping by the skin of their teeth, following a deep overgrown field drain that took them within yards of the soldiers who were surrounding the farm and then out beyond them into the safety of the countryside.

It was after that episode that Heaney took over the American operation. He found it easy to work in America. He fitted in well. People respected him. Several times he declined the offer of plastic surgery to remove his scar. The drink was plentiful, the women were there for the taking. But it wasn't home. And after seven years of the easy life Heaney was glad to be going home.

Bob Stone bought six separate packs of self-assembly model railway buildings in the toy department of a big Princes Street store one lunchtime when he slipped away from his office. They were the stiff cardboard type he found most convenient to work with. Each brick, each roof tile was individually outlined on the models. The windows were tiny pieces of perspex. The overall effect was quite realistic.

The store was busy and Stone had to wait patiently in a queue for more than ten minutes before he could hand over the money for his purchases to the salesgirl at the counter. She was a short, dumpy girl with spikey hair, wearing a brown and white staff uniform that was at least one size too small for her. She had not spoken to any of the other customers in the queue but for some reason decided it was time to be friendly and outgoing when Stone appeared in front of her.

'Who's the railway buff in the family then, sir? Is it yourself or your son?'

Stone took a few seconds to realise that the question was directed at him. The girl was pushing the model packs into a plastic bag. He wanted to grab it and run. He felt that everybody in the store was watching him, waiting for him to answer the question.

'I don't have a son,' he said quickly.

The girl nodded as if she was perfectly aware of the real reason he was buying the models. The till played its tune of computer music. She smiled pleasantly at him and held out her hand. Stone thought for a moment that she was blackmailing him, demanding payment to stop her telling the whole world exactly what he was up to.

'Your change, sir.'

'Thank you, thank you,' he stammered, taking the offered money and snatching the bag from the counter. 'Actually, they are presents. For my nephew. Yes, my little nephew.'

'I hope he enjoys them.'

'I'm sure he will. He lives in Dublin, you know.'

That night Stone sat at his kitchen table with a modelling knife and the contents of the packs spread out in front of him. He had selected the models he needed very carefully from the maker's catalogue before going in to buy them. He now had the constituent parts of four different station buildings, a two-storey stationmaster's house, and a signal box chosen for the pitch of its roof.

Stone used the sharp knife to cut into the stiff cardboard as he created one model from the six packs, working from memory to shape the buildings into the form he wanted. It was intricate, painstaking work and it was after midnight before he was satisfied with the result of his labours. His back was sore from being hunched over the table. He had a headache from concentrating so hard.

He stood up to admire the station he had put together. He walked round the table, viewing it from every angle. It was a very good likeness, he told himself. Very good indeed. He found it easy to project himself down to its scale, to im-agine himself walking on one of the platforms or standing outside the ticket office or under the platform canopy opposite.

Stone began to dismantle the model of Kingsbank Station. He had numbered the parts so that he could quickly rebuild it again at any time. When it was folded down he removed some papers from his briefcase and put it in there. It seemed to him appropriate that he should carry Kingsbank around with him until such time as it was needed.

It had been a wild night on the Falls Road in Belfast and it wasn't over yet. A burned-out laundry van lay on its side, half on the road and half on the pavement, flames flickering round the remnants of one tyre. The ground was strewn with bricks and boulders and other debris. The rain was teeming down, water sweeping in great sheets across the city. Inches deep, it filled the gutters and lay in rippling puddles where holes had been torn in the road surface. Twice the soldiers had bulldozed their way past hastily erected barricades that night. Five times the snatch squads had managed to lay their hands on rioters and drag them back behind the mobile wall of protective shields. Rubber bullets whirred through the air and kept the crowds out of petrol bomb range. A sniper had hit one soldier in the neck. But it had been the sudden downpour which had emptied the streets. Like a dissatisfied football crowd, the mob of people had decided to go home, drenched by the rain and frustrated by the effective containment tactics of the soldiers.

It was just after midnight and the few remaining groups of persistent rioters, mostly young boys, were being driven up the road by the soldiers. From the rear seat of a stolen Ford Granada parked near the corner of a narrow side street, John McCook saw the Pig, a Saracen armoured troop carrier, emerge through a shining curtain of rain and nose its way slowly along the road, the two black oblong sight slits like screwed-up eyes.

McCook cursed under his breath and opened the back door of the car, nudging it outwards with the bulbous, red-painted tip of the rocket that was locked on to the portable launcher he carried. He swore again as he swung his legs down on to the ground. The riot should still have been going on to cover his escape route but the bastards had faded away because of the rain. However, there was no question in his mind about abandoning the attack. Not when he was this close.

The Pig lumbered over the rubble scattered across the road. The road of its engine grew as it approached the junction. Black smoke belched from its exhaust. Elongated raindrops flashed across McCook's line of vision making the scene look like a bad television picture. He turned and tapped the car driver on the shoulder. He felt the vibration as the car engine started up. McCook breathed deeply through his nose to calm himself. Three times he sucked air right to the very bottom of his lungs. Then, he stood up and walked quickly to the corner of the street.

The Pig was drawing level with the junction, barely twenty yards away. It was swinging round to face him, tilting as it ran over the frame of a bus shelter that had been used in the barricade building. The screech of its engine rose to a crescendo as the tyres slipped and spun on the smooth metal.

McCook went down on one knee and took aim unhurriedly. In the grid pattern of the rocket launcher's sight the Pig was like a grey thumbmark. Raindrops spat into his face. He used three fingers to squeeze the stiff trigger. A yellow flash washed over him. His shoulder was shaken roughly as the side of his face grew hot. There was a giant rushing round in his ear and the smell of burning. He rocked backwards as the rocket hissed away from him. The backblast reached as far as one side of the Granada's boot, partly melting the plastic light covers and singeing the paintwork.

He regained his balance just in time to see the orange tail of the rocket strike the Pig low down, slicing through the thick steel of the offside wheel arch with a massive thump. The vehicle reared several inches off the ground and slumped heavily back down again. The doors at the back flew open and a soldier fell out, his rifle skittering away from him across the rain-soaked road. Three more soldiers jumped down and helped the first one to his feet. They all ran for cover, crouching low as if the pelting rain were lethal bullets. Another soldier scrambled down from the driver's side of the Pig. He stopped and turned and appeared to be leaning back inside to help someone else. Flames were beginning to take hold of the underside. The glaring headlights suddenly went out. Close by, the crack of a rifle shot sounded.

McCook saw no more. He dived full-length onto the back seat of the Granada. The door slammed shut by itself as the driver accelerated sharply away. McCook lay clutching the still warm launcher to his chest. He wiped the rain from his face. It had not been as good a shot as he might have hoped but at least it had hit the target. That had been his fifth rocket attack. He had yet to miss. He allowed himself a satisfied smile.

Violence was a way of life for John McCook. His father had told him how his grandfather had died at the hands of the Black and Tans. His father was to die in a Proddy ambush. One brother was killed in a car bomb explosion. The other was shot by soldiers after a bank raid. The three funerals of his father and his brothers had all seemed strangely identical. The coffin on trestles in the front room of the terraced house in Belfast holding the body dressed in its best suit with the hands carefully crossed over the stomach and the closed eyes in the white, bloodless face. The little groups of relatives and friends standing around and pretending not to stare too much at the body. The smell of whisky and beer and the tiny sandwiches with no crusts his mother always insisted on, and the rock cakes and the shortbread that Mrs Miller next door always made. The polished coffin lid leaning against the wall like an extra door in the room.

Then there was the funeral procession: a slow, impressive, stately affair, following the flag-draped coffin. He held his mother's arm at the head of the procession, not that she needed supporting, and the crowds of mourners – always there were crowds – would follow silently behind all the way to the cemetery with the soldiers watching from a safe distance. The last time, for his brother Bobby, the television cameras had been there and they had seen themselves go through it all again later that night. At the graveside, after the priest had done his bit, six masked men would suddenly appear and fire a volley of pistol shots as a military salute before quickly melting into the

61

anonymity of the crowd again. The soldiers could only look on from a distance. At Bobby's funeral he had been old enough to fire one of the pistols.

Funerals used to take up a large part of his young life. Hardly a week seemed to pass without the dark suit and the black tie coming out of the wardrobe. He did not know a single family that had not lost someone in the Troubles. The will to fight was inbred in him; it was as natural as the instinct to breathe. There was no other way he could live. He hoped there would be huge crowds at his funeral and that the volley of shots over his grave would somehow take out another six British soldiers.

John McCook had been underground for three years. He had not seen his mother nor his wife and two children in that time. Their only contact was birthday cards and a phone call on Christmas Day. He had to be careful and they were watched all the time. He was wanted for the shooting of two Brits. It had been three years ago but they were still hounding him. If they caught him, he knew they had enough evidence from that one job to put him away for a good twenty years. That had been the one and only time he had allowed his temper to get the better of him and found himself laying into the dead body of a soldier he had just executed by a bullet in the back of the head. It had been the smug, self-satisfied smile on the Brit's face that had really touched a raw nerve inside McCook. He was stone dead but there he was, smiling away. A smile that was the manifestation of how superior the English thought themselves. His hatred of all things English boiled to the surface, annoyance changed to blind rage in the space of a few seconds. He savagely attacked the dead body, kicking and punching it. He kept it up until he was physically exhausted and the stupidity of his actions became obvious to him. Close to panic at his loss of self control, he fled from the flat, leaving behind the gun he had used to kill the soldier. The gun was plastered with fingerprints the Brits had taken from him during his six months in internment. It was a damning piece of evidence.

The episode had been a foolish, totally unnecessary mistake. But he was always quick to learn from his mistakes and he never repeated them. He quietly resolved to control his temper, to harness the aggression and make it work productively for him. To the people who mattered, he became an even more formidable figure. He was an ugly man with wiry red hair and a pug nose and a well-muscled body he kept in fighting trim. The small hint of madness he had displayed made him a legend inside the tight circles of the IRA.

There had been many jobs since that one, but they had all been much more tidy, much more professional. In twelve years he had been involved in no outright failures. He was firmly established as the IRA's most dedicated, most reliable operator. When a job needed doing they said, 'Give it to McCook,' and it was as good as done.

It was Friday night and Bob Stone was in a hurry to get home. He had been forced to stay late because of a derailment outside Dalmeny that had caused chaos by blocking the line in both directions just before a peak period. It had taken ages to reroute services until the line could be cleared and the backlog shifted. Stone had been sorely tempted to delegate responsibility to one of his junior managers and let him take care of the situation, as any of them was capable of doing. He had stayed on himself, however, because that was what was expected of him by his staff. They all regarded him as a diligent, if boring, workaholic who liked always to be in charge. It had been true of him in the past, but it was no longer. Now more urgent, more important things exercised his mind. He was careful not to show any outward change. His cousin John had advised him to carry on working exactly as he had always done. That was why he had felt obliged to stay on. Everybody had to be convinced that he was the same old Bob Stone, conscientious employee of British Rail. It would be soon enough that they would discover the truth about him.

Stone walked quickly along George IV Bridge, head down in his usual manner, paying little attention to what was going on around him. The street was relatively quiet with only a handful of people on the pavements. He was absorbed in thinking of the weekend and how he was to go to Glenrothes to check that the plane had been serviced properly. That would give him another opportunity to visit Kingsbank.

Something else had been troubling him slightly over the last few days. He was sure the anniversary of his first meeting with his wife Caroline was around this time of year but he could not remember when. He was not even sure if it was the sixth or seventh anniversary of that meeting. Her divorce lawyers kept trying to contact him. They sent him letters he ignored, and made phone calls he hung up on. In the beginning it had annoyed him, but he had persuaded himself that it was good to know that Caroline was still thinking about him. The last thing he wanted was for her to forget him.

A shadow fell in front of him. He stepped to one side to walk round whoever was casting it. The shadow moved with him to block his path. Stone looked up, stepping back the other way, ready to apologise for the confusion over who should give way. The man in front of him moved again to head him off. Stone found himself right up against the man's chest, his forehead brushed an unshaven chin. He tried to go backwards but the man had seized his arm and was forcing him sideways into a doorway, pressing him with his body against the glass. Stone's face was forced to one side. An unpleasant, musty smell came from the man's clothing. He could not see his face, but looking down he noticed that there were no socks under the scuffed suede shoes.

'Got any money for a cup of tea, pal?' the man demanded in a growling voice.

Stone tried to shake his head but could not move it. The glass of the door was cold against his cheek. Across the street he could see a group of youngsters walking past. If he shouted to them they would fetch the police, but he did not want the police. The police might ask awkward questions, might want to know why he had a model of Kingsbank Station in his briefcase; might want to know where he got the money to buy a plane; might insist on searching his flat; might want to know about his cousin in Ireland.

'Come on pal, give's the money,' the man growled. 'I've got a knife here in this pocket. I'll stick it in you.'

Stone felt something poking into his ribs. Panic began to well up inside him. He shoved a hand into his trouser pocket and it closed on half a dozen coins he did not know he had. The man was pressing against him so hard it was difficult to get his hand out again. It came away suddenly and the coins flew from his grasp, scattering on the ground. Stone immediately felt himself being released as his attacker went down on his knees to frantically gather them up.

Quickly regaining his composure, Stone stepped past him on to the pavement and began walking away. A woman outside the public library was looking at him curiously but he ignored her. His legs were weak with fear; his shoulder blades ached in anticipation of a knife thrust that never came. He did not once look back, just kept going, wondering how much it had cost him to save his life. Probably less than fifty pence.

When he reached the flat, Stone locked the door behind him and went straight to the bathroom to be sick. His whole body trembled uncontrollably as he retched again and again until there was nothing more to come up. Then he went to his bed and lay down.

The thought of how close he had come to dying at the hands of some drunk or junkie in the street in broad daylight terrified him. If he had died, his plan would have died with him. But he had survived, and he had not got involved with the police. He had handled the situation well, he decided. His cousin John would approve of the way he had done it, if he should ever tell him. John would laugh if he knew how little it had cost to ensure that the plan went ahead.

Eugene Pearson lay on his bunk in the upturned shoe box of a hut that had been his home for the past month. It was the coolest part of the day, just before darkness set in and brought with it the chill of an Arabian night. It was still hot enough for him to be wearing only a pair of shorts, ignoring the flies that buzzed incessantly round his head as best he could. He watched a huge spider scuttle up the wall, sit for a moment on the window ledge, then disappear. He turned over on to his back and stared at the low ceiling. With his left hand, he pulled the string that operated a simple cardboard flap to create a draught. The flies were blown away for a moment then they settled back round his head.

The Mukalla training camp in South Yemen consisted of about fifty white-plaster huts arranged in a rough square in scrubland at the foot of a small range of hills. They encircled two long wooden buildings with corrugated-iron roofs and a flattened expanse of cleared ground. There were four bunks to each hut but only about half were occupied by four Irishmen, twelve Arabs, eight Japanese, thirty-eight Africans, sixteen South Americans, two Dutchmen and three West Germans. Every person there was a committed terrorist, mostly young men thought highly enough of by their organisations to pay the fees for a six-week training course in basic technique. The food was greasy and the entertainment was non-existent. There was no drink and no women. Only a belief that they had been chosen to right the wrongs of an unjust world sustained the men.

The instructors were Cubans and East Europeans who shuttled by helicopter between Mukalla and the island of Socotra where another camp offered similar training. All lessons were conducted in English which posed difficulties for a lot of the trainees, but it was a strict rule. English was apparently the international language of terrorism.

Pearson had been taught to strip down and reassemble an AK 47 rifle blindfold. He learned quickly, unlike many of the others who seemed to have the greatest difficulty in grasping the simplest concept. He had thought he was pretty proficient at putting together bombs, but the Russian who specialised in that area was able to show him a thing or two. The psychological warfare training was not very ambitious, confined to things like don't let the hostages go to the toilet, don't let women hostages use make-up, kill any hostage who displays signs of a dominant personality. It was all pretty straightforward stuff that could be found in a dozen different text books.

Every day, in the early morning before breakfast, all trainees at the camp were required to attend an hour-long Marxist indoctrination lecture which took place in the open air before the sun rose too high in the sky. Speakers would stand on tables and harangue against the capitalist system and preach the imminence of world revolution. The Africans and the South Americans, in particular, responded like children in a pantomime audience, booing the villains, cheering the heroes. Pearson found it all faintly amusing. He always stood at the rear of the cluster of people and gave a few half-hearted cheers just in case anybody was watching him.

None of the IRA men had known each other before being chosen for Mukalla. Pearson was the only one from the Republic and he knew the others resented the fact that he was the son of Frank Pearson, a member of the high command. They believed he was there not because of what he had done but because of who he was. They were right, though Pearson would never give them the satisfaction of admitting it. He was not there on merit. His father had pulled rank to have him sent out. His father liked to relive his youth through his son. When he volunteered his son for a job, he was really volunteering himself.

A low chant began to rise slowly through the still air. Voices murmured harmoniously in a strange language. It was the Africans singing their revolutionary songs as they did every evening and every morning. Pearson swung his feet down to the ground and walked to the door of the hut. About forty yards away he could see the group of black figures squatting round a fire. Their song began to get louder, then abruptly stopped. A single voice sang out. The others replied in chorus. They stamped their feet in time to the rhythm, stirring up clouds of dust that hung like smoke around their waists. The song was about the crushing of tyrants and the imposition of a new order where everyone would live as equals, one of them had told him in broken English while his eyes shone like a little boy in an ice cream factory. A pile of burning wood collapsed in the middle of the fire sending a shower of sparks spiralling upwards. The chanting swelled to a peak, fell away and began again as a whisper.

Pearson lit a cigarette and looked up at the dark blue velvet of the sky. Stars appeared as he watched. Something passed through the bushes at the side of the hut. He went back inside and drank lukewarm water from a bottle, spitting most of it out on the floor. The previous day had been his twenty-first birthday. He had anticipated it eagerly, imagining that he would somehow be different afterwards. But he didn't feel any

67

different and the world outside was just the same as it had always been. It had been his brother Eddie's birthday as well. He had tried to get permission to use the camp radio to send some kind of message but they wouldn't let him. It didn't matter. The world would also be the same for Eddie today. Nothing would have changed for him.

Mrs Monica Pearson had an uneventful pregnancy. She did not show very much, certainly not as much as she had done for her three daughters. The doctors discovered she was carrying twins in the fifth month. No problem they said. The labour began right on schedule and the first baby was born normally within four hours. That was when things began to go wrong. The second baby was stuck in the birth canal and would not budge. Contractions continued and the doctors waited but after twenty minutes they were increasingly concerned and were forced to do an emergency Caesarian section to get him out. It took them another ten minutes to get him to breathe on his own.

The Pearsons were delighted to have two new sons after three girls. They called them Eugene and Edward and learned to tell them apart by the tiny strawberry birth mark almost hidden behind Eugene's left ear. The boys were identical twins. They had developed from the same egg which had split in two. Apart from the birthmark they were mirror images of each other.

Eugene was always the more lively and attentive baby. Suspicions that Edward had suffered extensive brain damage at birth were not fully confirmed for two years. Eugene was walking and talking by that time. Edward, who was all right physically, was still only able to lie on his back and stare upwards with largely unseeing eyes. It took him four years to be able to hold his head up and another four years after that to learn to walk. The doctors said that speech was completely beyond him. Edward was permanently locked into a world of his own. There but for the grace of God go you, Eugene's mother kept reminding him.

When Eugene was old enough to really understand what was wrong with his brother he became obsessed with what might have been. What if he had been the second child to be born, he asked himself What if their names had been changed round? Would that have made any difference? They had grown from the same egg, did that mean that Eddie was part of him? That he was part of Eddie? His young mind twisted this way and that in tortuous logic as he tried to make sense of it all, but everything always came back to the fact that he and Eddie shared the same blood. They were the same height, although Eddie was much thinner because he took hardly any exercise; they looked exactly alike, with thick luxuriant fair hair framing their faces. But a closer look showed the slack jaw and continual drool of Eddie, whose green eyes showed not the slightest spark of life.

As a teenager, Eugene spent hours sitting beside his brother telling him about what he had been doing, reading to him, listening to the radio with him. Frequently he would support Eddie's limp body with an arm round his shoulders and stand with him in front of the full-length bedroom mirror, trying to imagine just what was going on inside his brother's head.

Their father was a distant, domineering figure. He made little effort to get to know his children as they grew up but expected them to obey him without question. He ignored Eddie.

Eugene had an irrational fear of his father. He often found himself staring at his face while the family watched television in a darkened room, telling himself that this was the man who had given life to the two of them. His mother was different because he saw her every day, but his father was a far off, almost mystical person who held the power of life and death. He had chosen to make Eddie as he was and that terrified Eugene.

Frank Pearson was jailed for five years for possession of firearms when Eugene and Eddie were ten years old. Eugene, who knew all about the IRA and the words of all the songs, was shocked when he discovered that his father was a high ranking member of the Provisionals. His mother tried to hide the newspaper containing details of the court case but Eugene got hold of a copy and read it to Eddie that night. He was proud enough for both of them.

Eugene visited his father regularly in prison and saw his attitude change from one of lofty off-handedness to one of warm affection. Frank Pearson was realising that there was a lot of himself in his son. Eugene looked and behaved just as he had at that age. The instinctive rejection of both boys because of Eddie's handicap quickly disappeared and he even began to write letters to Eugene from prison phrased in a careful code that only father and son could fully understand. The new relationship between them grew stronger and stronger when the prison sentence was completed and as Eugene approached maturity. Eugene told his brother all about it.

Eugene's first job for the IRA was as a driver. He stole a car and picked up two men at a prearranged point. Then he drove to a quiet stretch of country road, following his instructions to the letter, and parked in the overgrown driveway of a derelict mansion house. At exactly the time he was expected, a man cycled past the end of the driveway. Eugene felt somebody tap his shoulder and, with his hands trembling, he turned on the ignition and slipped the car into gear. He swung out on to the road and accelerated past the cyclist who had been identified as an off-duty policeman. He cut sharply in front of him, knocking him off his bike. The man hurriedly staggered to his feet and began to run back down the road. There was the sharp crack of a pistol shot and hundreds of crows rose suddenly into the air from the surrounding trees, cawing frantically. Eugene watched transfixed in the rear-view mirror as the policeman fell forward on to his face in the road and writhed there. Two men appeared, one on either side of him. They kicked him and rolled him onto the grass verge. One of them grabbed his hair and pulled his head back, standing with one foot in the small of his back. The other pointed the gun. Another sharp crack and the shadows of the circling crows sweeping over the car. Then the doors were slamming shut, the car was rocking, he was being shaken by the shoulder, the engine was racing, and they were speeding away from the dead man towards the safety of the border crossing. His two companions congratulated him on his part in the job. He dropped them and dumped the car. Later he was terribly sick. The next day his father phoned him to say how proud he was.

The horror of the cold-blooded killing left a numbness inside him that did not wear off for weeks. He detested the mechanics

70

of violence. The sight of a fellow human being suffering pain or death left him as weak as a kitten. He controlled his feelings as best he could and managed to get by in half a dozen jobs with no one suspecting him, least of all his father. But all the time he was manoeuvring himself into a position that would keep him in the background. He decided the safest thing was for him to set himself up as an expert in bomb-making. It did not take him long to learn the basics about explosives and detonators. He showed genuine inventiveness. He made himself too valuable to waste on routine assignments. His father acknowledged the important contribution he made but Eugene sensed that he would have preferred an active, more glamorous role for his son.

At the age of nineteen Eddie had to be confined to a mental hospital. For a number of years he had been susceptible to occasional fits which meant that every muscle in his body twitched uncontrollably. It was frightening to watch but practically harmless until increasing co-ordination during the fits began to make him dangerous. He would batter his head against the wall till it bled. He would punch windows, smashing them with his bare fist. He would gouge at his own eyes with his thumbs. He would tip his head back and his throat would vibrate in a dramatically silent howl. He was committed to hospital after he broke his mother's wrist as she tried to calm him down.

The hospital was a depressing place with corridors peopled by weird figures from a thousand different nightmares. On his first visit Eugene found his brother in a room by himself, tied to his bed by wrists and ankles, and wearing a sort of padded crash helmet buckled under the chin. His bruised and blood-shot eyes rolled very slowly from side to side. Tears gathered like rainpools in the sockets and overflowed down the side of his face. The bandages on one arm were pink with seeping blood.

Eugene sat for hours but did not speak. There seemed little point now. He thought how the policeman who had been shot was lucky compared to the living death being suffered by his twin brother. He was ashamed of himself for not taking full advantage of his good health, for being so weak and unable to

71

fully satisfy the demands of a father who asked only that his son should follow in his footsteps.

After that, Eugene faithfully visited his brother for at least an hour every week, getting back into the habit of telling him about everything as if he could understand what he was being told. The month at the Mukalla camp had been the longest time he had gone without seeing him since he first went into hospital.

The large, empty room was almost completely dark. The heavy curtains drawn across the semi-circular space of the window alcove allowed only a very meagre grey light to spill round their edges.

Bob Stone sat in the corner of the room, his head and back supported by the angle of the walls, his legs straight out, feet pointing outwards, his hands resting lightly on his knees. His eyes were tightly closed. In front of him a model train, invisible in the darkness, was constantly circling on forty-four feet of track. An electric wire ran from the track connection to the gently humming transformer between Stone's legs and a thicker wire ran over his ankle to the plug socket in the wall. The railway track was laid directly on to the bare floorboards of the room. It described a simple oval with slight zig-zagging at one end to accommodate it all in the space. He had once owned a much more elaborate layout with papier-mâché hills painted green, and plastic trees, and an extensive station complex thronged with miniature people. But that had been destroyed and he had never got beyond the basic track in building up a new layout.

Stone liked to sit for hours in the darkness following the train by the low rumbling noise that accompanied it round the track. If he sat with his eyes open, he could follow it by the occasional spray of tiny sparks thrown out by the wheels. He preferred to keep his eyes shut. That way he could more easily imagine that he was controlling the train, that it was he who provided the energy to turn the wheels and drive the locomotive. He could imagine that he was in total command of everything that happened in the room, in the darkness. It was a pleasing sensation which gave him confidence for what he would soon be doing outside the room. He was flying to Dublin the next day. Terror and pleasure mingled in his blood at the prospect of what was to come. He wished he had done it years before.

The seaward wall of the tiny harbour was crumbling. Handfuls of small stones were being washed away on each swell of the incoming Atlantic tide as the sea surged and sucked and lapped against the wall. There was no moon, but a pale, grey light washed the entire sky and distant white horses rose and fell beneath the thin streaks of cloud on the horizon. On the finger of land stretching out from the south west coast of Ireland it was very dark, as if a black fog was hanging over it.

Big John Colquhoun leaned on the tumbledown walls of a ruined stone cottage which stood at the edge of the disused harbour. His hands were plunged deep into the pockets of his brown duffle coat and the hood was pulled tightly round his face. He was a large man, once muscular but now running to fat. Broken veins glowed on his ruddy cheeks. His small eyes were almost lost in the fleshy folds of his face as he narrowed them to look directly into the salt-tinged breeze.

Beside Colquhoun another man was squatting on his haunches, almost completely enveloped in a green quilted anorak. He too was staring out to sea and taking occasional puffs from a cigarette sheltered in the cupped palm of his gloved hand. A third man was standing out on the breakwater, within a few feet of the waves. His hair streamed back from his head, outlining a profile dominated by a huge Roman nose.

Behind the men, on the rough track of a road which petered out about ten yards from the harbour, sat a transit van and a Volvo estate car. Above them, on the brow of the hill which ran into sheer cliffs along the coast, were the patchwork lights of a little group of houses. All the curtains were firmly closed.

The man standing on the breakwater suddenly pointed out over the sea and shouted softly. John Colquhoun straightened up and peered into the lightening darkness. He made out a dark shape floating away from the corner of the headland lying to the north. As he watched, the shape gradually resolved itself into

73

an inshore fishing boat and the steady chug-chug of the diesel-powered engine became audible and began to grow louder. Colquhoun took a hand from his pocket and looked at his watch. The change-over had been completed and they were exactly on time. That had to be a good omen.

The rust-streaked sides of the small fishing boat slipped through the harbour entrance with only inches to spare. The engine noise died as she swung broadside on to the inside of the breakwater and nudged up against it. An old piece of sacking obscured the boat's name. Rubber tyres on the side squeaked as she rode the swell she had created in the calm water. Ropes were thrown up to be attached to ancient mooring rings at bow and stern to hold her steady. The deck was a few feet below the level of the breakwater.

There were about a dozen wooden packing cases laid out haphazardly on the deck. They had been transferred from the Liberian registered freighter which had brought them across the Atlantic from Boston at a rendezvous point twenty miles due west of the old harbour just over two hours previously. The freighter, now continuing its journey to Hamburg with an innocent cargo of timber, had also delivered Brian Heaney. He was standing in the door of the trawler's wheelhouse waiting for the deck to be cleared. The fur-edged hood of his anorak hid his face but Colquhoun was in no doubt that it was him.

Three men on the boat's deck began lifting the cases on to the shore. The scraping sound as they were pushed up on to the stone platform of the breakwater seemed inordinately loud. The transit van reversed slowly towards them, its rear doors propped open. The two men with Colquhoun began piling them inside. In all, the loading and unloading operation took slightly more than ten minutes with everyone working in total silence. As soon as it was finished the van doors were shut and it drove away, mounting the hill leading up and away from the harbour.

Heaney stepped forward from the wheelhouse, threw a bulging holdall up on to the breakwater and climbed after it. A tremendous feeling of satisfaction rushed through him as he stood up on dry land. He had been at sea for more than a month and had anticipated his arrival in Ireland as a starving man looks forward to a feast.

'Welcome home,' Colquhoun said as they shook hands.

'It's good to be back,' Heaney replied.

'No problems with the transfer?'

Heaney shook his head. 'Smooth as you like.'

'Is that all you have?' Colquhoun asked, indicating the bag.

'That contains all my worldly goods.'

The boat's engine revved up as the crew cast off and jumped back on board. The hull swung away from the wall and she nosed round to head out through the harbour entrance and off to the north. By the time it was fully light she would be working her normal fishing grounds. One of the men waved from the stern. Colquhoun acknowledged him.

'Not as good a run as I would have liked, a few cases of rifles but mostly ammunition,' Heaney said, picking up his bag and walking with Colquhoun towards the car. 'There are four automatic machine pistols though, special prototypes that aren't even on the American market yet. Deadly stuff.'

'That's good. But you're the most important cargo at the moment, Brian. Everything is well on schedule.' Colquhoun had an incongruous high-pitched voice for such a big man.

'When am I going to be let in on the secret?'

'As soon as I introduce you to the others. It will take us a good few hours to drive there. They'll be waiting for us.'

Heaney got into the passenger seat. Colquhoun took off his duffel coat and threw it in the back before squeezing in behind the steering wheel. He was wearing an open necked shirt. He had so many chins it was like a flight of steps leading up from his chest.

'Aren't you at least going to give me a hint of what I'm letting myself in for?'

'You'll know soon enough Brian. But I can tell you it's something really big. Really big.'

The car crested the brow of the hill and the undulating farmland spread out all around them. Daylight was just beginning to flood over it. The colours brightened as Heaney watched.

'I was beginning to worry that we were in danger of losing

momentum,' Colquhoun was saying, speaking more to himself than to Heaney. 'After the deaths of the hunger strikers what could we do to top it? The bombings went on, of course, and we would shoot the occasional soldier or policeman but nobody seemed to be paying any attention to us. We were pissing in the wind.'

The powerful car engine purred quietly as they drove rapidly along narrow country roads. The sun rose above the horizon. Heaney had to adjust the sunshade to keep it out of his eyes.

'The hunger strikers were great for us. They got us world-wide publicity. People sat up and took notice because they saw that men were prepared to die for what they believed in. The whole episode advanced the cause ten years at least.'

Colquhoun was becoming more and more animated. The car swerved across the road as he glanced sideways at Heaney. Heaney nodded approvingly, worried that he had been ear-marked for a suicide mission. He might have taken it on as a young man but he was too old to be a martyr now.

'I'm a great advocate of the spectacular gesture,' Colquhoun continued, his eyes on the road again. 'I think that things like the Harrods bomb do the cause more harm than good. It's cowardly to plant a bomb and then run away. I've always argued that. Ordinary folk see it as cowardly, that was why we had to issue a statement denying responsibility – for all the good that did us. There are too many stupid bastards working on their own, who don't seem to realise it's the ones who are blown up who are made out to be the heroes. It's about time we brought them into line again, began to exercise proper control.'

'You've been responsible for a few bombs in your time, Big John. So have I.'

'Oh bombs can be useful in maintaining a campaign of terror but we have to look beyond that. The Provos have always had more bombs than brains. You know that. And we can't all be hunger strikers. That could only ever be a short term thing. It became self-defeating because we let it go on too long.'

'Just as well you're not asking me to be a hunger striker,' Heaney said. 'Because I'm starving now. We had just about run out of food on that bloody boat.'

Colquhoun laughed. 'There are some sandwiches and a Thermos of coffee on the back seat there. Help yourself.'

'Thanks. I will,' Heaney said, leaning back to get them.

'Anyway,' Colquhoun went on, keen to tell his story. 'I was getting more and more depressed about the state of the Provos: too many splinter groups, fading public support, lack of co-ordination in everything we did do. Then, out of the blue, I got a phone call that was the answer to my prayers.'

'What?' Heaney asked through a mouthful of ham sandwich.

'It was a call from my cousin, Bob Stone. It was completely unexpected. We only ever get a Christmas card from him. That has been about the extent of our contact since his parents took him to Scotland when he was ten years old to get him away from Belfast. He's my mum's sister's boy.'

'What did he say?'

Colquhoun smiled secretively. 'I'll let him tell you that. You'll be meeting him soon. But I can tell you that when I heard what he had to say I immediately recognised it as a big chance for us. A chance we mustn't allow ourselves to miss.'

'A spectacular gesture?' Heaney suggested.

'Exactly. Something that will stir the imagination of the world. Something that will get us on every front page from here to China. Tell me, Brian, what is it that people admire most of all?'

'Well, it isn't your sandwiches.'

Colquhoun was being very serious. He ignored the joke. 'I'll tell you. They admire courage. They admire daring. They admire someone who puts his head in the lion's mouth. They admire someone who puts himself at risk deliberately in order to achieve something he believes in. It isn't bombers who slink away and hide, or snipers who pick off soldiers from a safe distance. It's the people who get right in there and risk everything.'

'This isn't a suicide squad you're putting me in charge of?' Heaney asked.

'No. Not at all. Because another thing people admire is the gambler who risks everything and comes out on top. We have to get away with it. That's all part of the plan.'

Heaney relaxed a little. The way Big John was talking was

getting him increasingly excited. The old familiar feeling of light-headedness that he always used to get during the run-up to a job returned. Big John was brimming over with enthusiasm. Whatever the job was, it had to be good.

'I hope your cousin can impress me as much as he seems to have impressed you,' Heaney said.

'I'm sure he will.'

'What caused the mysterious rush of blood to the head that turned him into a Provo radical?'

'That I don't know,' Colquhoun replied. 'I've only met him a couple of times and can't really remember him as a kid. He's very quiet, very shy. I think he went a bit queer when his wife left him. She ran off with some oilman. They lived in Aberdeen.'

'How old is he?'

'A little older than me. Mid forties. But his reasons don't really matter. He has come up with this idea, that's what matters.'

'There's a reason for everything but I suppose you're right. It doesn't matter if it isn't relevant. I would be better placed to judge if you would tell me what this is all about.'

'Patience, Brian. Patience.' Colquhoun was smiling again. He accelerated to overtake a slow-moving tractor. The car shaved the high grass verge. 'Only seven people know about this operation. Bob Stone, me and the other two members of the high command, yourself and the other two men who have been selected to carry it out.'

'Only three of us?' Heaney mused. 'Do I know them?'

'There's a reason for the numbers. You'll know John McCook.' Heaney nodded. 'The other one is Frank Pearson's boy, Eugene.'

'I take it his father chose him?'

'Each member of the high command selected their own man. You were my choice.'

'It's nice to feel wanted Big John. Thanks for the compliment.'

Heaney balanced the plastic Thermos cup on his knee and poured steaming black coffee into it. He sipped it and relished the bitter taste. McCook was a reliable professional. Frank

78

Pearson's boy could well be, too. He had to be given a chance.

Heaney's curiosity nagged at him, but he knew it was useless trying to get any more out of Big John. He would just have to wait. After seven years that should not be too difficult.

He held up the coffee cup so that the early morning sunlight through the windscreen made the plastic semi-transparent and sparkled on the smooth pink curves of his fingernails. The cup looked huge in his small hand.

He made a slight gesture towards Colquhoun. 'Cheers,' he said. 'Here's to success.'

Bob Stone had gone for an early morning walk. He had been unable to sleep at all during the night. Nervousness made him feel permanently sick. His armpits were damp with sweat. He was out of his depth, but he could not go back now. The men he was dealing with were ruthless killers. Even his cousin, Big John, for all his amiable nature was responsible for the death of God knows how many people. He had gone into this willingly. No one had forced him. But now that things were beginning to happen fast, the idea that had seemed so attractive when it had first occurred to him had become a heavy burden to bear. It had been foolish of him to contact his cousin, but he had been so angry at the time and the desire for some form of revenge on that bitch Caroline had blinded him to the consequences of what he was doing.

If only Big John had not answered the phone that night, by the next day his anger would have passed and he would still be the same ordinary man he had been all his life. He would have brooded about it, he would have cursed and swore, but eventually he would have got over it. It was too late for that to happen now. He was irretrievably committed. He was caught up in a chain of events of his own making and, like a swimmer being sucked down into a whirlpool, he could struggle for all he was worth but he could not break free.

A fresh wind ruffled the sparse grey hairs he had carefully combed over the crown of his head. His face was red; the eyebrows like two white chalk marks. He walked briskly, head down, along the avenue of tall trees leading up to the house they had brought him to last night. He had no idea where he was and he had no intention of finding out. There was nothing to be seen for miles around but fields and forests. By tonight he would be on his way home again. Then another few months and he would have to uproot himself permanently. When the time came he would have no choice.

The trees in the avenue were heavy with their summer growth. The high branches swayed in the wind. Birds sang among the rustling leaves. A thousand different smells competed for his attention. The regular tap of his metal-studded heels on the tarmac of the driveway fixed itself in his mind like a metronome. Wet grass stuck to the soles and the toes of his shoes. The morning sunshine quickly dried the footprints he left behind him.

He should never have married Caroline. It was obvious now. She had been completely wrong for him. She was far too young and far too attractive for a man like him. He had been astonished when she showed interest, almost incredulous when she agreed to marry him. The first night they slept together he could not stop himself crying silently as they lay together in the darkness after making love. He was thirty-eight and a virgin until then. Caroline changed his life totally.

Stone considered himself to be an unremarkable, boring man with few friends. He rarely went out, devoting all his energy to his work as a traffic controller for British Rail at Aberdeen Station. As a teenager, steam trains had kindled a love of railways that manifested itself in his adulthood by the creation of a sophisticated model train layout that took up an entire room of his Rosemount flat. Each week he allowed himself to buy a new addition for the layout. It was his only indulgence. He did not spend much money on anything else, only the necessities of life like food and clothes. He knew that the people at work thought of him as a rich miser, hoarding every penny he earned. It had long since ceased to bother him. He was content supervising the movements of real trains during the day and operating his immaculately maintained models at night.

Caroline was a secretary in his office. She had long red hair, rosebud lips and pale blue eyes. She wore fashionable clothes

80

designed to show off her figure and moved around in a cloud of perfume. He hardly noticed her at first and it was she who had to make all the running. She invited him for lunch, she hung around at night so they could be alone when he worked late, she brushed his fingers whenever she handed him a piece of paper. Suddenly, Stone began to realise what was happening. At first he dismissed it as wild fantasy on his part. Why should a girl like Caroline be attracted to someone like him? He felt it was vaguely ridiculous for him to entertain any hopes but dormant instincts were starting to emerge. He would try to work but achieve nothing because he was aware of her presence close behind him. Finally he took the plunge and accepted her invitation to have lunch. From then on she had him where she wanted him.

She took him with her to pubs and parties. She seemed to have hundreds of friends, all, like her, in their early twenties, all of them leading interesting lives. He felt uncomfortable with them and got the impression that they were all laughing at him behind his back, sneering at him as Caroline's sugar daddy. He was sensitive about it at first but quickly learned to shrug it off. After all, it was his hand she held so lovingly, it was him she went home with, it was him she slept with. Nobody else. They could laugh all they liked.

After a few months they got engaged and she wanted to get married straight away. He hesitated for some reason he could not quite put into words but she kept on at him until he gave in. They set the date to coincide with the eight month anniversary of the first time they went out together.

He was doing things he would never previously have contemplated because of Caroline's influence. She was always urging him to be more outgoing, to be more spontaneous. As a birthday present, she booked flying lessons for him. He was terrified at the prospect and the expense, but she urged him on and, to his great surprise, he found that he enjoyed it and quickly became addicted to it. He booked a luxury cruise on the Nile and arranged for her to have a credit card so that she could furnish the flat more comfortably.

Caroline had very expensive tastes. He thought she was spending too much on clothes for herself and too little on actual furniture but he did not challenge her over it. He told himself he was being too mean. He had always been reluctant to part with his money. Things had changed. Caroline was entitled to good clothes. He liked to see her in them. How could he argue? Even so, her extravagance worried him. He secretly opened a savings account and began to transfer his money in dribs and drabs. She had no head for figures and did not notice what was happening. Stone felt a lot better with a thick cushion of money in the bank.

She was, in many ways, just like a little girl. Often, when they were alone together, she would sit at his feet as they watched the television, or she would suddenly insist that they go for a walk together: just to see that the rest of the world was still alive, she would say. She had a childish fascination for pictures and stories about the Royal Family. She religiously cut them out of newspapers and magazines and stuck them in large scrapbooks. Her eyes would glow with excitement as she looked through her scrapbooks. He often teased her about her obsession but she was sensitive about it and quick to take offence, so he never kept it up for long. 'You have your trains,' she would say, 'and I have my Royal Family.'

There was no single turning point that marked the time when things began to go wrong with their marriage. The atmosphere between them gradually seemed to grow colder. She had no enthusiasm for doing things with him any longer. She began to go out more on her own, saying that she was with girlfriends. But unwelcome suspicions were already forming in Stone's head. When he proudly showed her his private pilot's licence, her display of congratulations was so obviously false it frightened him. She became sulky and withdrawn. She appeared to lose interest in sex and taunted him about his poor performance in bed. He could hardly say a word to her without being shouted down. And, like a fool, he meekly accepted all the insults and never answered back, worried that if he did she might perhaps leave him. He carried on as usual outside the home, giving no clue that anything might be wrong, but all the time he was fantasising about what he would like to do to her. He would like to slap her firmly on the face when she screamed at him. He would like to throw her on her back and rape her when she taunted him about sex. He would like her to obey his commands unquestioningly. It was all fantasy though. He knew it would never happen.

He came home one night after a long day at work with a thumping headache. He hung up his coat and threw down his briefcase. He went through to the bedroom to get his slippers and froze in the doorway at the sight which confronted him. Caroline was in bed with another man. Both of them were completely naked. The man was lying on top of her, his bare backside rising quickly up and down, the crumpled bedclothes wrapped round his ankles. She had her legs curled tightly round his waist and her hands were kneading at his hairy back. She saw Stone clearly over her lover's shoulder but she didn't show any surprise. Instead she just smiled at him, a smile like the one she gave as he had slipped the wedding ring on her finger the day they were married. She smiled and then she groaned softly. Her eyes rolled upwards to expose the whites. Her legs squeezed even tighter. The man snorted like a horse and then lay still. She looked back up at Stone and smiled again. The smell of them filled the room and all he could do was stand and stare as the pain inside his head steadily worsened till he felt sure his skull was about to burst. Then everything around him dissolved into a featureless blur and there was a cold wind in his face and cold air filling his lungs and he thought he would never be warm again.

He did not go home for three days after that. The third day he stood for five hours on the pavement opposite the flat to be certain she was not there before he would go in. She was long gone. She had taken all her belongings and everything that could be carried easily. As a parting gesture, she had ripped up the track of his model train set and smashed most of the carriages and equipment he so cherished.

He was seized by a fit of uncharacteristic rage that moved him to violence for the first time in his life. He grabbed a kitchen knife and went through to the bedroom to slash furiously at the mattress where he had seen them together, imagining all the time that it was their bodies under the flailing knife. His rage slowly died inside him as he ripped at the bed till he was left standing motionless, breathing hard, looking down impotently.

His anger curled up inside him and lay there heavily. He knew it would never leave him until he had worked out some satisfactory way of getting his own back on Caroline. The cruel bitch should suffer for what she had done to him.

He was offered promotion to traffic controller for the whole east coast system. It meant moving south to Edinburgh. He did not hesitate, glad to get away from the haunting memories of his old home. He bought himself a big Victorian flat in Edinburgh, choosing it because there was a large spare room just perfect for the layout of the new model train collection he was putting together.

He immersed himself in his new job, maintaining a polite off-handedness with his new colleagues, making no friends, preferring to be alone as often as possible. Night after night he would sit on the bare wooden floorboards of his spare room operating his trains; trying to resist the temptation to think about Caroline as she had been when he first met her; strangely soothed by the constantly circulating procession of electric sparks from the train wheels.

It was the night after a lawyer's letter arrived informing him that Caroline was instigating divorce proceedings that the germ of an idea formed in his head.

He ignored it for a while but it would not go away. It was like having somebody constantly whispering in his ear, urging him on. He studied maps, telling himself it was all an academic exercise, and checked details of past timetables. It was all so beautifully feasible. Everything slotted into place so very naturally, as if events had been leading up to the fulfilment of his idea in a logical sequence. The whisper in his ear became steadily more insistent.

He had never cut himself off from his Irish roots, making a point of going back to visit relatives every few years even after his parents had died. He had lost his early Irish accent but was proud of his origins and well aware that all his cousins were active IRA or Sinn Fein men. Big John, he knew, was a very high ranking commander. Stone supposed he himself was a Republican. He had lived such a reclusive life that the question had never really arisen for him. His new workmates in Edinburgh were not even aware that he had been born in

Ireland but he realised that it made him the one person in the country, probably in the world, who could successfully carry out the plan he had constructed so carefully in just over a week. His access to a man like Big John was the key. Other people could only dream about it, he could actually get it done. And when it was done he would like to see Caroline's face then. He would like to see what pictures she stuck in her scrapbooks then. The whisper in his ear grew into a loud voice, a voice he heard speaking over the telephone to his cousin in Ireland.

Bob Stone looked up as he rounded the final bend in the driveway and saw the house. It was a nineteenth-century mansion house owned by a rich businessman who had diplomatically gone abroad for a while, he had been told. An undulating lawn followed the drive up to where it curved round the front of the house. The warm sunshine on the dewy grass made it steam as if it were smouldering. Two marble lions guarded the bottom of the wide steps leading up to the tall arch of the main door. Stone felt his chest tighten slightly as he saw the car parked at the foot of the steps. Big John was back. That meant that all three men were now present. It really was going to happen. Caroline was going to be paid back in a way she would never dream him capable of. He licked his lips and swallowed hard as he began to walk towards the house. Revenge would be so sweet.

Bob Stone waited in what must have been the mansion's library. Two walls of the room were lined with books from floor to ceiling. The spines of the books were nearly all unbroken, indicating that they were there for show rather than for reading. Two large windows looked out over the front lawn to the trees beyond. A fire had been laid but not yet lit in the huge marble fireplace, above which hunting trophies and horse brasses vied for wall space. Chairs and sofas were scattered about the floor. A leather-topped desk stood in one corner beside the window with the line of sunlight slowly creeping over it. In the middle of the room was an oblong dark mahogany table holding the two neat rows of model buildings Stone had set up. He paced back and forward in front of it, stopping to check it every few minutes, opening up and then refolding the map that lay beside it. Everything was ready. What was keeping them? He was impatient to get on with it and terrified to begin. A turmoil of emotion was fermenting in his head and the most powerful emotion there was fear.

The door to the library swung open and Big John Colquhoun came in followed by three other men. Stone suppressed the urge to smile in welcome. He waited uncertainly, wondering if he should offer to shake hands.

'This is Bob Stone,' Colquhoun said to his companions. Then he turned to face Stone. 'This is Brian, John and Eugene. You don't need to know their second names.' He pointed to each man as he was named.

Stone was suddenly seized by a sense of the ridiculous. Big John looked just like a jolly fat man on a seaside postcard. The three men stood in a line like a queue for tickets. The feeling rapidly drained away as he studied their faces. He felt a coldness affect him as if he were being immersed in freezing water. These were dangerous men. Killers without consciences. They seemed to sneer at him with their eyes. The one with the scar on his cheek held his gaze and Stone swallowed repeatedly to keep his throat clear of saliva. If he could have walked out the door and gone home he would have done it. But they would not allow him to leave now. The sweat lying in the palms of his hands might just as well be blood. For the hundredth time that day he told himself that there could be no going back now.

Colquhoun directed the three men to seats and eased his own massive body into the high-winged armchair in front of the fireplace. 'All right, Bob,' he said. 'Let's have the full story. Just as we worked it out.'

Stone nodded. He was glad finally to have to do something. They were all watching him now, he could feel their eyes burning into him. For a brief moment he could see Caroline's smiling face float in front of him then he was back in the present and he could hear a strong, clear voice speaking. He was surprised to realise it was him. It did not sound like him at all.

86

Brian Heaney slept soundly towards the end of the journey and had to be shaken awake after the car drew up in front of the house. He was pleasantly surprised by the opulence of the surroundings, the antique grandfather clocks and the suits of armour in the high-ceilinged hallway. It was far superior to the smokey back rooms of terraced houses he had been used to in his day. He told Colquhoun as much. 'It belongs to a generous benefactor,' Colquhoun said. 'He likes to live dangerously by giving us the run of his house when he is out of the country.'

An elderly woman with snow-white hair cooked him scrambled eggs and toast for his breakfast. She and her husband, who acted as gardener and chauffeur, were the only domestic staff. They were both sympathisers. Heaney ate hungrily and washed it down with strong black coffee, a habit he had picked up in America. He had a shower and changed into clean clothes. Colquhoun came back to collect him and led him through the long corridors to meet the other two.

McCook greeted him enthusiastically, enveloping his hand in a giant fist. He had met him before apparently. Heaney did not remember his face but pretended to do so to please him. McCook fairly glowed with gratitude, like a faithful dog thankful for being remembered. Pearson was more restrained. He looked like a sullen teenager. His bottom lip pouted temperamentally. Heaney realised he would have to watch him carefully.

Colquohoun introduced Heaney as the leader of their little band. Heaney quickly established himself as the dominant personality by asking the other two about their IRA careers. He told them nothing about himself. His reputation went before him. McCook submitted readily to his dominance. Pearson did so grudgingly. The pattern was set.

They went through to the room where Bob Stone was waiting for him. Heaney knew at once that the man was terrified. He had about him the smell of fear, something he was well acquainted with. They all sat down in comfortable chairs and Colquhoun prompted Stone to begin speaking. Heaney listened carefully, never once taking his eyes off the man.

'My job involves coordinating the train timetables for the

east coast of Scotland. I am responsible for everything that moves between Berwick and Inverness.'

Stone paused to unfold the ordnance survey map that was lying on the table. He held it in front of him and indicated the east coast line.

'At the beginning of October one of the things that will be moving will be the Royal Train when it leaves Aberdeen to take the Queen and other members of the Royal family south to London. My idea is that we should hijack the train, kidnap the Queen and hold her to ransom.'

There was no reaction. They all sat there staring at him. He felt the blood rush to his face. Only Big John Colquhoun was smiling and nodding to encourage him to continue.

'The Royal Train has special adaptations which make such an attack particularly difficult. The Queen's favourite method of travel is by train and it is considered to be a vulnerable target so a lot of effort and thought has had to be put into security.

'For example, an ordinary railway carriage weigh about thirty tons. A Royal carriage weighs much more. They are specially built from thick toughened steel with windows of armoured glass. They are said to be bomb proof, missile proof and able to withstand the most modern armour-piercing shell fired at close range. They can be totally sealed off from the outside environment in case of a crash into water, or a fire or gas attack. They carry an independent oxygen supply . . .'

Colquhoun piped up excitedly, his voice even more high-pitched than usual. 'We might be able to derail the train but we could never get inside it. At the most we would shake Queenie up a bit. But that's the beauty of Bob's plan. Tell them, Bob.'

Stone waited patiently for Colquhoun to finish. He was aware that the man with the scar on his cheek was staring straight through him. He could practically hear the man's brain ticking over, seeking ways to ridicule the plan. But Stone was confident he had all the answers.

'The only way to get inside that train is to have it stopped somewhere with no security blanket like they have at Aberdeen Station before a departure. We need it to stop in the middle of nowhere. I can get it to do that.'

He pointed to an area of the map that was shaped like a dog's head. 'This is Fife and here,' his finger tapped the paper, 'is the village of Kingsbank. It is on the main Aberdeen to London railway line and has a quiet country station ideal for our purposes. Big John and I have chosen it carefully.'

Colquhoun nodded vigorously. 'It's perfect, perfect,' he said.

Stone turned to indicate the model buildings set up on the table. 'These models are an almost exact representation of Kingsbank Station. It sits on an embankment with a clear view of the track for at least a mile in both directions.'

Heaney pushed himself to his feet and walked over to the table. Stone heard him coming and did not turn round. He lined up the model train against the edge of one cardboard platform. McCook also stood up and came over to the table. Pearson leaned forward curiously in his chair to peer at the models. Colquhoun lit a fat cigar and sucked at it deeply.

'How do you get the train to stop?' Heaney asked.

Stone smiled nervously. 'As traffic controller I send a message to the driver instructing him to stop at Kingsbank. He will do so.'

'Why? Why should he? Will he not be suspicious?'

Stone's smile grew wider. He shook his head. 'The Royals traditionally go to Balmoral on Deeside for their annual holiday in the middle of August. They stay there until the beginning of October when they have to return to Buckingham Palace again. For security reasons no more than three of them can travel together at one time, and the reigning monarch and heir to the throne are never allowed to travel together. For the last week at Balmoral nearly all the Royal Family are at Balmoral. The Queen insists on it. She likes to have all her family around her. It is usually on Friday or Saturday they disperse depending on what their programme is. They have the choice of flying or using the Royal Train. The Queen always takes the train overnight to London. Five years ago she left Aberdeen on the Royal Yacht but that was exceptional. She always takes the train and likes to have at least one of her sons with her on the journey. Prince Philip as well. Two years ago the Prime Minister travelled south on the train. We cannot be certain who exactly will be on board but the Queen can virtually be guaranteed. Others will be icing on the cake.'

Stone silently thanked Caroline for her constant chatter about the Royals that had been impossible for him to ignore. If only she had known what she was doing at the time: setting them up nicely.

'OK, OK,' Heaney said impatiently. 'But why should the bloody train stop at Kingsbank?'

'Part of the tradition of the last week at Balmoral is that the princes should invite their current girlfriends to meet the family. It started with Prince Charles, Prince Andrew has continued it, and no doubt Prince Edward will, too, in his turn. That's fine. The boys bring home the girls to meet mum and dad, just like anyone else. But you know how any Royal girlfriend tends to attract Press photographers like flies round a cow's arse.' Stone had chosen the comparison as being suitably coarse for the company. 'The newspapers then begin to speculate on what her chances are of becoming a princess. It all grates on the Queen's nerves.

'So, when the time comes for the journey south the girlfriends are either smuggled out anonymously and flown or driven away. But now and then the Royal Train is asked to make a special stop to pick them up. They cannot board the train at Aberdeen because that is a public event, but a detective motors down the road a bit to a quiet station with no one around and the train stops for a moment before getting underway again. All this is worked out weeks in advance so the stopping place can be checked out by security men on the night.'

'We simply tell the train to stop at Kingsbank,' Colquhoun said from his chair. 'There is nothing suspicious about it. The driver won't be surprised.'

'The driver does not know he will be required to stop anywhere until he gets into the cab of the locomotive fifteen minutes before the departure time,' Stone went on, gaining confidence with every word. 'It is my responsibility to have a special stop order there for him if he is required to stop.'

Heaney studied the map, deep in thought. 'Kingsbank is pretty far to the south. Too far maybe?'

'No. Not really. It is just over one hundred miles. The train has been asked to stop in Fife previously. Then it was at

Leuchars station. A plane had flown down from Aberdeen with the girl and landed at the RAF base there. Kingsbank is ten miles from Leuchars. It would have been just as reasonable a choice.'

Stone pointed to the map again. 'This used to be the favourite rendezvous point. Laurencekirk, a station closed down in the Beeching cuts of the sixties. It still had serviceable platforms, if a little overgrown, until a few years ago when they ripped them out and demolished the place. Quite a few of Prince Charles's lady friends shivered in the cold there waiting for the train to arrive.'

Heaney nodded, shifting his attention from the map to the model buildings on the table. 'OK, so we get the train to stop,' he said slowly. 'You've made it out to be virtually impregnable. What good does it do us?'

'You're right, the train is virtually impregnable while it is on the move and while it is sealed,' Stone confirmed. 'But there is a way to get inside. We wait for them to open the door.'

Only Colquhoun laughed.

'It will be very late at night or very early in the morning,' Stone said, speaking quickly. 'Kingsbank Station will be deserted. There won't be a soul around. The driver and his mate are expressly forbidden to leave their cab while passengers are on board: security again. And there is no means of communication between the carriages and the locomotive.'

'No radio?' said Pearson.

'None,' Stone replied firmly. 'There are a few radiophones actually in the carriages but no direct link to the driver's cab. Usually when the train stops the place is crawling with police and security people. Plenty of people to wave it on. If the bodyguards travelling inside the train want to tell the driver to get underway again they are going to have to get out and go round and shout in his ear.'

'Why can't they just open a window and shout from there?' Heaney asked.

'The windows don't open.'

'They could use the radiophones to call in the local police,' Pearson suggested.

Stone swallowed hard. This was where he had to move from

91

hard facts to possibilities. 'That is true. They could do that. But I believe it is highly unlikely that they would take that course of action.' Pearson tried to interrupt but Stone kept talking. 'Think of the scene as the bodyguards on board the train will see it. The train has stopped unexpectedly in the middle of nowhere at some unearthly hour. It is as quiet as the grave outside. They cannot open the window to look forward and they know the driver can't come back to them. The reasonable assumption has to be that they open the door and run along to see what is happening. After all, in that situation what would you do?'

Colquhoun heaved himself to his feet and flicked the cigar butt into the fireplace. 'If they call out the local police and it's only a temporary delay the people on the train are going to look pretty silly. And the newspapers will inevitably find out and kick up the kind of fuss that the Royals hate.'

'It's human nature,' Stone said, picking up from Colquhoun. 'When the train stops their first thought isn't going to be that they are being hijacked by the IRA. They are going to think there is some kind of hold-up on the line ahead.'

'You said earlier that the train had absolute priority,' Heaney reminded him.

'It does. It does. But no system is perfect, far less British Rail. The Royal Train has been held up before now.' Stone suddenly realised he had made a joke and allowed himself a self-conscious smile. 'Not in the way we intend to hold it up, of course.'

'What happened then, when the train was stopped?' Heaney asked.

'It was a couple of years ago. A faulty signal north of Peterborough stopped the train. After five minutes the body-guards were out telling the driver to ignore it and carry on. He refused to move until the signal was at clear. I know this because the driver concerned was hauled up before an internal disciplinary tribunal where he won his case and ended up with a commendation for sticking to official procedure.'

Nobody spoke for a few minutes. Heaney was looking at the map. Pearson and McCook were fingering the models. Out-side, the gardener was standing on a ladder to reach the top of a tall hedge with an electric trimmer that buzzed like a wasp. A long orange flex stretched across the lawn behind him.

'No guarantees, Brian,' Colquhoun said softly to break the silence. 'But it will happen that way. If it doesn't you'll still have time to get out anyway.'

'A spectacular failure, eh?' Heaney said.

Colquhoun shrugged. 'Not so spectacular. But at least we'll have tried.'

'OK. I would open the door if it was me. I think it will happen that way,' Heaney said, looking over at Pearson. Pearson nodded in agreement. McCook did so as well.

Pearson said, 'Won't the bodyguards check with the driver before the train leaves Aberdeen in the first place?'

Stone felt a great sense of relief. He envisaged no other difficulties in convincing them of the competency of his plan. He knew he had all the answers.

'That can't happen,' he said confidently. 'The driver is not supposed to open the sealed envelope containing instructions for any halts until the train is underway. Security regulations again.'

'But supposing he does open it before they leave,' Pearson persisted.

'He won't. And even if he does, it does not matter. It is not unusual for the train to be required to stop as I have explained. He will think nothing of it.' Stone hesitated, then went on. 'The instructions in the envelope which will have been relayed by me will tell the driver to stop at Kingsbank. You three will be hidden at strategic points in the station.' He waved a hand over the models. 'It will be up to you to choose them when you actually see the station for yourself but, believe me, there are plenty of suitable places. Then, when a door opens, you rush it. Before you know it, you're inside . . .'

'Hold on a minute. It can't be as easy as that,' Heaney said. Behind him, McCook picked up the model train and nodded in agreement as he examined it. 'Suppose we don't get to the door before they manage to shut it again?'

'You will,' Stone said confidently.

'What makes you so sure?' It was Pearson's turn to ask the question. 'It doesn't look like a racing certainty from my angle.'

'I can be so certain because of the design of the train,' Stone replied. 'Remember I told you about the abnormal weight of the coaches, well the doors would be too heavy to open and close normally by hand. They operate on a hydraulic system which needs to go through a full cycle before it can be reversed.'

'What does that mean?' Heaney asked quickly.

'It means that when the train door is being opened it has to pass through one hundred and seventy degrees before the hydraulic system automatically cuts out. That takes approximately five seconds; five seconds to open, five seconds to close. There is no way of speeding up the process. Once the door begins to swing open there will be a period of ten seconds when it will remain open to some extent. The system can easily be jammed by inserting any solid object.'

'People can run a hundred yards in ten seconds,' Colquhoun said, spreading his arms wide to emphasise the words. 'It's an eternity.'

'We'll need to make it in the first five seconds when the door is fully open,' Heaney said softly as he traced his fingers along the cardboard platform. He looked up at Stone. 'And then?'

'And then you do what you have to do,' Colquhoun said, a great smile carving itself into his fat cheeks. 'And come home again.'

Stone continued, 'Kingsbank was chosen for two reasons: its relative remoteness and its proximity to a small grass airstrip at the town of Glenrothes. The airstrip is less than six minutes' drive away. We drive there and I fly you home.'

'You can fly?' Heaney asked. He would never have guessed.

'Yes,' Stone replied proudly, thinking that he had Caroline to thank for tying up all the loose ends of his plan so neatly. 'A few months ago I bought a light aircraft, a pretty ancient Piper Comanche, with a little financial help from yourselves. She is a little dented here and there and could do with a new coat of paint but she's in beautiful mechanical condition.'

Colquhoun interrupted. 'The plane is a four-seater with a baggage compartment which will take a nice bundled-up member of Royalty. I would have liked at least six of you on the actual job at Kingsbank but we have had to restrict it to you three –' he nodded at the three men in turn – 'and Bob here because it is essential that you all get away. This is no suicide mission. We don't want any dead heroes. What we want is the world sitting up and saying, "Bloody Hell it took some nerve to get away with that." '

'I have already rented a house beside Kingsbank Station,' Stone said after making sure that Colquhoun had finished speaking. 'You will stay there perhaps four weeks, perhaps longer. It will be around the beginning of October sometime but I will only have three days' notice so you must be ready to act quickly.

'Kingsbank is a small village with its share of gossips and nosey parkers. Your cover will be that you are employees of an electronics firm here in Ireland looking for markets for your goods in Scotland. Fife is a major centre for that kind of thing. Electronics people are coming and going all the time. Nobody should give you a second glance.

'From Kingsbank to Glenrothes it is a six minute drive. From the airfield at Glenrothes to the landing site John and I have identified just north of Roscommon it will be a two hour flight given ideal conditions, certainly no longer than two hours twenty minutes.'

Colquhoun's whole body seemed to quiver with excitement. His small eyes shone luridly out of the folds of fat on his face. 'The Brits will have barely had time to work out what has happened when you will be sitting with your feet up back home,' he said. 'What do you think, Brian? Sounds good, doesn't it?'

Everybody in the room watched Heaney as he walked round the table to view the model buildings from the other side. McCook replaced the train in the space between the cardboard platforms.

'It will be this side,' Stone corrected, moving the model over.

Pearson got up from his seat for the first time since Stone had begun speaking and examined the table carefully. Stone stood back reverentially to let him past.

After a few minutes of total silence Colquhoun spoke. 'Our propaganda boys will have a field day. We'll be on every front page from New York to Vladivostock. You just have to say the word, Brian.'

95

There were another few minutes of silence in the room then Heaney looked up from the models and nodded to Colquhoun.

'It sounds good,' he said finally. 'But there is one thing I'd like to ask Bob. Just to clear the air.'

Stone, who had been leaning with his back against the wall of books, stood bolt upright as Heaney turned his deep-set eyes on him, like a soldier coming to attention. 'Why are you doing this?' Heaney asked simply.

'All my life I've been content to let things pass me by,' Stone said quickly, the words pouring out in their well-rehearsed sentences. 'I've never really done anything of any great significance. I've always taken the easy way out, never caused anyone any trouble. I must have said sorry a million times. I decided it was time to stop saying sorry and make my mark on the world.'

As he listened to the words of his carefully prepared explanation Stone suddenly realised that it had become true for him. It had been Caroline who had started him off initially, who had shaken him out of his lethargy, but things had changed drastically since his desire for revenge had got the better of him. He had responded to her being unfaithful and to her needless, childish destruction of his cherished model railway layout with the unthinking instinct to retaliate in kind. What better retaliation than to hit back at her beloved Royal Family: provide her with a picture and story for her scrapbooks she would never be able to forget? When he first contacted Big John Colquhoun he had been frightened and the fear had held him in its tight grip ever since. It was a fear that often left him weak-legged and breathless but combined with it was an incredible feeling of exhilaration. He enjoyed the danger. It made his life more vivid, more intense. Now he was standing in a room a few feet from a professional killer and he could almost have cried with the joy of it. He craved fear like a drug.

Heaney held out his hand. 'Welcome to the real world,' he said and Stone felt their skin come together. A sharp thrill of pleasure shot through him. Now he knew why he had deliberately put on a thick Irish accent when he had rented the house at Kingsbank. There had been no need for it but he had done it, glorying in the association with the infamous IRA. And there had been the secret smiles he was unable to suppress when people looked at him in the street or at work: people who thought him to be the same self-effacing, inconsequential person he had always been; people who were blissfully unaware of exactly what he was capable of. And there was the ever-present, stomach-churning fear that had begun with the first stirring of the idea in his brain as he watched the circling electric sparks from the model train: the fear that he would be found out; the fear that one day he would be brought to heel like a misbehaving child.

But it wasn't like that. He wasn't a child. The world outside had no idea of what was being plotted in this house. He was the architect and now he had handed the plans over to the professional builders. He couldn't stop it happening now even if he wanted to. Caroline would soon be pasting a new story into her beloved scrapbooks. He shivered at the thought of her and anger seethed to the surface out of the conflicting mass of emotions swirling inside him. He imagined Caroline looking up at him over the stranger's shoulder and, with a great effort of will, he imagined himself returning her smile.

Heaney was relieved to feel the old hunger for action begin to burn inside him. All the way across the Atlantic, cooped up in his tiny bunk on the freighter, he had been dogged by an almost overpowering sense of weariness and detachment. He kept thinking that he had grown too old and too soft to return to his former life. His reflexes had been dulled by too much good living in America, too much drink and too many women. He no longer hated as he used to do. He was no longer driven by primitive instincts that required him to kill as dispassionately as a thirsty man will drink water. He had lost his commitment to the cause. But as he listened to Stone outlining his plan, the strange lethargy of the sea crossing lifted from him. He felt refreshed and invigorated, as if he had just plunged his head into ice-cold water. It sounded good, it felt good. He could hardly wait to get started.

As Heaney began questioning Stone closely on the detailed working of the plan, he noticed Stone had hands even smaller than his own. Hands not like a woman's, but more like those of a little girl.

Heaney's questions tried to anticipate every eventuality. Stone had a ready answer for every one. Occasionally Pearson threw in a question. McCook and Colquhoun sat on the sidelines and watched. The more he heard, the more Heaney's enthusiasm for the job grew. He was eager to see this Kingsbank Station for himself so that he could work out positions and angles and escape routes and vantage points. Already he had a picture of it in his head, created from the model buildings on the table and Stone's painstaking description. It looked like a familiar place, somewhere he had seen before. He shrugged off the feeling.

The housekeeper knocked politely at the door and called them to lunch. The questioning continued over the meal and into the afternoon when they went back into the library. It was late evening when Stone was finally allowed to leave.

Heaney was satisfied apart from a few niggling worries. He was not too happy about Stone, a rank amateur, being in at the kill. He would probably panic when the shooting started so he would have to be confined to the driving and the flying, no more. There were no question marks over McCook but Pearson was a different matter. Heaney didn't like the look of him and suspected he was in the team because of who he was rather than what he could do. The points he had put to Stone had been useful and constructive, however, and perhaps the boy deserved to be judged less harshly. They were stuck with him anyway, so they would just have to make the best of it. Heaney silently decided to keep a close eye on him. Then there was the actual frontal assault on the train door as it swung open. Stone said the platform was twelve paces wide. That was a lot of ground to be covered; a lot of time in the open. He would have to consider very carefully the best way to tackle that problem. And he doubted very much if they should bother with hostages, even if one was the bloody Queen of England. No, it would be much easier and safer just to kill anything that breathed inside the train, corgis and all.

The job itself was a beauty. The Brits would choke on the news of the Queen being blown away in their own backyard.

The world would look on amazed and enthralled by the most spectacular of gestures.

Eugene Pearson quickly realised that Stone's plan was not as crazy and wild as he had first thought. Kidnap the Queen? Every punk cutting his teeth for the cause came up with that idea. But none of them had the means to deliver. That was the ingredient which made Stone so special.

His heart sank but he was careful to maintain an outward façade of enthusiasm. He had hoped the thing would be so outrageous he could have pulled it apart, but Stone had an answer for everything. Pearson grudgingly admitted to himself that he was impressed, even if he did believe that any attack on the Royals would be counter-productive in producing a backlash the like of which would make the Black and Tans seem positively benevolent. He could not actually voice his beliefs because such talk was considered defeatist and almost treacherous. All he could do was go along with the scheme. After all, it was his own father who had volunteered him and he could not disappoint his father. It was a high risk enterprise: death or glory. He doubted if his father really cared which as long as it was one or the other.

Pearson had been depressed since returning from the training camp. His brother, Eddie, was as bad as ever. He just lay still all the time showing the whites of his eyes, all yellow and lined with veins. A shake of the arm or a slap on the cheek would bring the eyes rolling down into place momentarily but they were filmed over, dull and lifeless, like every other patient's in the God-forsaken place. He might just as well have been dead and buried. The doctors said they had to keep him heavily sedated to prevent him from injuring himself. Every pill that went down his throat was like a spadeful of dirt into his grave.

Pearson suddenly felt very cold as he thought of his twin brother lying in that hospital bed. The doctors kept him drugged to stop him hurting himself. He smiled ironically and held a hand up to his face to hide it from the others. No one was going to drug him to stop him being part of the elaborate plan that he was helping to construct. No one would try to stop him from doing something which inevitably carried a good chance of him ending up dead. Who was the real mental defective then?

He shivered at the thought of his own mortality and wondered vaguely what he would have been doing now if he had not been born in Ireland, or what he would have been thinking if *he* had been brain damaged at birth instead of Eddie.

Each person, it seemed, had his own destiny. It stretched out, prepared in every detail, just like Bob Stone's plan. Pearson could only hope that he was destined to survive. If not, what could he do about it? His eyes surveyed the cardboard buildings of the model station on the table and he imagined himself to be standing on one of the platforms, a toy for the pleasure of other people, to be moved here and there as they saw fit, and utterly powerless to stop them. He was a child of his father and of his country. That was the way things were. He had to accept them.

The small market garden occupied just under three acres of land in the hills fifty miles south-west of Dublin. Its perimeter was clearly marked on three sides by a tall, untidy hedge and on the other by a row of mature trees whose branches were all tangled up in each other. The two-storey house was set in one corner. It was a rambling affair with a fairly modern extension at the back which had added two bedrooms. In the corner of the market garden diagonally opposite the house were two old railway carriages. They had originally been put there as kennels when the owners had bred labradors, then another owner had used them as hen-houses. Now they lay derelict and unused with their wooden frames rotting, all glass gone from the windows, and what little paint remained flaking off in large patches.

Daniel Grogan had taken over the business from his father eighteen months previously after serving three years for possession of explosives. He had been completely legitimate since coming out of prison, forsaking all his old friends and concentrating solely on growing his carrots and cauliflowers. It pleased his wife that he was no longer on active service and he had his four daughters to think of as well. He wanted to see them grow up. He had already missed enough. The youngest was nine, the eldest sixteen. Beautiful girls they were, all blonde curls and bright smiles.

It was because of them that Grogan had thought twice when Big John Colquhoun had contacted him asking for the use of the place as a safe house for a while for himself and three men. Of course, he knew he could not refuse. The hesitation lasted no longer than the time it took to draw breath to say yes. Big John had used the house before – a long time ago when Grogan's father had been living there. He remembered the old railway carriages. They hadn't been knocked down or anything like that, he asked. No, Grogan replied, he had been meaning to do something about them but had never got round to it. Don't do anything until we get there, Colquhoun said cryptically.

Grogan's wife did not argue. She never argued about anything to do with what she called official business. She just nodded silently and made arrangements to take the girls to stay elsewhere during the specified period. She stocked up the freezer and the drinks cupboard and left Grogan to it.

It was late at night when the headlights of a car swept over the living-room walls and woke Grogan from the doze he had fallen into in an armchair. He rushed to the front door. He had been waiting patiently for them all day and was in time to open the driver's door of the Volvo estate as it drew to a halt.

'How are you, Danny?' Colquhoun enquired as he hauled his massive bulk out of the narrow door. 'This is Brian, John and Eugene,' he added nodding at the others as they got out of the car. 'Your guests for a while.'

'Glad to have you all,' Grogan said, acknowledging each in turn and suddenly breaking into a wide smile when he saw Heaney. He went quickly round the car and grabbed his hand to shake it firmly. 'Brian Heaney, it is. Well, Mr Heaney, do you not remember me?'

Heaney studied Grogan carefully. The man was of average height and build, with jet black hair, greying at the temples. His face was deeply lined and gave an impression of great age. Heaney did not recognise him at all but out of politeness pretended to be thinking hard. As he did so, Grogan pressed his

101

finger against the back of Heaney's hand and cocked his thumb like the hammer of a pistol. 'Hands,' he said, smiling hugely. He pointed his hand down at Heaney's knee. 'Knees,' he said. Then he pointed his hand up at Heaney's forehead and let his thumb fall to the horizontal position. 'And Boomps-a-Daisy.'

'Of course, of course,' Heaney said. 'Danny Grogan. You were with me a few times'.

'That's right. How long ago is that now? Five years is it?'

'Seven years. A long time. You look older, Danny.'

'I'm the father of four daughters. You would look older too.'

Colquhoun interrupted them with a hand on Grogan's shoulder. 'I didn't realise you knew Brian, Danny. It's supposed to be a strictly first names basis.'

'Sorry about that Big John, but you know you can trust me,' Grogan said. 'I worked under Brian Heaney in one of our interrogation teams. I was only with him about two weeks before he had to leave the country with the Brits breathing down his neck.'

'Quite a coincidence us meeting up like this so many years later,' Heaney said, feeling unaccountably disturbed by Grogan's friendly greetings. He still could not place him. There had been so many back up boys, always there, almost always efficient and reliable. He could not remember them all, but they would probably remember him. He did not like people having the advantage on him. He liked always to be in control of what was happening around him.

'If you'll all come into the house now,' Grogan was saying. 'I've got food and drink if you're hungry, and your rooms are all ready.'

'Anyone else here?' Heaney asked, asserting his leadership.

'Just me and the cats,' Grogan replied good-humouredly, holding out an arm to indicate the front door. McCook and Pearson led the way towards it carrying the bags from the rear of the car. Colquhoun and Heaney followed with Grogan falling into step beside them.

'You went to the States then?' Grogan said as if talking to himself.

'No questions just now, Danny,' Colquhoun cut in sharply. 'You should know the rules.'

102

Grogan nodded and held a finger to his lips to show that he understood. When he took his hand away he cocked his thumb pistol-fashion again and pointed his finger at the side of his head. 'Boomps-a-Daisy,' he said, laughing out loud at the memory. 'That was a good game. You should have seen them shivering in their boots and crying for their mummies.'

'I saw them,' Heaney said, beginning to enjoy Grogan's adulation. 'Every one was a born loser.'

'That's right. Every one but the last one.'

'What do you mean?' Heaney asked, turning to face Grogan from the doorway and almost forcing Colquhoun against the wall.

Grogan stepped back, surprised at the reaction. 'The last one in the barn. His friend went Boomps-a-Daisy but we only had time to drop him in the hole with the bloody soldiers swarming round us. They found him.'

'You're sure?' A strange sense of fear passed over him and he had to breathe deeply so that it wouldn't show. It doesn't matter, he told himself. It was seven years ago. Who cares now? 'I always thought of that last one as dead,' he added.

'No.' Grogan shook his head. 'He's alive. At least he was then. They took him to the Belfast Royal to patch him up. Their was some talk of sending in a man to finish the job in case he was able to identify you. But with you baling out for the States and him not having seen any of the rest of us, it was decided to forget him. I don't know what happened to him after that. He certainly was a lucky bastard, I'll say that for him.'

'The only survivor,' said Heaney, embarrassed that he should have taken the news so seriously and trying to make light of it now. 'He ruined my average. I always aim for one hundred per cent efficiency.'

'It's history now,' Grogan said with a shrug of his shoulders and a half step forward that got all three of them moving into the house.

'You don't remember his name, do you?' Heaney asked.

'Too long ago,' Grogan replied with a shake of his head. 'Why? You planning to look him up some time?'

It was Heaney's turn to laugh. 'No. But just in case I ever do run across him, I'd like to know his name.' He held up his forefinger and thumb in the shape of a pistol. 'Then I can finish the job properly.' He dropped the thumb and smiled at Grogan. 'Boomps-a-Daisy,' he said.

The next day Heaney was quick to forget about Grogan and the one soldier who had got away from him and concentrated all his attention on the job in hand. He had been thinking about nothing else since the meeting with Stone. Using the model station, he filled out the outline of the basic plan, working out positions and strategies and deciding what weaponry they needed. McCook was the kind that would go along with anything provided all the thinking was done for him but Pearson threw in a few useful ideas. In particular, Pearson came up with the idea of a flame-thrower. The original intention of rushing the train door with all guns blazing carried quite a high risk that maybe one of the bodyguards would be able to struggle back inside, maybe even get the door shut behind him or get himself into a position where he could do a lot of damage. The flame-thrower solved that problem. It would burn up everything in front of it. It was not as selective as a bullet. None of the guards would have a prayer against it.

At first Pearson had had difficulty getting the mechanics of the thing right and Colquhoun had to call in the help of an engineer to get it operating properly. The trouble was maintaining a pressurised flow of petrol to get an adequate reach with the flames. The final result was a fearsome machine that could spit a tight bunch of flames almost thirty yards. When they hit a target, the fire splashed outwards like a bucketful of water hitting a wall. Pearson said he had seen a flame-thrower like it demonstrated at the Arab training camp he had attended. It looks as if it was money well spent to send him there then, Colquhoun had commented.

It was September. There was a week to go before they were due to take up residence in Kingsbank to await the call to action. Colquhoun had decided to bring them to this particular safe house after weapons training sessions in the remote west of Ireland because he knew about the old railway carriages that would allow Heaney to put his theories into practice on a lifesize scale.

104

The old carriages lying in an overgrown corner of Grogan's neatly-cultivated market garden were several feet shorter than the Royal coaches but exactly the same width. Heaney paced out the length of Kingsbank Station platform beside them, trampling down the long grass as he went, and worked out where the station buildings would stand in relation to them. He put McCook towards the front, Pearson approximately in the middle, and himself at the bottom end from where the actual locomotive would stop. They all crouched down in their allotted places as if they were hiding from someone in the ramshackle shells of the old carriages.

Colquhoun sat watching them from the rear of the small pick-up truck Grogan used to deliver vegetables to local hotels. He sat on the very edge of the back platform and his weight tilted it very close to the ground. His short legs were splayed in front of him, his heels were dug in to prevent him slipping forward, his hands rested on his knees. He chewed on an unlit cigar. The elaborate pantomime unfolded in front of him and he used his imagination to project the happenings into the near future when it would no longer be a rehearsal, and when it would most definitely be for real.

All three men rose at the same time on Heaney's shouted command. Pearson stood his ground, holding the imaginary flame-thrower. McCook and Heaney began moving in towards him.

According to Stone, the Royal Train would consist of the locomotive and five carriages. There were occasionally extra carriages, never fewer. The first carriage was where the bodyguards ate and slept. The second was a sitting and dining area for the Royals, and the third was divided into their sleeping accommodation. The fourth was used by equerries and ladies-in-waiting and any administrative staff that might be travelling. The final carriage contained the kitchens and beds for the chef and other servants lower down the pecking order like the footmen.

A corridor ran the entire length of one side of the train, the side that would be towards the south-bound platform at Kingsbank. That corridor was sectioned off by doors in the middle and at each end of the carriages. The doors were merely

105

firestops and could not be locked. There were no windows in the interior walls separating the corridor from the living quarters in any of the carriages. The exception was the last carriage with the kitchens where the corridor was wider for half the length and there was a large hatch in the wall for passing out the food. The doors into the interior compartments were electronically operated and flush-fitting. According to Stone – and there was no reason to doubt him – the thick steel forming the exterior of the carriages was considered to be a sufficient barrier to any possible exterior force that might reasonably be brought to bear on it. As a result, the interior walls were a mere two inches thick and the access doors were half of that thickness to allow them to slide open and shut. A medium size explosive charge placed at the weakest point, where the door rested against the frame, would have little difficulty in blowing it apart. Heaney would carry five charges with detonators, each one capable of blasting a door open. McCook would carry the same amount of explosive as a back-up.

Because there was no radio link between the train drivers and the people on the train, someone – one or more of the bodyguards – would have to get out of the train to tell the drivers to get going again. According to Stone, there was no chance of the drivers and the bodyguards getting together to compare notes on the journey before leaving Aberdeen because the security procedures demanded that the drivers were settled in their places at least fifteen minutes before departure time. In the cab was an envelope which was not to be opened until the train was underway. The envelope contained details of any stops to be made during the trip, the details having been forwarded by telex to Edinburgh and on to Aberdeen using a code number known only to the security services and senior controllers who had to alter timings of other trains if necessary.

The one assumption in Stone's plan was that the bodyguards would come out of the train. It seemed inevitable because it was inconceivable that the train driver would take it upon himself to leave the station without being ordered to continue. That could only be done by the spoken word. When the bodyguards

106

emerged it was likely to be from one of the doors at either end of the first carriage. That was why Pearson was positioned directly opposite where that carriage would come to a halt. Whenever the door began to swing open, that was the sign for action. Pearson would send a jet of flames in through the opening and burn up anybody standing there. Meanwhile, McCook would take out the drivers by shooting them, or lobbing in a grenade if the side window was open. The locomotive's windscreen was an ordinary one and not armoured in any way like the carriage windows. Heaney would put a metal bar in the door hinge to jam the hydraulic mechanism. Pearson would go into the train and smoke out anybody who might be in the corridors. Then he would come out and cover the doors while Heaney and McCook went in and blasted their way through to the big prize. Then it was turn and run for the night flight back home.

Heaney was looking over at Colquhoun and giving the thumbs up sign. Colquhoun returned the gesture. Heaney, McCook and Pearson returned to their positions and crouched down again. Practice makes perfect, Colquhoun thought.

Everything was arranged. They were leaving at the end of the week by fishing boat which would put into Oban, ostensibly for repairs to her engines. There was no check at Oban on who came or went by the fishing boats. It was a simple way into the country. All the equipment would follow in another fishing boat a few days later to be picked up from a Glasgow address at their convenience.

Stone did not expect the Royal Train to be in operation until at least three weeks after their date of arrival, but it had been decided – Colquhoun had decided – that Kingsbank was the best place for them to be. They could get familiar with the lie of the land, make any changes in plan that might prove necessary. And, in the event that the train left early for some reason, they would be ready and waiting. Kingsbank was the back of beyond. No one would recognise them. They might be conspicuous in the house there, but it was only for three weeks. If they kept their heads down, people would gossip but they wouldn't do anything. It would probably be the biggest excitement in the village for years to have three mysterious

107

Irishmen living there. By the time the real excitement started they would be long gone.

Colquhoun noticed that Danny Grogan was standing behind him at the side of the truck watching what was happening round the railway carriages.

'How are you, Danny?' asked Colquhoun. 'Did you sleep well?'

'I did,' he replied. 'I trust you did yourself. I'm sorry to disturb you, Big John, but I need the van here.'

'Of course. Of course,' Colquhoun said, shifting his feet to get into a position to rise. Grogan came round in front of him and helped pull him upright. The little pick-up truck bobbed on its springs like a cork surfacing on the water once it had been relieved of Colquhoun's weight.

'Is it a mail train they're going to rob then, Big John?' Grogan asked in a matter-of-fact tone.

'No it's not that. And I told you, no questions, Danny.'

'I can't think of what else it could be,' Grogan continued, ignoring the implied warning.

'You'll known soon enough,' Colquhoun said, getting drawn into the conversation despite himself. 'The whole country will know soon enough. The whole world will know soon enough.'

'It's to be a big job then?'

'The biggest,' Colquhoun confirmed, warming to his theme. 'The most spectacular gesture.'

'I hope it goes well,' Grogan said seriously.

'It will,' Colquhoun said. 'We've thought of everything. Nothing can go wrong.'

Part Three

AUTUMN

It wasn't a secret any more. The whole village knew that Kathy Manders had moved in to live with Jim Anderson. Her husband had not been seen for months and no lights burned in the empty windows of the old manse at night. She drove Anderson's car. She went into his house laden with shopping bags. A few weeks ago they had announced it to the world by going hand in hand to the lounge of the Station Inn for a quiet drink. People smiled to their faces and whispered behind their backs. It was the best scandal the village had seen since the minister's daughter got herself pregnant and had to get married. There were some who believed that Jim Anderson had been responsible for that scandal as well.

Jock Shaw did not look up as he pushed the change and the single ticket to Edinburgh through the gap in the ticket window which was cracked down one side and held together by brown sticky paper. Anderson took them and walked out of the narrow wooden corridor, where his footsteps echoed hollowly past tattered railway posters at least ten years out of date, to emerge into the soft evening sunlight on the north-bound platform at Kingsbank Station.

He saw Kathy standing on the other side; her arms were folded tightly under her breasts; a large suitcase was at her feet. The stiff wind funnelling through the station moulded her thin dress against her body, outlining her legs and hips. Her blonde hair floated around her face. Occasionally she put up a hand to brush it back. He reached down to rub his knee.

She was going south to her parents' silver wedding. She had pleaded with him to go with her but he had resolutely refused, not only embarrassed at being the cause of her marriage break-up but also reluctant to travel far away from his home for any length of time. Morbid thoughts had been troubling him with sickening regularity recently. He could not kiss Kathy on the lips without remembering his ordeal in Northern Ireland and once, when he was digging out the roots of a dead rose-bush in the garden, he had been mesmerised by imagining what it was like to be laid to rest in the earth. That had really shaken him. He was aware of the physical weight of the soil on his chest and the shadows flickering over his field of vision became the soil being tossed down on top of him.

His grave was waiting for him. Bought and paid for, it lay undisturbed in the village cemetery: plot number 1176. It was topped with lush green grass and sprinkled with white and yellow daisies which hid the cold, forbidding slice of ground in which he would lie like a stone. He could not bear the thought of being cremated like his parents. Heat and flames terrified him.

Kathy had taken the decision to move in with him. She had not asked him. She had simply arrived one night and had not left the next day. She had taken his car up to the manse to collect her clothes and a few personal odds and ends. She had organised a domestic routine and had hot meals on the table when he returned home from work. He took her for a weekend at a remote Perthshire hotel, signing them in as Mr and Mrs Smith. In bed she was tireless and inventive. She constantly told him that she loved him, leaving a heavy silence hanging in the air as she patiently waited for the response that never came.

He was glad when she came to live with him. He had wanted to suggest it for a long while but had never been able to. The words always stuck in his throat, held back by some half-acknowledged, semi-conscious fear. It was the same thing which stopped him telling her just how much he loved her. It was as if he were a policeman charged with the duty of informing her about the death of her lover. He knew it was irrational to look at it like that. He knew that one day he would have to tell her, but that did not make the telling any the easier.

He looked across at Kathy where she stood on the platform

110

and was not surprised to feel his insides churn because of the intensity of his love for her. The few months they had spent living together as man and wife had flown past at lightning speed. Their relationship seemed to him to be gaining momentum, flinging the days behind them like mud off a spinning wheel. He ought to tell her he loved her. He ought to ask her to marry him. There was no logical reason why he should not do so. But a thousand other reasons prevented him.

Anderson ignored the signs commanding him to cross the line by the subway under the bridge and lowered himself down on to the pathway of old wooden sleepers that ran over the stony bed supporting the double lines of railway track that rested on modern concrete sleepers. The edge of the south-bound platform came up to his chest. It took him two attempts to swing his bad leg up on to the surface and push himself clumsily to his feet. He brushed the dirt from the palms of his hands and limped over to Kathy.

She took the ticket from him without a word, staring past him at the swaying branches of the mature trees towering above the ticket office and the derelict stationmaster's house. It had been a long, hot summer and the leaves had only just turned to their autumn colours of red, yellow and brown. They bobbed and weaved in the wind. Handfuls broke away like spots of paint tearing free from an unsettled canvas.

'It is such a shame that beautiful things have to die,' Kathy said.

'Yes. But don't they die gloriously?' Anderson said in a rare moment of open emotion inspired by the swirling heads of the trees. Trees that were already steadily casting off their leaves to stand thin and emaciated like skeletons throughout the winter.

Kathy looked at him curiously. Anderson shifted uncertainly under her gaze. He had not meant to speak out loud. That was the kind of thing he thought but never said. He searched around for some way to change the subject. He saw the deep black shadow of the old parcel-office canopy had spilled over the edge of the platform and was creeping imperceptibly over the stones.

'I used to stand here every Saturday night about this time

111

waiting for the train from Dundee to deliver our batch of *Sporting Posts*.' He spoke quickly, recalling the childhood memories with great pleasure. 'I took them round to the newsagents and got one free for my trouble.'

Kathy smiled indulgently. She liked to hear about his past. She seized on the tiniest scraps of information and repeated them to him weeks later.

'There is a loose flagstone somewhere about here. Yes, this is it.' He stood on the corners of a flagstone and tilted it one way, then the other. It rose and fell a couple of inches each time. 'I used to stand here as a boy and rock back and forward watching for the train to arrive. They were steam trains in those days and you could see the firebox glowing miles down the track, long before you heard the huge steaming monster.

'It would pull up here with a lot of hissing of steam and grating of metal on metal, and the guard would lean out and toss a bundle of papers on to the platform and I would tuck them under my arm and run off round the corner with them. I was always down the steps and away before the whistle went and the great monster got going again.'

Kathy laughed and held out her hand to him. He stepped off the loose flagstone and stood close up against her. She kissed him on the tip of his nose.

'This station is pretty famous, you know,' he continued. 'The train that fell off the end of the Tay Bridge in the disaster there last century stopped here. The local minister got on it. Just imagine, he stepped off that platform over there. Pretty exciting, eh?'

'Fascinating. Absolutely fascinating,' Kathy said and kissed him again. He squeezed her hand tightly. The wind whipped her hair against his cheek.

Jock Shaw came out of the side door of the ticket office pulling his cap down firmly over his forehead. He scrambled inelegantly down on to the sleeper pathway and up again at the other side. He nodded briefly to Anderson and Kathy and went to stand at the gate at the top of the steps, studiously ignoring them.

Anderson saw the train approaching in the distance. The evening sun glanced off the metal tracks and left them

112

shimmering like the strings of a musical instrument. The train grew rapidly as it approached in complete silence then the rails began to sing and there was the whine of the diesel engine and the metallic screeching of the brakes. He bent down to lift the heavy suitcase.

One person got off the train. Mrs Wilson smiled benignly at them both as Kathy held the door for her to descend and then got in herself. Anderson placed the suitcase in after her. She swung the door shut and pulled down the window.

It was a three-carriage train with a driver's cab at the front and rear. She had got into the last carriage, the last door. The smell of hot oil and diesel fumes rose around them.

'See you in a couple of weeks then,' Kathy said, leaning out of the window to rest lightly on her elbows. There was a gold chain with a small, oval locket round her neck. It swung freely, casting a sharply defined shadow on the skin above the low-cut neckline of her pale blue dress.

He kissed her softly on the cheek and she touched the back of his hand. The train started off with a jerk and he stepped back from the edge of the platform. The train drew clear of the station buildings and the sunlight suddenly smacked against its side, flashing and sparkling on the glass and metal as it gathered speed on the mile-long, level straight leading to the south. It seemed to grow smaller, as if it were deflating like a burst balloon, rather than get further away. Its shadow rippled along beside it, falling away down the steep slope of the embankment. Anderson shaded his eyes to watch it as far as the distant cutting where the embankment petered out and where it disappeared like a swimmer diving under the water. Almost at exactly the same second as it disappeared he saw another train emerge and begin to approach, swelling slowly in size from its toy-like proportions.

He was suddenly aware of Jock Shaw at his shoulder and wondered how long he had been there. Each separate grey hair standing out stiffly on the old man's jaw seemed to throw its own individual shadow across the lower half of his face.

'Your ladyfriend's away then?' he asked unnecessarily, moving off at once.

'She'll be back,' Anderson replied defensively, watching Jock

113

Shaw scramble down on to the sleeper pathway and hurry across to the other side to be in position to meet the oncoming train. By the time he had got to his feet on the opposite plat-form Anderson had walked to the top of the steps curving down to street level. The railway lines were just beginning to sing to announce the imminent arrival of the train as he went down, leaning on the iron handrail to take the weight off his bad knee.

Brian Heaney stepped down from the train as it rolled to a halt at Kingsbank Station. He pushed the door shut behind him and his eyes automatically began to rove around the features of the station that had grown so familiar to him over the past six weeks.

He was standing on the north-bound platform facing the entry and exit corridor where Jock Shaw stood waiting to check his ticket. He was the only passenger to disembark. To his left, the boarded windows of the old stationmaster's house were beginning to take on the same colour as the smoke-blackened stone surrounding them. The derelict house jutted out, narrow-ing the platform, and towered above the single-level of the wooden ticket office. He knew that the house had been built on to the side of the embankment and the foundations were at street level. A garden marked out by a rotting fence hugged the base, still retaining the impression of a geometrical pattern despite being long-abandoned to the wild.

To his right, connected by the ceiling of the ticket office corridor, was a symmetrical single-storey building with a rusting iron sign designating it as a ladies waiting room. At the edge of its roof a brick chimney stack rose, incongruously tall. Three chimney pots were at the top, one lay on its side like a giant bird's egg in a nest. Beyond the waiting room was the parapet of the bridge hidden behind a picket fence, stained brown with creosote. The platform itself stretched out a few yards beyond the bridge before sloping down to the railway track. A rectangular concrete box containing telephone and power cables followed the track into the distance, the patch-work fields of the valley flattening out on either side. In front of the buildings the platform consisted of large flagstones, worn and uneven after many decades of travelling feet. Moss and grass had established themselves in some of the cracks. At the outer edges, past the bridge parapet and past the old house, the platform was made of hard-packed ash except for the stone lip which overhung the track bed.

Heaney turned casually as the train moved out of the station. His eyes swept rapidly over the opposite side. The platform there was almost identical except that it was shorter and did not extend beyond the bridge before sloping down sharply. There were four ornate gas lamps, matched by four on his side, spaced out evenly along its length. They had long since been converted to electricity. They glowed yellow in the soft evening haze but were always turned off when the station was locked up for the night. The drivers of trains knew to use the third lamp as their checkpoint for stopping the locomotive when driving a three or four carriage train.

There was a continuous row of what seemed to be three separate, self-contained units: a waiting room, a parcels office, and an unidentified set of rooms offering no clue to their original purpose. Only the waiting room was still used regularly. The doors to the other two were secured with large padlocks, grown rusty over the years. Three chimney stacks on the roof threw long, narrow shadows down on to the wooden canopy which reached out to cover half the breadth of the platform and was supported on thin pillars. The canopy had a fussily carved fringe which hung downwards like folded curtains waiting to be unrolled.

Heaney's concentration dwelled momentarily on the padlock holding the double doors of the former parcels office. Letters engraved on to the opaque glass of the windows on either side of the doors declared its function. It had taken them almost three hours a few weeks ago to prise off that padlock and gain access to the place without leaving any obvious marks. The inside had proved to be completely empty apart from a solitary chair and a bad oil painting of Wexford Bay, of all places, screwed to the wall. It's as if they want us to feel at home, Heaney had joked. His grandmother came from County Wexford. The floor was smothered in thick layers of dust.

115

When they walked over it it seemed to rise around them like millions of tiny flies. Pearson would wait in there with the flame-thrower.

To the right of the row of buildings, opposite the fourth lamp, was an ugly square block of undressed brick without a roof. It was a basic urinal with a shallow earth ditch leading out through a hole in the bottom of the wall on to the embankment. The ground around it was permeated with the stink of urine. McCook would be there.

To the left of the waiting room door was a waist-high wrought iron gate. It stood open at the top of the steps from the street. Between that and the point where the picket fence started on the parapet of the bridge was what had once been a narrow flower bed. There were no flowers in it now, instead an untidy jumble of grass and weeds climbing halfway up the low wall at the back almost totally obscured the whitewashed stones, grey and flaking, that spelled out the station's name. In the small space between the far edge of the flower bed and the beginning of the fence was an old bench with iron legs moulded into the shape of lions' feet. The back and the seat were made from wide planks of wood, rotted at the ends as if an army of mice had been nibbling away. Behind the bench was a four-foot tall electrical junction box which stood out a little from the wall. It was there that Heaney had decided to conceal himself as the train approached. He would be ready for anyone who tried to escape from the rearmost carriages.

Heaney took only a matter of seconds to complete his survey of the station. He had done the same thing almost every night for the past three weeks, usually in the early hours of the morning in the darkness, standing waiting for his eyes to grow accustomed to the gloom after climbing up the embankment. It was like a film set and he half expected a steam train to come puffing through at any second. The only thing that detracted from the impression was the abundance of little, oblong blue and white signs carrying the station's name. They were bright and modern and were screwed to almost every available flat surface, contrasting sharply with the dowdy paintwork peeling off the wooden window frames and the carved canopy with ancient birds' nests occupying several convenient corners.

116

The sun reflected into his eyes off the grey-slated roof of the ticket office. The trees rustled in the breeze beyond it. Dust swirled above the ash at the ends of the platforms. Jock Shaw stood waiting for him, waistcoat unbuttoned, cap tipped back on his silvery hair. Heaney handed him the ticket and nodded curtly as he went past, his footsteps cracking like pistol shots on the wooden floor of the exit corridor. It was best not to get friendly with the locals. They would not be here much longer now.

Heaney had been to Edinburgh to meet Stone. He could have phoned him but he preferred to make contact personally, just to check. The man had been as nervous as a schoolboy on his first date. They had rendezvoused in Princes Street Gardens and joined the tourists straining their necks to look up at the castle perched on top of its massive rock. It would not be long now, Stone whispered dramatically. Nothing definite yet, but probably this weekend. Confirmation would come tonight or tomorrow. He would phone immediately. He was sure it would be this weekend. It was October. It was time.

Stone was a weak link in Heaney's carefully rehearsed sequence of events. He was an amateur they were being forced to play in a professional game. His early wariness about Pearson had been misplaced, he now admitted. The boy had shaped up well. He was keen to get the job underway. He had proved himself in the short training sessions they had held. But it was different with Stone. He looked and acted unstable, as if he was on the edge of a nervous breakdown, and would bring them all down with him if he cracked. Yet he was indispensable. Without him they could not stop the train. Without him they could not fly out of the country. They had no choice but to rely on him. Heaney studied the little man carefully as he stared up the castle. The lump in his throat bobbed up and down in his scrawny neck. The collar of his shirt was dirty. The man was fraying at the edges. They could only pray he could hold himself together long enough to deliver the goods.

Heaney went down the station steps and out on to the pavement. His blood fairly tingled with anticipation as he forced himself, with a conscious effort, to think positively. Stone would deliver. For his own reasons, he wanted the job to

117

happen successfully. The reasons had taken him this far. There was a tough streak in the little man. He would deliver.

The doorway of the pub opposite was wedged open. The lights inside burned fiercely in the gathering darkness. He could see people moving at the bar. His mouth was dry. He would have liked a drink but he had made the strict rules of no fraternisation with the villagers. They had hired a car in Glasgow, paying cash for a month in advance, and used it to travel to outlying towns with big, anonymous supermarkets where Jesus Christ himself would not rate a second look even if the blood was still dripping from the holes in his hands.

He and McCook had gone down to Glenrothes one evening for a few drinks. That had been a mistake which would not be repeated. McCook's appearance was too distinctive for comfort with his shock of carrot red hair. Heaney had felt they were being watched all the time. They had not stayed long.

Tonight they would repeat the journey but only to check on the timings of the various routes to the airfield. All the equipment they needed had been smuggled across the water and dumped in a lock-up garage in Glasgow. It had been arranged for them to pick it up there themselves so that none of the couriers knew its ultimate destination.

Back in Ireland, Big John Colquhoun was paranoid about secrecy. He was seeing traitors and new supergrasses in his sleep. Only a handful of people actually knew what was going on and there was no let up in activity in the six counties. One soldier had been shot dead and another seriously wounded by snipers in Belfast. An IRA man had been killed when an ambush on two policemen in Londonderry went wrong, and a planted tip-off had got rid of some sweating gelignite that was more dangerous than it was worth. All this had happened in the last seven days. There was to be no lull before the storm.

The firearms had been taken apart, cleaned, oiled and reassembled hundreds of times since arriving at the house. There were the automatic machine pistols Heaney himself had brought back from the States. They took a magazine of fifty-four soft nosed bullets and, with their integral silencers as quiet as a baby's cough, were a real joy to handle. Compared to them the .357 Magnum handguns were cumbersome things,

118

but just as effective. The explosive was split up into two pound blocks the size of cigarette packets and wrapped in greaseproof paper. There were twenty blocks and twice as many detonators shaped like pencils. There were two dozen Bulgarian-made grenades, supplied with special chest harnesses with clips to hold them.

The most unwieldy part of the armoury was the custom-built flame-thrower. Pearson had shown a great talent for its use during their arms training sessions, though McCook had tried to muscle in on him. Pearson could send a concentrated tongue of flame through the centre of a car tyre from thirty yards, almost without singeing the sides. Given that kind of accuracy any target only ten yards away would be like aiming at a barn door. So Pearson got the job. When the Royal Train's door swung open he would roast the bastards alive, burn neat holes in their guts and let them watch themselves fry. Once the heavies had been eliminated, Heaney and McCook would move in to do their part. Heaney had decided that the idea of hostage-taking was no longer feasible. It was to be hit and run. That shortened the odds even further in their favour.

The gate to the house was stiff. Heaney had to use his foot to kick it open and then two hands to push it shut behind him. He frowned at the wilderness of the garden. It could conceivably attract curiosity by its very untidiness when the one next door was all short grass and nicely-dug borders. They couldn't work in the garden themselves because, in a small village like Kingsbank, that was almost an invitation to the locals to stop and chat. Heaney had considered getting the halfwit who did all the work next door to come and do theirs. There would be no danger in that. He couldn't even talk properly. They were supposed to be Irish businessmen using the house as a base to establish contacts for their electronics firm in Scotland. Perhaps businessmen like that would get their garden seen to. Heaney decided that if they had to stay beyond the weekend he would get something done.

The sycamore tree overhanging the boundary hedge was shedding occasional leaves in the light breeze, like pieces of dandruff being brushed off its shoulders. They spun down to land across the doorstep. Heaney kicked a pile of them to one side. He noticed McCook's hairy face grinning at him from a corner of the living-room window. McCook had grown a straggly beard that was deeper red in colour than his hair. It made him look more conspicuous than ever. He had tried to dye his hair black but the stuff sprouted out of him so quickly the roots were red again before twenty-four hours were up.

This would definitely be his last job, Heaney told himself as he had been doing since first setting foot back in Ireland. He would probably end up back in the States. It would not take him long to pick up the threads of the gun-running operation. Younger men could take their turn to have their moment of glory. He was getting too old. It would be better for him to go out at the peak of his powers. Besides, after knocking off the Queen of England everything else had to be an anti-climax.

It was Pearson who unbolted the door and stood back to let him in. In the living room McCook was slouched comfortably in an armchair in front of the television set watching a video film.

He was naked from the waist up. Blue tattoos twisted their way up both his arms. On his right shoulder the snarling head of a leopard looked as if it was bursting out from under his skin. Beside the chair a stack of video cassettes in black boxes had fallen to one side and lay in a line along the floor. Pearson bolted the door and came into the room behind Heaney. He stretched out on the sofa, feet on one arm, and resumed the paperback book he had been reading.

'Any messages, Cookie?' Heaney asked.

'None,' McCook replied without looking away from the film. A woman was spreadeagled on a bed, wrists and ankles tied to the posts. A man was standing over her fondling the barrel of a gun suggestively. The woman's eyes were wild with fear. She thrashed uselessly from side to side. It was the kind of film McCook enjoyed.

The living room was sparsely furnished. There was just the sofa and two old armchairs and a table with three straight-back chairs. On the table was a half-empty milk bottle, a crumpled bag of sugar, and a teapot encircled by three mugs. Everything is done in threes, Heaney thought. Just like the three bears, that's what we are.

On the film the woman was being raped clumsily and noisily.

120

McCook had turned up the sound to get the full benefit. Heaney realised that he had not had a woman since the prostitute Colquhoun had supplied the night before they left Ireland.

There was a scrap of carpet in front of the gently hissing gas fire. All the curtains were drawn despite the lightness of the evening and the bare bulb hanging from the centre of the ceiling was not strong enough to dispel all the shadows crowding along the top of the walls. Pearson had to squint closely at his book to be able to read it.

There were three bedrooms, two upstairs and one downstairs. They were the only private places they could retreat to when the others began to get on their nerves. It had been claustrophobic living together so closely for three weeks. Each of them had to have some privacy. The kitchen door led directly off the living room; the tins of food on the shelves gave the kitchen a splash of colour that was lacking everywhere else but the television screen.

The telephone was balanced on the mantelpiece, one third of it sticking out. Heaney picked it up carefully in two hands and put it on the floor. He stared at it, willing it to ring. 'No calls, I suppose?' he asked. Nobody answered. There was nothing to do now but wait, he reminded himself.

'How about something to eat before we go down to the airfield, Eugene?' he asked, this time making it clear he required an answer.

'Sure,' Pearson said, folding down the corner of the page and getting to his feet. 'Hamburgers and beans do?'

'Fine.'

'How about you, Cookie?'

'Fine. That'll do.'

Heaney watched Pearson go to the kitchen. The boy always went without complaint; always did exactly as he was told. The son of Frank Pearson might reasonably be expected to be a little big-headed, or at least think himself above making the tea all the time. Not young Eugene Pearson though. Heaney sat down in the spare armchair. McCook was engrossed in the film, sitting on the edge of his seat, rocking back and forth, his hands clasped tightly between his legs. On the screen the rape was

121

over. The woman, still tied to the bed, was smeared with blood. The man was standing over her fondling the gun again. He pressed the barrel against her forehead. Heaney nodded approvingly. He fired. The camera zoomed in on the resulting little round hole, smoke rising from its blackened edges. Very realistic, Heaney thought. And the entire back of the skull would disintegrate as well from that range.

'There's one of them,' said Pete Guthrie, pointing through the open door with his walking stick. 'One of your neighbours, Jim,' he explained.

The five men in the public bar of the Station Inn followed the line of the pointing stick to watch as the man came down the steps from the ticket office and stood momentarily at the bottom looking across at the pub. Anderson turned round and moved to his right to get a clear view. Daft Davie shuffled to the door and peered suspiciously round the side of it. Digger, drying glasses at the sink behind the bar, leaned sideways from the waist to see him. Even Pete Guthrie's grey-muzzled mongrel, lying peacefully at his feet, lifted its head and seemed to be looking too.

'Haven't seen that one before,' Anderson said, shaking his head slowly. The man was standing in shadow. His face was a black smudge. 'Mind you, there might be half a dozen of them living there and I wouldn't know about it. They're certainly keen on keeping themselves to themselves.'

'That's one of them,' Pete Guthrie insisted. 'I've seen him driving around with the red-haired one that looks like the wild man of Borneo. And there's a young lad who never leaves the house, and an older man who visits regularly. He's the one Mrs Beaton rented the place to. Doesn't stay there himself, though.'

'You been spying on them, old Pete?' Digger asked jokingly.

'I just keep my eyes open,' the old man replied, his nostrils flaring proudly. He placed the tip of his walking stick back on the floor between his legs and rested his hands on top of it. 'And if you ask me there's something funny going on in there.' He took a drink of his whisky and sucked thoughtfully at his top lip. 'Something funny,' he repeated slowly.

Anderson had hardly noticed his new neighbours. They had

not disturbed him once since they moved in and anyway he and Kathy had been too wrapped up in their own problems to bother with strangers. He turned round to face the bar, shrugging his shoulders. It was none of his business.

'What do you mean, Pete?' prompted Donald Williamson in a voice that tailed off in a hacking cough. He took a draw of his untipped cigarette to cure it.

'Well, you know what Irishmen are like,' Guthrie said steadily as he opened the tin of tobacco on his table and began rolling himself a cigarette. 'Put two of them together and they'll start plotting something.'

He noticed that Anderson had unconsciously begun to rub his knee. 'You of all people should know that, Jim. After what they did to you.'

Anderson felt his face turn red. He gripped his glass more tightly. He refused to be goaded. Why did they always have to bring that subject up?

'He's right you know, Jim,' said Williamson coming over to the bar to get another drink. The skin around his face was a mass of deep wrinkles, so deep they looked like cuts. His fingers were knotted like willow twigs. Christ, I don't want to grow old, Anderson thought suddenly.

'You lot are getting as daft as Davie there,' Digger interrupted. 'What the hell are they plotting in Kingsbank of all places? Tell me that. Well?'

He gave Williamson his drink and hitched up the metal armbands on his sleeves. Pete Guthrie carefully licked the edge of his cigarette paper and rolled the finished product between thumb and forefinger. Daft Davie had pricked up his ears at the sound of his name and come away from the door, allowing it to swing shut, to stand beside Anderson at the bar. Williamson had a coughing attack on his way back to his seat and had to steady himself against the fireplace before sitting down.

'Lots of things,' Pete Guthrie said confidently. 'They could be plotting lots of things.' He struck a match, lit his cigarette, then held the burning match between two fingers and flicked it with his thumb to put it out. The flames immediately disappeared to be replaced by a thin spiral of white smoke. He threw it on the floor.

'Such as?' Digger persisted, going back to drying glasses. It was Wednesday night and the lounge was closed. The voices echoed through its empty space.

Pete Guthrie placed his cigarette in the corner of his mouth and returned his hands to their position on top of his walking stick which had been lying against his waist. 'Lots of things,' he repeated.

'They're probably building a guided missile in the back garden. Going to aim it at Buckingham Palace,' Anderson said sharply. Digger laughed. Daft Davie smiled hugely. Williamson coughed.

'Why don't we send Davie round to ask them just what they're up to?' Digger suggested. Daft Davie brayed like a donkey at the mention of his name.

'You mark my words. There's something funny going on there,' Guthrie said quietly to himself, effectively ending the conversation.

Digger turned his full attention to Anderson. He refilled the whisky glass without being asked and gave Davie a tonic water. Anderson paid for them. 'You going on this shoot on Saturday morning then, Jim?' Digger asked as he rang up the money on the old-fashioned till that still recorded the amount in shillings and pence.

'I suppose so,' Anderson replied off-handedly. 'I've looked out my shotgun and bought a couple of boxes of cartridges.'

'I got an invitation from Lord Drummey himself. He's a member of the licensed trade association; owns the Highfield Hotel.'

'You'll be with the top party then. My boss will be with you. I'll be following behind with the gamie's bunch. We'll pick off what you miss. Bert says it's been a good year: still plenty of birds, and hares as big as ponies.'

Anderson was not really concentrating on what he was saying. His thoughts were on Kathy and how much he already missed her. What would it be like for him after a few weeks? Loneliness sucked at him like quicksand, pulling him down towards depression. He fought it half-heartedly. Time would pass more quickly if he kept busy. He should never have let her go.

124

Daft Davie was holding up his empty glass. A vast smile, all teeth, enveloped his face. Anderson nodded and handed over the money for another drink for him. Davie waggled his ears in appreciation.

'That's your reward for doing my garden,' Anderson said in an attempt at humour.

'He made a fine job of it,' Digger said.

'Aye, but it will need a few more times before the winter.'

The small talk petered out. Digger went through the back to change a beer barrel. Anderson found himself staring at the side of Davie's head, watching the skin around his eyes twitch as if it had a life of its own, and the thick lips moving constantly up and down over the yellow and brown teeth. He smelled the faint hint of dampness that always seemed to hang over him. It struck Anderson that, apart from Kathy, the poor blighted creature standing beside him was the only person in the world that he felt any affection for. It really mattered to him whether Davie lived or died, probably more than it mattered to Davie himself.

An express train thundered over the bridge and through the station. The spirit bottles on the shelves rattled gently together like a crowd murmuring quietly in anticipation of a great event about to unfold. Jock Shaw would be closing up the station for the night soon. Then he would come down into the pub and spread the story about Anderson's woman leaving that day. He would have to be gone by then, Anderson decided. He couldn't face that.

All the old men had gathered round Pete Guthrie's table. His dog had been forced to move. It was lying on its side in the fireplace, legs sticking out at right angles, dead to the world. They were talking about their favourite subject: the last war and the fact that the youth of today hardly knew they were alive. Anderson did not consider himself young. Kathy was young. But to them he was a little boy. Everything is relative, he thought.

'The trouble with young folk today is that they've never had to fight a real war,' Pete Guthrie said imperiously, the cigarette in the corner of his mouth bobbing up and down in time to the words. 'A real war, I mean, not a flea-bite like the Falklands or

125

a dog's breakfast of a thing like Northern Ireland. A real war where your entire way of life is under threat, where it's kill or be killed, survive or perish. That's right isn't it, Jim?'

Anderson made no reply. He could not admit to them that he agreed with all that was being said. When he had just joined the army he had often lain awake at nights hoping that a war would break out, a real war where a young boy would quickly become a man. He had been young then, young and eager, anxious to prove himself. But he still thought the same way all these years later, despite all that had happened to him. When the task force had sailed for the South Atlantic, he had been immensely jealous. He longed to go with them. He longed to be young again, to be given another chance. He threw back his glass of whisky and rapped on the bar to attract Digger's attention.

'Every generation needs a war to teach them what the world is all about,' Guthrie was saying. 'Young folk have had it too easy. They're ungrateful bastards because everything is handed to them on a plate.'

If there had been a war, Anderson thought, perhaps he would have been killed in battle. Perhaps they would have been talking about him. 'Remember young Jim Anderson?' they would be saying. 'Killed in the war. Brave lad, young Jim. None finer.' And then they would toast his health. Anderson toasted himself and drank the nip of whisky in one gulp. Digger gave him a refill.

Of course he had had his chance, he couldn't help thinking. He had had his chance and been proved wanting. His time in Ulster had cured him of his glamorous vision of the soldier's life, and also cured him of his glamorous vision of himself. There was no bravery in him. He had watched his best friend die. He had wanted him to die so that he might be saved. There had been no question of self-sacrifice when it came to the crunch. No hesitation in making the choice to save himself. He was a live coward, not a dead hero. And he was glad that no one knew the truth except himself.

He ordered a round of drinks and the old grey heads nodded in appreciation. Despite what he had done, Anderson thought, despite who he was and what he knew he still hankered after glory on the battlefield. Ireland wasn't a proper war. A dog's breakfast of a war, Pete Guthrie called it. He should be entitled to another chance.

The old men had somehow got back to the subject of the mysterious Irishmen. Donald Williamson was holding court this time, his sentences punctuated with throaty coughs.

'I agree with Pete,' he said. 'They haven't opened the curtains in that house since they moved in. Definitely something funny going on.'

Two hours later, Anderson stepped back from the bar and swayed unsteadily so that he had to grab the edge to stop himself staggering. He realised he was more drunk than he expected. He had been drinking too quickly. It had made him very tired. He rubbed his eyes to wipe away the weariness. He wanted to stay in the warm security of the pub but he needed to be alone. The house would be empty and cold without Kathy. That would suit his mood. He said his goodnights and went to the door.

A glance back imprinted the scene on his mind like a snapshot and, for some totally incomprehensible reason, he knew that he would never forget it. Digger was smiling at him with the palms of his hands resting on the bar, arms bowed round, fingers facing each other, metal armbands glinting. The group of old men were huddled together, witches over their cauldron, a huge cloud of cigarette smoke hanging over their heads like a storm cloud. Daft Davie was looking across at him, his glass suspended halfway to his mouth, a tiny trickle of saliva was running down his chin, his dull eyes reflected the lights so that they looked blank and lifeless like those of a statue.

The cold night air clamped itself around him as he stepped outside. The freshness of the wind in his face made him feel dizzy. He sucked air deep into his lungs and rubbed his eyes again. He stood for a few moments telling himself to sober up, but when he tried to walk he misjudged his first step and jolted his foot hard into the ground as if he had been trying to mount a staircase that wasn't there. He massaged his knee and kept hold of it as he started home.

The darkness was patchy. Wispy grey clouds chased each other over a predominantly light sky although there was no moon to be seen. The wind rustled the long grass of the railway

127

embankment. The lights of the station were like fat stars fallen to earth. Beneath the bridge it was pitch dark and he imagined he had become invisible. He held up his hand in front of his face and could not see it.

There was a coloured halo round the top of the street-light on the pavement outside his gate. The brightness of the light dazzled him and flooded the ground below it, picking out objects with an intense clarity. A stone on the pavement was like a huge boulder. The waving shadows of the sycamore branches were writhing snakes. A car approached. Its head-lights swept over him and he instinctively flattened himself against the damp wall of the underside of the bridge. The car, a white Cortina, drew up alongside the lamp-post. Two men were inside, indistinct shapes. One got out and dragged open the driveway gate of the Fraser house. The car went past him, headlights swinging away, leaving Anderson once more in total darkness. The man closed the gate from the pavement side of the wall so that he had to walk a few yards to the small garden gate to get back over. As he covered those few yards he was looking directly towards Anderson. A gust of wind dispersed the shadows like a flock of birds and exposed his face clearly under the full glare of the light. Anderson stiffened. A terrible coldness gripped his whole body. A thumping pulse of blood began to beat hard above his left eye. The face seemed to swoop straight at him. He saw the dark curly hair, the deep set eyes, and the thin lips. He saw the scar on his cheek and terrible memories at once stalked into his mind. For several, endless seconds their eyes were locked then Brian Heaney tilted his head and seemed to be looking up at the station. A moment later he was gone. A car door slammed with a noise like a gun shot. Anderson jumped. The world was spinning around him. He stood with his weight supported by the wall, his breathing rasping loudly, and stared at the spot where Brian Heaney had been.

Eugene Pearson lifted the curtain from the corner of the living room window and watched Brian Heaney open the gate for the car. The lights blinded him as it came up the driveway and he let the curtain fall back into place. Outside, he heard McCook

128

get out of the car and go to open the garage door. He moved through the house to unbolt the front door. As he opened it he saw Heaney walking towards him up the garden path which was little more than a gap in the knee-high grass.

'Any messages?' Heaney asked as he went past.

'None.'

Pearson waited for McCook to come round from the garage and carefully locked the door again. Like a dutiful wife he had the kettle boiling for tea, and cheese and biscuits were laid out on the table. He filled the teapot and took a fresh pint of milk from the fridge. He carried the things through to the living room. The gas fire had filled the room with a pleasant warmth. McCook was crouching in front of the television inserting a video tape. Loud music began to blare out. Heaney had taken one of the machine pistols from the cupboard where all the equipment was stored and was staring at it as if he had never seen it before.

'Everything all right?' Pearson asked, having to shout above the noise of the film.

'Fine,' Heaney replied, sitting at the table and starting on the biscuits.

'I'll go to bed then. Good night.'

Pearson filled his own mug with tea and took it upstairs to his bedroom. He cherished his privacy. Without the sanctuary of his own room to retreat to he would have gone mad during the three long weeks he had been cooped up in the house with Heaney and McCook. All McCook did was watch bloody films on the video machine. All Heaney did was sit and file his bloody nails. He had never seen anyone so obsessed with keeping his fingernails clean. Any conversation that did get going was inevitably staccato and limited. For the other two the whole affair seemed to be as simple and straightforward as waiting for a bus. When the time came it would arrive and they would get on it. They did not seem nearly so nervous or anxious as Pearson felt. Their confidence reassured him, but at the same time it also terrified him. It was a mad scheme, a lunatic idea; bumping off the Queen of England. But it was not like that. It was all engagingly simple. It was all perfectly logical. It was going to happen. There was nothing to stop them.

129

Pearson had realised immediately on learning of the plan that he had little or no chance of extricating himself from the situation he had been landed in by his father's vicarious ambition. Therefore, as he had done since first joining the IRA, he resolved to make the best of it and try to ensure that he at least came out alive. It was obvious from the start that Heaney was suspicious of him because of his parentage. Despite the fact that Heaney was absolutely correct in his original assumption, Pearson won him round by suggesting the idea of the flame-thrower. It came to him in a flash of inspiration when he discovered to his horror that they were planning to charge the train with all guns blazing: a good old-fashioned recipe for someone on their side ending up dead. Pearson reasoned that with the flame-thrower he could stand back and burn up the opposition from a safe distance. Heaney was impressed. Any lingering doubts he had about Pearson's ability to do the job vanished. The three of them were a true team – killers all.

Pearson had never killed anyone before, not face to face. He had no doubt that he would do so without hesitation if it meant his own survival. No one questioned his lack of experience in that line. No one even asked about it. Heaney and McCook never mentioned the killings they had taken part in, and he knew there had to be dozens of them. Like wishing an actor all the best before he goes on the stage, it appeared to be considered bad luck. McCook had a reputation of being a real mad bastard, and it was fairly obvious why. Even when he was asleep he looked violent. Heaney was different. He was an intelligent hard man, smart enough to raise wagon loads of money for the cause over in America, but some of the stories Pearson had heard about his cruelty to informers and prisoners made him almost physically sick. It was not healthy honest-to-goodness violence, it was sadistic stuff done as much for pleasure as for results. There was no shortage of sadists in the IRA ranks, so to come top of that league you had to be something special. And the third member of the trio was Pearson himself. He wondered what the other two thought of him.

Pearson took a drink from his mug of tea. It was lukewarm by now. He grimaced and put the mug down. He thought how nice it would be to get completely and hopelessly drunk; to sit down with a full bottle of whisky or work his way slowly through a tableful of pints of Guinness. But no alcohol was allowed in the house. Another of Heaney's rules.

Instead, Pearson got down on his knees beside the bed, elbows resting on the covers, and pressed his hands together in front of his face. It was done on impulse. He had not said his prayers properly since leaving school and religion to him was like an insurance policy – he had it only because he might need it some day. The music rising up from below was a background rumble as he closed his eyes and politely asked God to watch over him and see that he came to no harm, the same for his mother and father, and a special mention for his twin brother, Eddie. As an after-thought he threw in Heaney and McCook, and immediately regretted doing so because it probably made the other requests invalid. The prayer was short and to the point. He crossed himself and got to his feet hurriedly, almost as if he was embarrassed to find himself in such a position. He wondered if God would have any better luck trying to communicate with Eddie than he did. He wondered if Heaney and McCook were God-fearing men. If they were, they had a lot to be frightened of.

Pearson missed his weekly visits to the hell-hole of a hospital where Eddie was a patient. He had gone there on his last night in Ireland, driving Grogan's pick-up truck. On his way back, he stopped for more than an hour at the side of a road and sat in the darkness without really knowing why. He eventually got back so late the freckle-faced prostitute Colquhoun had arranged for him had fallen sound asleep in his bed. When he climbed in beside her, she did not wake up but put her arm over him and nestled her head against his shoulder as if they were an old married couple. In the morning she told him her name was Mary. But not the virgin one, she laughed.

He wished Mary was available to join him in his bed tonight, to sleep with her arm over his chest and her soft hair on his shoulder. But he had been taught as a child that was not the kind of thing a boy prayed to God for. He went to the window and looked out. The calm stillness of the village was rudely shattered as a train roared across the bridge. The house

131

trembled around him, shock waves coming up through the soles of his feet all the way to the top of his head. Then everything quietened down, disappearing with the faraway sound of the train whistling, a high pitched note and then a low pitched one. Pearson suddenly remembered the lines of a poem he had learned by heart at school. 'I balanced all, brought all to mind/The years to come seemed waste of breath/A waste of breath the years behind/In balance with this life, this death.' The lines had seemed strangely prophetic to his young imagination. The rhythm of their message had struck home deep inside him. They came back to trouble him now as he stood unbuttoning his shirt and the cold air seeping through cracks in the window frame settled on his bare skin. He repeated the lines softly to himself over and over again and thought about his brother lying in hospital hundreds of miles away.

He did not know how long he stood like that staring out the window. A movement outside brought him sharply out of his trance. A man was walking past. He was walking quickly but unsteadily. Pearson watched him swerve out into the middle of the road almost as if he was trying to avoid the house altogether, and then back onto the pavement again. A drunk on his way home from the local pub, Pearson thought, turning back into the bedroom. Lucky bastard.

He finished undressing and slipped naked between the sheets. Lying on his back with his hands tucked comfortably behind his head, he wondered what he would have become, what he would have been doing now, if he had had the good fortune to be born and brought up in a place like Kingsbank.

Anderson stood transfixed, leaning on the wall. His eyes grew accustomed to the darkness until he was able to make out the ground beneath his feet. His jaw moved restlessly as if he was trying to speak. He rubbed at his knee with a circular motion of his hand. A confusion of thoughts whirled uncontrollably inside his head. He was reliving the whole Brian Heaney episode of seven years before.

A series of jerky flashbacks came flying at him like bullets to

132

smack into the soft mass of his defenceless consciousness. He was in the hospital bed identifying Heaney's picture. He was in the Mess drinking with Bill Lowrie. He was face down in the dirt beside a parked car and feet were tramping all around him. He was in total darkness, inside some kind of box, and there was another body lashed tightly against his. Someone opened the box and the light flooded in. He saw that he was tied to the pretty red-haired nurse and she was kissing him on the lips. He looked up and saw that it was Bill Lowrie who had opened the lid of the box and that he had a small, round hole in the centre of his forehead. Then he was tied to a chair and Lowrie was tied to a chair beside him. The ropes were tight, biting into the flesh. Somewhere in the background he could hear somebody humming a tune. The humming got louder. He recognised the tune. It was an old nursery rhyme tune. Hands-Knees-and-Boomps-a-Daisy. And then somebody was pressing a gun barrel against Lowrie's forehead and he, Anderson, was shouting, 'Yes. Yes.' And he was falling, spiralling downwards into the very mouth of the gun barrel, into the black hole in Lowrie's forehead. But the face below it wasn't Lowrie's. It belonged to Heaney and dark shadows moved and shifted on it like living animals. And he was falling into the V-shaped scar on Heaney's cheek. It opened wide, like lips parting. And a hand touched his shoulder . . .

A hand did fall heavily on his shoulder. Anderson spun round instinctively, screaming in a sudden release of terror. A long, loud scream that was drowned by the noise of the train thundering across the bridge overhead. He saw that it was Daft Davie, crouching away from the unexpected violent reaction of his friend, cowering like a dog waiting to be whipped. Anderson sighed and the sound was amplified by the wind and he imagined it being carried miles beyond the village eventually to die out in the empty countryside.

'It's OK, Davie,' he said wearily, reaching down to touch his head and ruffle his hair. 'You took me by surprise. Go home now.'

Anderson turned and began to walk home. He looked straight ahead, feeling the presence of the house Heaney had entered as a prickly heat on the side of his face. He was emotionally drained. He walked like a zombie. Daft Davie watched him from the shelter of the bridge, a stupid grin imprinted on his gawky features. As Anderson turned into his garden, Davie waggled his ears and giggled. Then he sighed deeply as he had heard his friend do and climbed the fence to cross the fields to get home to his own house.

Anderson went directly to his bed. Daft Davie had broken the spell. He was able to think about what he had just seen in a detached and impersonal manner. But he was virtually in a state of shock and sweat pouring from him rapidly soaked the bedclothes. Perhaps it had not been Brian Heaney after all. It was a dark night. He had been quite far away. He could not be certain. He tried to convince himself but the heavy tightness in his stomach told him a different story. It had been Brian Heaney. There could be no mistake. He had seen him as clearly as if Heaney had been squatting in front of him in the pool of yellow light from the hurricane lamp.

There was no mistake. He had not changed. He could have pulled the trigger that killed Bill Lowrie only yesterday. Perhaps it had been yesterday, Anderson thought. Perhaps the last seven years had never happened. Perhaps he was still trapped in the airless pit beneath the pile of straw bales face to face with the lifeless corpse of his best friend. Everything had been an hallucination. He was still trapped. He was never going to be rescued. His mind was playing tricks on him, entertaining him as he waited to die. He dug his fingernails into the palm of his hand, drawing blood but feeling no pain. He licked the blood off and swallowed it. More oozed out of his skin to replace it. He sucked the palm clean until the bleeding stopped.

Pete Guthrie was right then, it suddenly occurred to him. Brian Heaney and his friends were plotting something in their house. He searched for some reason for them coming to Kingsbank. It could not be for him. They had been in residence three weeks now and could have picked him off a dozen times or more. There was nothing and nobody in the village itself. Nothing important, nobody famous or infamous. What did they want here?

He could not believe they were planning an attack on the

Leuchars air base. It was the only military establishment within a reasonable distance, but it housed the planes and pilots who would fight the Third World War. They could not possibly contemplate trying anything there. It was heavily protected by the latest security systems. But there was nothing else. Anderson knew the area intimately. Leuchars was the only target he could think of. Then he should tell somebody that there was an IRA threat. Maybe they were expecting to shoot down a plane or something like that. He should go to the police. Let them know who his neighbour really was. Or perhaps he should go straight to the military themselves. Major Henderson, his old squadron commander in Ulster, was now Colonel Henderson and fighting his battles from a desk at Whitehall. Every year Anderson got a Christmas card with a telephone number telling him to be sure to give him a ring if he was in London. Perhaps he should inform Colonel Henderson. Maybe they could set up a trap. Catch Heaney and his pals in the act. Phone them at the house and get them to agree to a meeting somewhere, then strip them and tie them to chairs and Anderson could play games with them, deadly games that always had to be played to a finish.

Anderson curled up into a loose ball in the bed. The house creaked gently around him as if it was deliberately trying to keep quiet to allow him to sleep. He heard what he thought was a footstep on the stairs. Immediately he sat up, his muscles tensed till they hurt. The silence bored into his head. He gasped suddenly when tree branches tapped at the window as they were caught by the wind and the absurdity of his action made him relax and fall back under the sheets.

He wanted Kathy to be beside him. She would have been able to comfort him properly. But, at the same time, he was glad she was away. Kathy would have sensed that something was wrong and would have wanted to know what it was. He could not have told her about Heaney. That would have meant sharing the secret. Only he and Heaney knew what the secret was. That was the bond between them. If Anderson informed on Heaney it would not be long before the whole world knew that James Anderson, DCM, hero of undercover operations in Northern Ireland, was nothing better than a selfish coward who had been responsible for the death of his friend. He could not turn Heaney in. The man still wielded as much power over him as he had when Anderson had been tied naked to that chair in that Irish barn.

Anderson must have dozed off because he was woken by the high-pitched whine of his alarm. He remembered waking at least once during the night, clawing the air like a drowning man, but he could not remember the nightmares that had caused him to wake. He remembered Heaney though, and the one-sided confrontation of the previous evening. He considered phoning in sick to his work but decided it would be better to keep himself as busy as possible to take his mind off the subject. Perhaps when he came home that night the Fraser house would be empty. Perhaps Brian Heaney would have disappeared as mysteriously as he had arrived. Then Anderson could continue his life as before.

As it was, even the early morning birdsong had taken on a sinister tone. There was a hint of rain in the air and the drops seemed to burn his face like acid as he went outside to get his car. He tried not to look at the house next door but could not stop himself. All the curtains were drawn. A carpet of dying leaves had collected overnight on the doorstep and it looked as if no one had passed through the doorway in the last hundred years.

Anderson's car was reluctant to start. Eventually the engine caught noisily. He eased it down the drive and out on to the road. As he drove away, the hairs on the back of his neck bristled. He was certain that Heaney was watching him, checking on him, silently taunting him. He accelerated fiercely to get away.

Waverley Station in Edinburgh was crammed with people. They milled around in seemingly aimless confusion under the great glass roof. The automatic sliding doors built into the Victorian stonework of the original terminus building were kept permanently open by the never-ending procession of travellers. There were families with babies in pushchairs and toddlers on reins; there were businessmen in smart suits carrying elegant briefcases; there were old folk in thick coats, and young folk with rucksacks on their backs and jeans cut off at the knees. A lot of them were tourists, struggling with giant suitcases or examining maps of the city to decide where to go first. Huge national flags of foreign countries hung motionless from the steel roof girders. They had been put there for the international festival and no one had yet got round to taking them down again. The taxi queue in front of the terminus never seemed to grow any smaller although a regular shuttle of taxis was constantly ferrying the people away in twos and threes. Only three taxis could stop at the rank at the same time, and a long tailback of the black cabs was forming on the ramp leading down into the station from Waverley Bridge. As soon as one cab left the front another two joined the rear. The drivers knew that a London train was due to arrive soon and that would mean an even greater demand for their services. The disembodied female voice of the station announcer heralded the arrival and departure of the trains. Each announcement was begun and ended by the sharp ding-dong of a bell. The silence in between usually lasted only a few seconds as if she was taking a deep breath before reading on.

Bob Stone was oblivious to the familiar background of incessant noise as he sat behind his big oak desk in his office in the terminus building and tried to concentrate on his work. The office was long and narrow and sparsely furnished with only the desk, an upright chair in front of it, and three filing cabinets along one wall. Shoulder-high oak panelling was hidden behind a chaotic jumble of papers and memos pinned one on top of the other. A modern electric clock was on the wall but the wire coming from its underside was curled neatly on top of one of the filing cabinets and the frayed ends were sealed with insulating tape. Behind Stone was an arched window with filthy panes that let through very little light. On the desk were an intercom, two phones and three filing trays. To his right was a mobile trolley with a video screen and keyboard.

Stone was supposed to be checking the timings listed on a computer print-out in front of him but experience had shown that the computer was never wrong and his examination was only a cursory one. When he reached the bottom of the list he realised that none of the figures on it had registered with him. 'Fuck it,' he said out loud in uncharacteristically colourful language and tossed the paper into a tray. He turned in his chair and leaned over to pull the video screen closer to him. He punched in a code number. Immediately rows of white figures and letters wrote themselves across the dark screen. He adjusted the brightness to make them easier to read and with his finger traced down the rows till he found the one he wanted. He cast a furtive glance at the door to make sure he was not being spied on. 'That's it,' he said as if informing someone standing beside him. 'That's the one.'

The information on the video screen read: Sat. ex Ab 22.27 to Lon via Ed. Newc. Goods (5) PR. The final letters gave the game away. PR meant priority status and that other trains were to be held or delayed to accommodate it. The description as goods was a poor attempt to conceal its true identity, and anyway everyone in British Rail knew that the Royal Train was the only reason priority status was ever implemented. So much for security, he thought smugly. Whoever heard of a goods train with only five wagons anyway. Stone had known since Tuesday when its journey north was logged, up the west coast line to Glasgow and across to Dundee and from there to Aberdeen, using track time as it was available and waiting in sidings when it was not. He had known it was the Royal Train running empty, but he had forced himself to wait for final confirmation. That had arrived first thing in the morning with the request for priority status on the weekend timetable. There could be no doubt after that. The Saturday night departure was easily arranged with minimal disruptions to other services; only a northbound cement train that would have to wait an extra ten minutes to let the Royal Train past on the single track viaduct at Montrose. There had been no additional requests for halts but that could come by telex tomorrow. If there were none, Stone would still be wiring Aberdeen with the request for at least one stop.

The timing meant that Kingsbank would be reached in two hours and one minute, giving an arrival time of 00.28. The last south train stopped at Kingsbank at 20.30 and the last north train stopped at 22.49. That gave Brian Heaney and friends plenty of time to move into position once the station was closed down. And by the time the sun rose on Sunday they would all be safe in Ireland and Caroline would probably still be totally unaware of what her husband had caused to happen to her beloved Royal Family.

Stone had been savouring his knowledge all day, continually calling it up on the video screen, reading it and re-reading it. It had been confirmed at such a perfect time. There had been another lawyer's letter delivered to his flat that morning: a registered letter he had to sign for, telling him that the divorce hearing was scheduled for a date in November. He had angrily torn it into small pieces and flushed them down the toilet, Oh, Caroline, he thought, how I will make you regret being unfaithful to me.

All of his money had already been transferred from his Edinburgh bank to an Irish one in the Republic. He had a new account there under the name of Robert Stark, the identity he had chosen for his new life. Australia attracted him, or perhaps Canada. He had not finally decided yet. Perhaps he might even grow a beard or get plastic surgery done and come back to Britain, find out where Caroline was living and move into the house next door so that he could keep an eye on her. Perhaps he might even make friends with her under his new name. If she was married again, perhaps he would sleep with her and get himself caught in the act by an outraged husband. Perhaps he would persuade her to show him the Royal scrap books she kept so faithfully and there would be tears in her eyes when she came to a certain page.

He should have phoned Heaney as soon as he had confirmed the time of the train, but he had been reluctant to do so, preferring instead to hold on to his little secret for a while like a boy cupping a butterfly between his hands. Heaney did not trust him, he suspected. That was why there had been the surprise visit the day before, probably to check that he was not having a nervous breakdown. Well, he wasn't having any kind of a breakdown. He had never felt so good and so confident in his whole life. He had told Heaney, without mentioning the five-wagon goods train running north, that he was convinced it would be this weekend. He could now inform Heaney that he

139

had been proved right. Events were fulfilling their ordained pattern. Everything Stone had promised and said had been shown to be accurate and credible. So it was right that Heaney should be made to wait as a punishment for his lack of faith. Meanwhile, the vital information belonged to Stone alone and if he did not choose to share it, what could Heaney do? He was like the boy holding the butterfly. He could crush it or free it. The decision was for him to make.

Stone pushed with his toes and the chair swivelled right round so that he was looking out the window and down on platform one. An Inter-City 125 was discharging its heavy load of passengers. He looked at his watch. Twenty-three minutes late, he observed; that would throw out a dozen other services.

On Saturday afternoon he would casually drop into the office to check that there were no last-minute changes to the timetable. Then he would drive to Glenrothes airfield to see that the plane was fuelled. It needed to be only three-quarters full for the flight they had to make, but he would have it filled completely anyway. He would pay by cheque and it would bounce on Monday because the account had been closed. Stone giggled and congratulated himself on his cleverness as he killed the display on the video screen. He would run the plane's engines but he would not take her up. He had been flying her regularly every weekend and had been disappointed when Heaney had declined to go up with him. He had had to take the gorilla, McCook, instead because Heaney lost interest when he found out that it was not possible to get air space over Kingsbank because the village was directly in the landing path for the Leuchars RAF base. Stone would have liked to demonstrate his flying skills to a more appreciative audience that McCook; that was another reason why Heaney should wait. He really would have been impressed, Stone felt sure.

There were five light aircraft, three of them Piper Cherokees, permanently based at Glenrothes and kept in their own fenced compound to discourage vandals. Stone had a key to the gates. There would be no problem in getting over the perimeter fence. It was only a token barrier. The difficult part of the getaway would be taking off in the darkness from the bumpy grass runway. Only Stone was able to do that. Heaney would have to appreciate his flying skills then, as well as the overall brilliance of the plan that had been accomplished.

Stone checked his watch again. He still had about half an hour to work but he could no longer contain himself. He quickly tidied his desk, locking the drawers. He got to his feet and took his raincoat from the mahogany stand behind the door. He draped it over his arm and went into the outer office. A glass wall with a skeletal diagram of railway lines in and around Edinburgh was flickering with dozens of red and yellow and green lights. In front of it, heads were bowed over video screens arranged like church pews three deep. His secretary sat up when she saw him come out of his office.

'I'm going home now, Sally,' he said cheerfully. 'You can pack up and leave whenever you like.'

'Thank you, Mr Stone. Good night.'

Sally was an attractive girl with long dark hair that flowed down over her shoulders and followed the curve of her breasts. Perhaps he would ask her out tomorrow night. Take her to a nice restaurant, wine and dine her and then bed her as a kind of farewell. Sally was younger than Caroline, barely out of school, but she was a full-grown woman and he had been aware of her looking at him in that curious way women had. Caroline had often looked at him like that when they were working together. There was a pink love-bite on Sally's neck. He let his eyes dwell on the cleavage shown by her dress and was amused when she pretended not to notice. She had no idea what he would be doing this weekend. None at all.

He walked briskly down the corridor and then down two twisting flights of steps to the staff door beside the left-luggage office. Someone said 'Good night, Bob,' but he was gone before Stone realised and tried to respond.

The station was like an anthill, he thought as he stepped outside. People were rushing in every direction. A convoy of eight parcel cages pulled by an electric trolley clattered past, the last in line zig-zagging wildly because of a jammed wheel.

He did not want to use his office phone to contact Heaney because he was sure the switchboard operator listened in on calls. That had worried him when Heaney had called the

141

previous day but they had said nothing incriminating, simply arranged to meet. Even so, there was no point in taking avoidable risks. He walked over to the row of fifteen public telephones. All were occupied except one which was fixed closer to the ground than the others and was intended for wheelchair users. He decided not to use it because he might have attracted unwelcome attention to himself crouching over it like an adult playing with a child's toy. He could wait. He rubbed the ten pence coin in his pocket against his thigh so that it grew warm. A man came off one of the phones and he started forward, but a middle-aged woman jumped in before him. He stepped back and collided with a little boy, almost knocking him over. 'Careful, clumsy,' the boy's mother warned sharply and Stone, mumbling his apologies and sidling away, did not know if she was talking to him or to her son. He walked up and down, stepping right and left to avoid contact with people. When he drew the palm of his hand over his forehead it came away glistening with sweat. There was no panic, he told himself. No hurry. He could just as easily go home and make the phone call. But he did not go home. It had become imperative for him to share his knowledge with Heaney. Heaney had to know as soon as possible. Two phones became vacant simultaneously. He ran forward, shouldering somebody out of the way, ignoring his cry of protest. He grabbed the receiver of the phone nearest him and balanced the ten pence coin in the slot of the money box. He repeated Heaney's number soundlessly with his lips as he dialled it. On one side of him a teenager who could have been a boy or a girl was jabbering away in a foreign language; on the other side an elderly woman had her back to him and was staring up at the pigeons sitting on the girders above platform one. There were no privacy hoods on the phones. The sound of people talking on them merged with the general uproar of noise in the station. He should have waited until he got home. But it was too late now. The number was ringing. He could feel the sweat standing out in big drops on his forehead. The receiver was moist in his hand. The coin had caused a red groove in the skin of his thumb. On the third ring the phone was answered.

The phone rang shrilly when the three of them were playing a bad-tempered game of cards. No bets of more than fifty pence. Another of the house rules. Heaney answered it and from the expression on his face it was obvious it was the call they had been waiting for. A smile slowly spread across his mouth and laughter lines appeared at his eyes. He listened for about a minute without saying anything then said, 'Right. Got it. Phone again tomorrow.' He put the phone down and turned towards Pearson and McCook who were still sitting holding their cards. He tried not to smile but his mouth refused to obey him. He sat down at the table again and began to write on a pad of paper.

'Well?' Pearson said eventually.

Heaney looked up, grinning hugely. 'Wrong number,' he said and burst into a loud guffaw of laughter. 'No. No,' he corrected himself quickly, holding up a hand like a policeman directing traffic. 'It's all set for Saturday night.' He paused to think for a moment. 'Or more like Sunday morning. We'll be home in good old Ireland in time for Mass.'

McCook grabbed Heaney's hand and shook it furiously. The pack of cards fluttered to the floor as the three men shook hands and hugged each other in the general release of tension. Pearson laughed the loudest, desperately trying to ignore the hollow emptiness in his stomach. Earlier that day he had been checking over his equipment and thinking how much the grenades really did resemble pineapples as they had been called in the Commando comics he had been addicted to as a boy. He had pictured himself as a cartoon character standing erect as he sprayed the train with his flame thrower, and with his free hand lobbing a pineapple through the open door. Guns blazed from the windows of the carriages and the bullets spattered the ground around his feet. 'Take that,' the balloon from his mouth was saying. Now the image moved on to the next frame of the story and another cartoon drew itself in his mind. In it the train was a burned out hulk and Pearson was being congratulated by his fellow soldiers as he stood holding a sparkling crown in his hands. 'We've done it, men,' he was saying.

The sound of Brian Heaney's voice woke Pearson from his

143

daydream. 'I'll have to phone Big John to let him know and make the arrangements for our welcome home,' Heaney said. 'First, I'll let you two in on the secret.'

Pearson and McCook leaned forward over the table like eager pupils over their desks.

Jim Anderson came home from his work with a fish supper and a bottle of whisky. The day had passed very quickly for him. It seemed only minutes before that he had left the house, he thought as he turned into the driveway past the spot where Brian Heaney had stood the previous night. The curtained windows of the Fraser house showed no change from the morning.

He had been distracted all day – to the extent that a few people at the factory had asked if he was all right. That bothered him. He wanted to keep up normal appearances. He had to act naturally, let no one guess what was troubling him. He said he must be developing a dose of the flu, had a headache, nothing serious, nothing that would stop him coming in to work.

All day he had silently tried to convince himself that it was not Brian Heaney he had seen. The excuses had lined up to offer themselves: he had been drunk; the light was not good; a jury would have laughed him out of court trying to make an identification like that stick; his eyes were playing tricks on him; it had been an hallucination conjured up by the wild talk of Pete Guthrie and his cronies; there must be hundreds of people in the world with little scars on their cheeks. He went over them again and again but he could get himself to accept none of the excuses. It had been Brian Heaney standing there. He knew that absolutely. Why he should be there, Anderson did not want to know.

He made himself comfortable in the armchair by the fire and ate his fish and chips. When he had finished, he screwed the greasy newspaper into a ball and threw it away from him across the room. He watched it curve through the air in seeming slow motion and take ages to reach the floor. His movements were slow and laboured. The whisky would only pour sluggishly

144

out of the bottle, like honey dripping from a spoon. He was surprised to see that the bottle was half empty. It was suddenly dark outside. A train sped through the station and he imagined the rhythm of the wheels was a whispered warning to him: He's coming to get you, to get you, to get you. He rested his head on the back of the chair and closed his eyes, but above him he could still see the ceiling. It pressed down on him, suffocating him, choking him, and the heat was all round his body. He woke with a start, leaning forward and flinging his hands up to his face as if to protect it from an invisible attacker. He looked at his watch and heard the bell in the church tower strike midnight. He counted the heavy chimes. The day was over. He was another day closer to his death.

Anderson got up and checked that all the doors were locked. He went up to his bedroom and pushed open the door and waited before entering, not knowing what he expected to happen. It was Friday already. He had to work today.

Bob Stone pressed down the intercom switch and spoke into the microphone. 'Can you come in for a moment please, Sally?'

Sally came through the door and up to his desk. Her hair was tied back in a pony tail. She was wearing a one-piece trouser suit and there was another pink love-bite on her neck. Stone decided that she did not look nearly so attractive today. Because of that, he would not ask her out.

'Have this telexed to Aberdeen straight away,' he said, handing her a piece of paper with a written message on it.

'Yes, Mr Stone.'

'You can read my writing?'

She studied the message. 'Yes, Mr Stone.'

'Good. Then on you go.'

She turned to leave. Stone rubbed his hands together as if he was washing them. Alone in his office again he called up the Aberdeen departure list on the video screen and stroked the warm glass with his fingers where the white letters and figures spelled out his future.

145

Brian Heaney had been restless all day. He had paced the floor of the living room backwards and forwards continually, punching his fist into the palm of his opposite hand at regular intervals. Whenever a train went past, he would freeze into immobility, like a gun dog pointing at the game, until the vibration had faded away. He had nothing to do but wait. Everything was prepared, everything was going smoothly. Nothing had been overlooked, nothing could go wrong. He polished his fingernails to a high gloss by rubbing them on his trousers. He ate standing up and drank as he walked.

The phone rang twice during the day and he pounced on it as if his life depended on stopping it ringing. The first time, in the early afternoon, it was Colquhoun ringing for no other purpose than to wish them luck. He said he would not speak to them again until they were reunited on Sunday morning. The second time, just after five o'clock, it was Stone to confirm that he had sent the necessary telex and that the train would stop as required.

McCook sat in front of the television set all day watching video films with the sound turned right down to little more than a whisper. He tumbled a copper-coloured bullet with the fingers of one hand, rolling it over and over.

Pearson tried to keep himself as busy as possible. The tension had returned to the atmosphere after the comradely back-slapping of the previous night. They were three strangers again, each containing the excitement and nervousness they felt in their own individual ways. Pearson did it by working away like a demented house-proud wife. He took all the tins and all the plates out of the kitchen cupboards to dust the insides, then he carefully replaced them. He washed the kitchen floor until he could see his face reflected in it. He tidied up his bedroom, then deliberately messed it up to give him something more to clean. When the others were not watching he stood at the back door and stared up at Kingsbank Station. He ground the soles of his feet into the dirt and trailed it over the kitchen floor so that he had to wash it again.

At seven-thirty, just as it was beginning to get dark, Heaney and McCook took the car and drove to the airfield at Glenrothes. It was an hour before they returned and they both

146

immediately settled into their former routines, Heaney pacing up and down, McCook slumped in the armchair. Pearson had run out of things to clean. He lay on his side on the sofa pretending to read a book. At eleven o'clock Heaney and McCook slipped out the back door to do a last reconnaissance of the station. Pearson was left in the house just in case there was an emergency and someone had to get in contact with them by phone.

Jim Anderson went drinking on his own after leaving work. He was determined not to allow himself to submit to the morbid thoughts that had taken possession of him the previous night. He did not want company but he did not want to be alone. He felt safe for a while surrounded by a crowd of strangers in a pub he had never been in before, but gradually the feeling wore off and the strange faces became menacing faces that leered at him and threatened him. Body contact became more physical. People were deliberately bumping into him, trying to goad him into a reaction. A woman's perfume filled his nostrils, her lips were wet on his ear, her hand was heavy on his inner thigh. With an effort, he concentrated on what was happening and discovered himself sitting beside a woman at a table in the corner of a pub. He did not know where he was or who she was. A long cigarette was stuck in one side of her mouth and the trail of smoke it gave off made her close her left eye in what looked to Anderson like a permanent wink at him.

He was trapped in the corner. The table would not budge. It must have been bolted to the floor. He got up and tried to excuse himself. She smiled up at him and her mouth was like a great gash across the bottom of her face. He squeezed out past her and looked around for the toilet. He could not see it and instead decided to make a quick exit. Once outside, he quickly found his car and drove off. He had to stop after half a mile and relieve himself behind a tree in a public park.

It was still only ten-thirty when he got home to Kingsbank. He scraped the side of his car trying to get it into the garage, and when he tried again he dented the bumper on the far wall. For at least four glorious hours his mind had been a complete

147

blank. It had recorded nothing, absolutely nothing, but now the memory of a certain Brian Heaney was creeping back in and depression was floating around him like a black fog.

He stumbled to his front door and almost screamed when he tripped over a body lying across the step. For a moment he was floundering on his knees, arms and hands flailing in all directions, then he was back on his feet and staring into the inane grinning face of Daft Davie.

'What the fuck are you doing here?' Anderson demanded, grabbing the idiot by the lapels of his jacket.

Daft Davie just laughed. His lips pouted as he tried to form words but all that came out were little puffs of breath in a meaningless jumble of sound. Anderson shook him violently so that his head flew from side to side and saliva streamed from his gaping mouth. Then he pushed him away and stood rubbing his eyes as Daft Davie regained his balance and stood a few yards from the door with his hands clasped in front of him and the collar of his jacket turned up round the back of his neck.

Anderson stuck out a hand and pushed him farther away. Davie moved and then stood his ground. Anderson sighed impatiently. 'Go home, Davie. Please go home,' he murmured. He walked over to Davie and took him by the shoulders, spinning him round. Davie allowed himself to be turned but his head remained in almost the same place, looking back over his shoulder at Anderson. The grin grew wider as if he was enjoying the game. Anderson swung his foot and sank the point of his toe into Davie's backside in a painful kick that hit the bone. Davie grunted and ran off across the garden into the darkness. Anderson immediately regretted his action and thought of running after Davie and apologising, but when he tried to move, his legs buckled under him and he fell to his knees. He had to crawl on all fours to the wall before he could get enough leverage to get himself back up on his feet. He stayed leaning against the wall for a while, his cheek flat against the cold stone. Then he began to rummage through his pockets for his front door key. He found it eventually and the metal felt thick and rubbery in his hand. Once inside the house he collapsed into a chair in the living room.

He could not summon the energy to go upstairs to his bed,

though the warmth and comfort of it beckoned to him. He did not deserve any warmth and comfort, he told himself. It was better that he should stay down in the cold and suffer a little. A big ball of wind gathered in his stomach and climbed his throat, escaping in a low croak. It was immediately followed by a rush of sickness leaping up his throat but he managed to hold it down. He closed his eyes and tried to sleep but could find no peace. Brian Heaney's face positioned itself a few inches from his and would not go away. Anderson rocked his head from side to side and squeezed his eyes as tightly shut as he could, yet still the face was in front of him. He gulped down great mouthfuls of air to ease the sudden dryness in his mouth. It seemed to him that it was only seconds before that he had stood under the railway bridge and had seen his torturer for the first time in seven years. The days in between had disintegrated into nothingness. Time was slipping like sand through his fingers. He curled his hands into fists but there was no stopping it.

Eugene Pearson watched from the kitchen window as Heaney and McCook walked along the edge of the field that led to the foot of the railway embankment. He could see them only as silhouettes passing between the thick black trunks of the trees. The moon was hidden behind clouds and its light only reached a small section of the sky off to Pearson's left. The effect was like a dim light bulb which did not have enough power to light up a large room.

Pearson's heart suddenly skipped a beat. A third silhouette had appeared, emerging from the dividing hedge into the garden in front of the window. He could see it quite clearly, up to its waist in overgrown grass and weeds, moving forward as a man wades through water. Pearson ducked to one side, sending a pile of plates crashing to the floor with a loud clatter. He held his breath and when he looked back the third silhouette had gone.

He was uncertain what to do. He couldn't shout to the others, that might alert other people. Already he could hear voices coming from the front. That would be people leaving the pub. It was around that time. He could see Heaney and

149

McCook beginning to climb the steep slope of the embankment. He had to do something. He couldn't allow the plan to be ruined now. He had to act on his own initiative.

He stepped backwards and crushed the shattered plates underfoot. He took two more slow steps backwards then he was running to the cupboard where the guns were kept. His machine pistol was ready, the pouch of loaded magazines lying on top of it. He snapped one in position and wasted a precious few seconds searching for the safety catch before he remembered that the guns were prototypes and did not have them.

He ran back to the kitchen and ducked below the sink that fronted the window. The door to the garden was still open, just as it had been left. A wide crack, untidily filled in with yellowing plaster, ran vertically down the wall beside it. Pearson slid on his backside across the floor until he was right next to the door. His finger was curled round the trigger of the gun. Already it was growing stiff. Who the hell was it, Pearson asked himself. Would he be armed? Would it be better to surrender now? Just walk out with his hands up. How had the bastards discovered what was going on? Someone must have shopped them. If he had seen Heaney and McCook leave, perhaps he did not know that there was somebody left in the house. If that was the case then Pearson had the advantage. If he did, he had to make use of it.

He moved his head sideways until he could see round the edge of the door about two feet above the level of the ground. There was enough light to allow him to see the vague outline of the garden. A harsh oblong of yellow light was splashed like fresh paint in the shape of the door; beyond that sharply-defined area everything merged into an amorphous grey mass. He could see nothing unusual. He strained his eyes to try and pick out dark shadows. Nothing. He listened intently. Dry leaves rustled over the ground nearby. Somewhere quite close by a dog barked.

Pearson drew his head back inside and crouched against the wall with the machine pistol held firmly against the side of his leg. His heart was thumping painfully and he was breathing in short, sharp gasps. He was not going to be a hero, he had decided. He was not going out there to be a sitting target for trigger happy soldiers. The house could well be surrounded by now. It would be pointless for him to get himself killed. If they had discovered the plot it was all over anyway. The best thing he could do was retreat to his bedroom and wait to be captured. He would not put up a fight. It was a lost cause. He should have known things were going too smoothly. How many years in prison would he get for this? He had no record. They could only get him on possession of firearms, possibly conspiracy. They could only stretch that to five, maybe six, years. He would be out in three, still a young man. That was infinitely preferable to dying for a lost cause. And he would still get the glory. It was not his fault that the job had been blown. He had done his best. They had come pretty close. It was a pity it had to end like this.

A new sound began to impose itself over the rustling leaves. It was a more purposeful sound. He thought of it like an orchestra playing music after the initial tuning of their instruments. He stiffened and pushed himself to his feet as he realised what the sound was. It was the sound of shuffling feet as they kicked aside the carpet of leaves. Somebody was coming towards the door, coming towards him. Pearson backed away. The corner of the sink stuck into his back and he slid himself round it. A shadow fell in the door, a few leaves followed it. Pearson lifted his gun, pressing the butt firmly against his shoulder, pushing it hard so that it hurt. He was glad to feel the pain because it told him he was still alive. It could be Heaney and McCook returning, he told himself. No, it could not. They had not been away long enough and, anyway, they would not sneak up quietly. They would call to him, let him know it was them. It had to be the man he had caught a glimpse of in the garden a few minutes before. He was going to come in the door shooting. He and his friends would have orders to take no prisoners. They did not want to fill the jails with IRA terrorists and run the risk of hostages being snatched as bargaining counters. That had been one of the lessons of the Arab training camp, Pearson remembered. Ruthlessness was not the sole prerogative of terrorist organisations, the instructor had said. The man was going to come through that door and blast the first thing he saw. But Pearson could use the element of surprise to his advantage. He wasn't dead yet.

151

Pearson backed up until he reached the far wall and could go no further. An arm swung over the threshhold, a leg followed it, the heel of a shoe clicked loudly on the floor. Pearson cocked the trigger. The man came into full view, looking across at Pearson, apparently frowning in puzzlement. Pearson recognised at once that it was the harmless half-wit he had seen working in the neighbouring garden and wandering about the village aimlessly. But, even though the recognition was virtually instantaneous, it was too late. Three bullets thudded into his stomach with neat precision and scarlet blood bubbled out. The man was lifted on to the points of his toes, spun round and thrown face-first against the door. The door slammed flat against the wall and he slowly crumpled up into a ball at the foot of it, leaving five vivid red streaks on the wooden surface as if a blood-stained hand had been drawn down it.

Pearson lowered the gun to his waist and then placed it carefully on the draining board of the sink. His hands were trembling badly. It was the first time he had killed a man and he had managed to kill the wrong man.

A deep-throated moan came from the body. He wasn't dead, Pearson realised, and went over to him, kneeling down and resting his head in his lap. The half-wit was clutching his stomach. Lumps of blood were oozing between his fingers. His teeth were clenched tightly in a gruesome smile, lips quivering pathetically around them. His eyes were wide open but strangely calm and peaceful behind the misty surface. There was certainly no pain or fear shown in them.

Pearson was astonished to see just how much the face he was looking at resembled that of his brother. He had noticed the strange fellowship of identity that seemed to be shared by subnormal people before. He had noticed it among the pupils of the school Eddie used to attend and among the inmates of the hospital he was in now. Every face was different but each blended into a single unit, like members of a football team who were recognised because they all wore the same strip. The man Pearson was holding was a member of that team. He had more in common with Eddie than Pearson could ever have. 'Oh Christ, I'm sorry. I'm sorry,' Pearson said softly as huge sobs

152

racked his body and tears fell onto the strange familiar face below him.

The half-wit passed into unconsciousness. His eyes rolled up to expose the whites in a movement that Pearson had seen happen to his brother a thousand times. He wasn't dead. Pearson could feel a strong pulse in his wrist and neck. The worst of the bleeding seemed to have stopped. Perhaps there might be a good chance of him pulling through if he got medical attention. Heaney wouldn't stand for it, of course. He would demand that he be finished off with a bullet in the brain. There was no other logical option with the job to be carried out tomorrow night. Pearson knew he was being ridiculous if he pretended otherwise. They were not going to abandon a carefully planned operation willingly when they were in sight of the winning post for the sake of an idiot who was probably better off dead than alive. But Pearson did not want him to die. He felt he owed it to his brother to try to keep him alive.

He had to think fast. Heaney would be back at any moment and then there could only be one outcome. He had to hide the man somewhere and then on Sunday morning he could phone up and have an ambulance sent round to collect him. It was less than two days. There had to be a good chance that he would still be alive then. That would not affect anything. Once the job was over and they were safe in Ireland he would make the phone call. But where could he put him till then? It could not be in the house. Heaney would kill him if he found him. That left only one possible place: the garden. It was so overgrown an army could hide in it.

Pearson worked quickly once he had made up his mind. He grabbed the body by the armpits and dragged him out of the kitchen. He followed the makeshift path to the fence which separated the garden from the fields. To one side was a clump of wild raspberry bushes, taller than Pearson and growing so thickly together that he had a struggle forcing a way through them. The thorns caught and plucked at his clothes. In the darkness a bush whipped across his face, cutting the side of his nose, and he tasted blood. He stumbled on a shallow ditch in front of the hedge. He heaved the unconscious body into it as gently as he could, laying him on his back. He checked his

153

heartbeat to make sure he was still alive. Then he scattered a covering of dead leaves over him and retraced his steps through the bushes. It was impossible to see if there was a visible trail leading to the spot. He stood for a while staring at the blackness. 'I'll send them to get you soon,' he whispered and the words came out more loudly than he had intended.

Back in the kitchen he replaced the gun in the cupboard after reloading the magazine. Then he sponged the blood off the door and filled a bucket to wash the floor. He had just finished when he heard the low voices of Heaney and McCook calling to him from the bottom of the garden. He could not see them properly but he knew they would be passing the raspberry bushes. What would happen if they heard a groan? How would he explain? He suddenly noticed that there was blood splattered on his forearm and he quickly plunged it into the bucket to clean it. The blood had congealed. It peeled off like paint.

'Washing the floor again?' Heaney said as he appeared in the doorway. 'You'll make a wonderful wife for someone.'

'I like to keep busy,' Pearson mumbled, responding to McCook's grin. 'Any problems?'

'Everything is in its place and all's quiet.' He looked at his watch. 'At this time tomorrow we'll be sitting up there waiting for our guests.'

Heaney and McCook left the kitchen and Pearson let out a sigh of relief. He closed the kitchen door and locked it. He lifted the bucket up to the edge of the sink and poured the blood-red water away. Outside the impenetrable darkness of the garden hid its secret. He is probably dead already, Pearson thought.

Pipe-major Tom Lang of the Scots Guards pulled his bagpipes across on to his knees as the Land-Rover stopped beside the east wing of Balmoral castle. He stubbed his half-smoked cigarette out in the ashtray, shoved the door open and stepped down to the ground. The wide expanse of lawn was awash with dew. The encircling boundary of trees was bright with autumn colours. The cold rays of the low October sun sparkled on the grey granite walls and the small-paned windows of the castle. In the distance, small white patches of snow guarded the smoothly rounded summit of Lochnagar.

154

Tom Lang ignored the cold air that made his cheeks and nose and fingers glow red and threw the pipes over his shoulder. He waded a few yards into the grass, leaving a darker line through the light green. He tucked the bag under his arm and placed the chanter between his lips. The tuneless wailing as the bag inflated resolved itself into a spirited marching tune and he began to stride forward. The music shattered the morning calm and penetrated to every corner of the castle.

Last month Tom Lang had done a stint as the lone piper on the battlements of Edinburgh Castle during the Tattoo. He vividly remembered how the lights had died on the esplanade, hiding the ranks of massed bands and the steep banks of spectators on either side. The spotlight swung on to him and he stood erect to play the lament for Sir James MacDonald of the Isles. Each night it had seemed to last for only the briefest of moments before it ended and the bands below were once more flooded with light as they picked up the tune of Scotland the Brave and began to march off the square. He had remained standing quietly in the darkness looking down on the scene as the wind tugged at his kilt and a great sense of pride swelled inside him. He thought how he would like to stand there for ever as, below him, the applause rose in a mighty wave to drown out the persistent howl of the wind. And he remembered how he looked out across the pin-prick lights of the city to the dark liquid band of the River Forth and the black hills of Fife beyond, solid and somehow sinister, under the red-bellied clouds of the night sky.

The pride Tom Lang felt then returned as he played for his Queen outside her castle. He had played at Balmoral every single morning for the last ten days. As he marched steadily up and down, little sprays of dew squirted from the soles of his black brogues to land on the white buttoned spats and drip back on to the sodden grass. This was to be the last morning. They were leaving for London that evening and Tom Lang was sad that his duty had come to an end.

Jim Anderson rested the butt of his shotgun on his thigh and put his free hand deep into the warmth of his shooting jacket pocket. The chill wind made him huddle further into the jacket, burying his chin into his chest. He had a splitting headache which seemed to be spreading slowly all over his body so that every joint and muscle was competing for his sympathy. He was weak and tired, and his mouth was dry and unpleasantly sticky from all the drink he had taken. He wished he had not come out on the shoot but it had been a different story when he woke up that morning after spending the night in the chair in the living room. Then he had been desperate to get away from the house, glad to flee from it. Now he was ready to go back. The only way to cure his headache was with a couple of drinks that would top up his alcohol level enough to relieve him of all the worries that continually snapped at his heels while he remained sober. He could stay drunk all Sunday as well. Monday was too far away to figure in his plans.

He shifted his weight by moving his feet slightly and his boots scraped up a miniature dust storm round his ankles. The ground was as parched as his mouth. There hadn't been any decent rain for a fortnight but it was definitely threatening now, he noticed, as he watched huge black clouds rolling into position on the horizon. Two Phantom jets flashed in front of him, flying very low. They were gone before he heard them. Their sound following on behind like the wake of a speedboat.

Anderson was standing at the extreme left of a line of four standing guns. Each man was about forty yards apart. Two of them had dogs lying obediently at their feet. In front of them the field rose gently, then more steeply, then dipped away and undulated into the distance through scores of larger and smaller fields. To Anderson's left there was a dense wood behind an ancient stone wall that marked the edge of the Drummey estate. He watched a fat wood pigeon fly in towards the trees, gliding low along the contours of the land then darting up to the highest branches at the last moment. It instantly became invisible there.

Approaching the standing guns, still out of sight, were half a dozen other men and as many dogs. They were strung out in a straggling line and working their way steadily, methodically and unhurriedly over the ground, driving all the game in front of them. Their progress was punctuated by the occasional blast of a shotgun and the more frequent shouted commands to over-excited dogs.

A rabbit came running fast over the hill. Anderson brought the shotgun up to his shoulder and thumbed off the safety catch in a single movement. The rabbit saw him and jinked to one side, scampering away so that he had to leave it for one of the other guns. It did not get far before there was a sharp bang and it suddenly crumpled into a heap of grey fur. It lay completely still. A dog ran out, picked up the rabbit in its mouth, and trotted back to the line. Anderson massaged his temples with the fingers of one hand and wished he was at home in bed.

Two large hares loped relatively slowly on to the brow of the hill and sat there sniffing the air. Anderson sighted on one of them along the barrels and curled his finger round the first trigger in readiness. They suddenly set off, running fast in opposite directions, tall ears laid back flat. He followed his as it ran towards the boundary wall. It tried to jump over it but could not manage to reach the top. It began to follow the wall, running in the shadow. Anderson followed with the shotgun, lining up on the head, then he smoothly moved the sighting forward and down and squeezed the first trigger. The recoil pushed his head up and sent the sharp crack of the shot echoing over the countryside. He felt a stabbing pain behind his eyes. The earth in front of the hare exploded upwards, stopping it in its tracks for a fraction of a second before it continued running.

Anderson let his finger slip back to touch the second trigger. He quickly sighted again. It was almost out of range. Once more he aimed just ahead and short of the target and fired the choke barrel. Again there was the stab of pain behind his eyes and his brain felt as if it was rattling against his skull. The hare jerked violently straight up in the air and its momentum sent it somersaulting down the hill for a few yards before it came to rest on its side with its feet thrashing wildly, spinning the broken body like a Catherine wheel at a fireworks display.

A young gun dog was on it as Anderson lowered his gun but the hare was a big one and the dog could not lift it. Anderson broke open his gun as he limped over to the spot and the cartridges were ejected over his shoulder. In the shadow the hare's eye looked up at him indifferently, neither sad nor scared. Its nose was still twitching and the two long, brown-stained teeth showed that it was an old animal. The young gun dog sat beside it panting happily with its little pink tongue hanging from the side of its mouth like a flag. The hare's hind legs were still vainly struggling to find some purchase, but more slowly now. It whimpered softly. Anderson bent down and gripped it by the hind legs and the back of the neck. There was blood on its fur and one front leg was broken in several places. He stretched it over his thigh and pulled hard on either end until he felt the spine break with a tiny crack and all life left the body with a sound like a muffled sigh. He checked the eyes. They had dulled almost imperceptibly. It was dead. He picked it up to carry back to the shooting party that was gathering in a group on the other side of the field. The hare's body was so big and heavy he could not prevent its nose from trailing in the dirt. The young gun dog leapt excitedly round him licking at the blood on the fur.

The guns were being rearranged by Willie Thornton, the gamekeeper, for a sweep down the side of Black Cow Wood. Anderson tossed the hare into the back of the gamekeeper's pick-up truck beside five rabbits, six pigeons, two pheasants, and another smaller hare.

'You'll be on the drive this time, Jim. OK?' Thornton said.

'If it's all the same to you, Willie, I think I'll give it a miss and go home. I'm not feeling up to it just now.'

Thornton was the same age as Anderson. They had been at school together and had been good friends at one time, but Thornton was married with two kids when Anderson came out of the army and the friendship had never been rekindled.

'Hard night?' Thornton suggested, tapping the side of his nose. Anderson nodded, smiling mischieviously because he thought it was expected of him. 'I'd take you back in the pick-up but we're meeting up with Lord Drummey and his party at the bottom of Grey's Hill after this drive.'

'That's OK. I'll manage.'

'It wouldn't do to walk out on the boss, would it now?'

Thornton got into the truck and drove off with four men crouched in the back, balancing themselves as best they could as they jolted over the unmade farm road. The other men were sitting on a grassy bank having a smoke as they waited to begin the next drive. The dogs sat around among them or sniffed at each other.

Anderson made his excuses to them as well and set off in the opposite direction from the truck. He walked with his gun broken over the crook of his arm. It was more than a mile to the big house where his car was parked, and his head was throbbing badly. Every step seemed to heighten the pain so that he had to walk with his eyes virtually screwed shut. Once a rabbit broke cover right under his foot and he automatically brought the gun up to the ready position, but the animal was long gone before he even thought of looking in his pockets for some cartridges.

By the time he got back to his car he was becoming desperate to get home to the safety of his own four walls. He threw his shotgun and the new sheath knife he had bought specially for the shoot on to the back seat and covered them with the shooting jacket. He sat quietly behind the steering wheel for a moment, hoping that the worst of the headache would subside. As it did, the spectre of Brian Heaney began to float in front of him, laughing at him, and depression seemed to settle down on top of him like a heavy weight.

He drove quickly back to Kingsbank on the narrow country roads, scraping the grass verges on corners and almost hitting his head on the car roof by taking the hump-back bridge over the River Eden at far too great a speed. He stopped at the Co-op in the village to buy two bottles of whisky and two dozen cans of beer. The woman who served him had been a few years below him at school. He had taken her to a barn dance once and remembered groping her outside against the wall in a long line of couples all doing the same thing. Her name was Marilyn something, but he saw she was wearing a wedding ring so her name would be different now.

'Do I get an invite, then?' she said as she packed the cans into a plastic bag.

'An invite?' he echoed stupidly.

'To the party. Surely you're not going to drink all this by yourself?'

159

She was small with big breasts and an attractive girlish face. For a moment Anderson considered taking her back to the house and spending the weekend in bed with her. The prospect appealed to him greatly.

'And what about your husband, Marilyn?' he said.

'He likes parties, too. He would love to come.'

People were queuing behind him to buy drink and she was the only person behind the counter. She flashed him a smile and moved to one side to take somebody else's order. He had lost his chance, he knew. If he was to have her, he should have asked her straight out there and then. It was too late now.

He left the shop with his carry-out in two plastic bags. He put them on the front passenger seat and drove the few hundred yards along the road to his house watching one of the small commuter trains drawing into the station. He turned sharp left into the driveway and saw a woman standing beside his front door. She had her back to him. Her manner stirred a remembrance in him and he felt the terrible coldness grip his body again, just as it had done when he saw Brian Heaney after seven long years. Were all his ghosts coming back to haunt him? The woman turned and he realised she was not Bill Lowrie's mother.

The woman was old and bowed. She was wearing a woollen cardigan that drooped to her knees, wrinkled stockings and slippers with fluffy ankle borders. Her face was framed by a plain brown headsquare. There was white gummy stuff at the corners of her eyes and mouth. She shuffled over to him as he got out of the car.

'What are you doing here, Mrs Caldwell?' he asked politely.

'I'm looking for Davie, Mr Anderson. You haven't seen him, have you?'

'Not for a while,' he said, almost immediately remembering what he had done to Daft Davie the night before. The drink had made him forget the incident until that moment.

'He didn't come home last night,' Mrs Caldwell was saying in her thin, tired voice. 'I thought he might be with you.'

'No. I haven't seen him. Have you tried the pub?'

'He left there last night,' she confirmed, nodding. 'But he didn't come home. I thought he might be with you.'

160

'No,' Anderson repeated.

'Well, I thought I'd just ask, Mr Anderson.' She began to shuffle away down the drive.

'I'm sure he'll be all right,' he shouted after her. It was not the first night Daft Davie had spent away from home. Every so often he took the inclination to sleep in the woods or under the little wooden bridge over the local burn. He had slept out on one of the coldest nights of the year last winter, no one knew where, and had come to no harm. He would be all right.

Mrs Caldwell reached the pavement at the bottom of the garden and turned to look back at Anderson. He shivered involuntarily. Davie's mother had never actually gone out looking for him before. Why was she doing it this time? Did her mother's intuition tell her that something was wrong? He was ashamed at having lied to the old woman but was too embarrassed now to own up. Davie would hold no grudge about getting his arse kicked. God knows, he had had worse done to him. He would turn up all right. Anderson had other things to feel guilty about anyway.

The distance between them made Mrs Caldwell's face little more than a grey blur, or perhaps it was the residue of alcohol in his blood affecting his sight. He started to wave but decided he would look foolish and changed the movement into a massaging of his forehead. He could feel the headache coming back. There was a gentle singing in his ears. He turned to get the carry-out from the car and when he looked round again Mrs Caldwell was gone. He walked towards the house. The sooner he got properly drunk the better, he told himself.

Bob Stone pulled the door of his flat shut with a satisfying click. Standing on the landing he could just hear the rumbling of the model train on the wooden floorboards of the spare bedroom. It would run in circles until someone broke down the door and stopped it. It had been running all night. He had been unable to sleep and had sat in the corner, in the darkness, following the erratic trail of sparks. It would be running when the Royal Train stopped at Kingsbank and it would be running when he landed the plane in Ireland to start his new life.

Stone was carrying two suitcases. They were stuffed with

161

clothes he had bought the previous day in a shopping spree in the centre of town, all paid for on a credit card bill that would never be settled. He took the cases down to his car and put them in the boot. The car was a two-month-old red Vauxhall Cavalier with an interior that still smelled of the factory. He had only removed the plastic covering from the driver's seat. The next payment on the car was due on Monday. It would never be paid.

He got into the car and started the engine. He had set himself a strict timetable which he intended to follow to the second. 'Remember,' he said out loud, 'tomorrow is the first day of the rest of your life.'

He drove carefully through the city, observing the speed limits and keeping his hands on the steering wheel at the ten-to-two position. He speeded up a little on the dual carriageway on the outskirts of the city because going too slow was as likely to attract as much unwelcome attention as going too fast. At the toll barrier of the Forth Bridge he had his thirty pence ready and his window wound down too early. It grew cold in the car as he waited in the queue to pay. Then he was through and winding up the window as he rejoined the stream of traffic. A yellow Citroen with anti-nuclear badges plastered over it tried to cut in front of him. He saw that the driver was a young woman, pretty looking with a thin purple ribbon in her blonde hair. He slowed and waved her on. A joke hand on the rear windscreen waved to him as he fell in line behind her. To his right a train heading towards Edinburgh on the railway bridge looked just like a tiny model as it threaded its way through the giant network of red girders.

He cruised up the motorway at a steady speed, not too fast, not too slow. He was warm again. The car engine purred. Every so often he felt himself trembling violently and gripped the steering wheel so that his knuckles turned white.

At junction five he turned off and immediately found himself on narrow, winding roads. He had to slow right down, almost to a crawl at one stage when he got stuck behind a big lorry loaded with rolls of paper. Eventually he managed to squeeze past and make up some time. He arrived at the airfield at exactly the time he had planned.

Three planes were up, but there were few people about on the ground apart from half a dozen doing elementary parachute training. Stone transferred his suitcases to the plane and made a show of doing all the pre-flight checks. They wouldn't have any time for that kind of thing later. He unhooked the wind-spoiling weights from under the wings and climbed into the pilot's seat. He turned on the ignition and depressed the starter. The engine burst into life first time. The bodywork of the plane shook furiously as if it was going to fall apart, then settled into a steady rhythm. He eased the throttle open and taxied out of the fenced compound. He steered with his eyes closed, swinging round to the left and counting off the seconds silently. Seven, eight . . . Now, he thought and opened his eyes to find himself in exactly the right place at the end of the runway. If he opened the throttle fully he would feel himself being pressed back in his seat and the plane would soar up into the sky. It can't be any darker than that tonight, he thought smugly and let out a nervous squeaky laugh.

He carried on over the grass runway towards the wooden hut that served as airfield terminal and control tower. As he approached, a middle-aged man, very like himself in appearance and manner, came out and stood beside the big tank of aviation fuel at the side of the hut. Above the tank a wind sock hung languidly. Stone stopped the plane beside it. By the time he had climbed down the man had opened the fuel inlet on the port wing and connected the flexible fuel pipe.

'How much do you want?' he asked curtly as he set the automatic pump.

'Just fill her up,' said Stone.

The man flicked a switch and a whining noise began. Above them the windsock blew out almost horizontally and then fell back against its pole. Stone took out his cheque book and filled in the date on the next cheque.

'Going up today?' the man asked disinterestedly.

'Maybe tomorrow,' Stone said truthfully.

The pump stopped. The man handed Stone the pink tear-off slip recording the number of litres and their price. He disconnected the fuel pipe as Stone wrote out a cheque. He took it without even bothering to glance at the banker's card and went inside without another word.

Stone taxied the plane back to the compound. He carefully locked it up and re-attached the weights to the wings. It wouldn't do to come back tonight and find it lying upside down. The nervous little laugh escaped his lips again.

He got into the car and noticed how quiet and smooth its engine was compared to the plane's. The windsock edged away from the pole. He drove past the group of amateur parachutists. The instructor was walking along the row and, as he tapped each one on the chest in turn, the men fell back into the grass as if they had been shot.

Brian Heaney would be waiting for him, as anxious as any father waiting up for his teenage daughter to come home after a first date. It would do him good to wait, Stone thought. It would give him time to think about just how important Stone was to the successful completion of this project. It could not be done without him. Nothing would happen if he suddenly decided to go home instead and simply abandoned the others. He could carry on as before, transfer all his money back, settle all his bills. He could deny everything, claim he was being framed if they tried to incriminate him. But he had already sent the telex to Aberdeen. The wheels were in motion. And somewhere Caroline was telling her latest boyfriend about her puny, pathetic husband. She did not know just how important he was.

He checked his watch and saw that he was right on schedule for his planned arrival at Kingsbank. His knuckles were white on the steering wheel.

Brian Heaney recognised the red Vauxhall and went out to meet Stone. He made him reverse the car into the drive. The white Cortina had been backed into the garage earlier. They would use both cars on the run to the airfield, two people in each. That way if there was an accident, or one broke down, they could all pile into the other.

Such fine details had taken on an all-consuming importance for Heaney now that the climax of the job was imminent. He had identified three alternative routes to the airfield. If a tree should blow down and block the road on one route they would take the second; if a water main burst and blocked that one they would take the third; if subsidence created a hole right across the third they would all get out and walk. He had not slept at all. All night he had tossed and turned thinking about all the different possibilities. He knew it was wrong to be over-confident so he conjured up the fantasies of blown-down trees and burst water mains. Otherwise he could not see any way they could fail to be successful.

Stone was a weak link until he arrived and came under Heaney's direct control. Now he was in front of him and another piece of the plan slotted smoothly into place.

'Everything OK?' Heaney asked putting a fatherly hand on his shoulder.

'Just fine. Excellent,' Stone replied with a nervous little laugh that ruined his carefully prepared air of indifference.

'You sent the telex to Aberdeen?'

'Of course.' The laugh came again, punctuating his sentence like a full stop.

'And the plane?'

'No problem.'

Heaney ushered Stone into the house. It was late afternoon and there was a strong smell of petrol in the living room because Pearson had spilled some of it while filling the two cylindrical tanks that looked very like divers' air bottles. They were propped below the window, a dark stain spreading outwards from them in an almost perfect semi-circle. McCook was sitting watching horse racing on the television, his machine pistol across his lap as he absent-mindedly snapped the magazine in and out of position. He looked up, registered Stone's presence, then ignored him.

Stone sat down on the sofa, his hands resting uneasily on the cushions, his legs crossed casually at the ankles. The commentator's voice on the television rose to a shout as a race came to its end. McCook was not listening. He seemed to be staring straight through the screen.

Stone looked at the short barrel of the gun in McCook's hands and felt the increasingly familiar twinge in his insides that could have been pain, or it could have been pleasure. He had yet to make up his mind which it was. He let his bottom jaw hang loose to be able to breathe more easily. There was a long time to wait still, but by this time tomorrow he would be home and free. He looked across at Heaney and his smile was acknowledged. His insides tightened of their own accord as his whole body went suddenly weak and he felt tears spring to his eyes. He was forced to look away quickly in case he made a fool of himself by crying. Not that it would have mattered, because by tomorrow the old Bob Stone would be left far behind and a new man would have emerged.

Heaney checked that Pearson was in his bedroom. The youngster had been acting pretty strangely all morning, but that was understandable. He stood and stared constantly out of the kitchen window and almost jumped through the roof when anyone spoke to him. He had not made any lunch but that did not matter because no one was hungry anyway. He had spent some time wandering about in the back garden, poking about in the tangled undergrowth. Heaney had ordered him inside. It was not really necessary, but Heaney was jumpy as well and got worried about a million to one chance that somebody would see Pearson in the garden and think he was a burglar and call the police. One nosey policeman could ruin the whole operation.

Pearson did not argue. He came straight inside, his face flushed bright red as though he had been caught in the act of doing something he shouldn't have been doing. Heaney worried that perhaps he was going to break down at the last moment and not be able to go through with the job. It was a passing worry. Of course, all three of them were living on their nerves. The hardest part was the waiting. Once things got moving there would be no time to worry.

Heaney went into the bathroom and saw himself in the mirror on the wall cupboard door. Earlier he had washed and shaved thoroughly and his hair was neatly combed. Lying on his bed were the dark cord trousers and the dark blue military style jersey with smooth shoulder patches he would wear that night. He grinned at his reflection and traced a finger over the scar on his cheek. He had even polished the boots he was to wear. It was just like getting ready for a wedding, he told himself. Or a funeral. The smile died on his lips. For at least the fifth time that day he picked up the brush and began to clean his fingernails.

More brown and yellow leaves had fallen during the night, filling the shallow ditch at the bottom of the garden so that it was completely invisible. Pearson could see no clothes or protruding arms or legs. He began to wonder if he had imagined last night's incident. Perhaps it had all been a dream. The halfwit had never come near the house. It had only happened in his mind. And yet it had all seemed so real. The gun, and the fear, and the blood, and the disinterested agony on the face that looked so like his brother's. It had happened. He could not escape it. The grave was in front of him, a few yards away behind the barrier of the thorn bushes. There was a body lying there below the leaves. He had put it there last night. He raised his fingers to his face and felt the tiny cut on the side of his nose with its ridge of dried blood. There could be no doubt.

Pearson pushed his way a few yards into the raspberry bushes. The thorns plucked at his jersey but the thickness of the bushes prevented him from getting very far. He retreated and tried another place, but once more he came up against a solid tangle of roots and branches through which it was impossible to pass. It had seemed so easy in the dark. Maybe they had grown during the night; grown more thickly the better to protect the body that had been entrusted to their care. He could find no way through so he stopped where he was and stared at the covering of dead leaves. Another yard and he would have been able to touch them, to scatter them and reveal what they were hiding. Perhaps the halfwit was suffocating under them, gasping for breath. A simple movement of the leaves would save his life, allow him to breathe. But Pearson could get no closer. The bushes held him back as effectively as strong hands on his shoulders. He could only stare down at the leaves, concentrating intently in the hope of seeing a slight rise and fall which would indicate that there was life below them. But there was nothing. Occasionally a single leaf would be caught in a little eddy of wind and would roll a short distance across the surface to settle in a different part. Otherwise there was nothing. Pearson closed his eyes and bowed his head as he began to say a prayer for the man's soul.

Heaney's shout took him so much by surprise that he stumbled backwards and almost fell. A thorn slashed across the back of his hand leaving a scarlet line.

'What are you doing out there?' Heaney shouted. 'Get back inside.'

Pearson moved quickly to obey, not looking back. An irrational fear seized him: that the halfwit would suddenly rise out of his bed of leaves to point an accusing finger at his murderer. His back between his shoulder blades burned red hot where the finger pointed. Heaney was staring past him, blocking the doorway. Pearson had to stop and wait for him to get out of the way.

'What were you looking at?' Heaney asked.

'Nothing. I was just looking,' Pearson managed to say. 'Just looking.'

Heaney looked past him again, his eyes narrowing to try and focus on the wild clutter of the garden. A crow flapped noisily in to land on the top branches of a tree over the bottom fence, making the whole thing shake with its weight. Pearson forced himself to turn round and look. There was nothing to be seen. Just the tangle of bushes, seemingly impenetrable. The leaves and the ditch could not be seen from the doorway.

'Just looking,' Pearson repeated.

'Yes,' Heaney said after a while, standing to one side to let him enter. 'I guess we're all a bit on edge. But I think it's safer if we all stay inside during the day. Just in case, you know.'

'Sure. You're right. It's better we stay inside. I'll stay inside.'

Pearson went into the living room and made a mess of filling up the flame-thrower tanks, losing what seemed like half a gallon on the floor. Heaney had made him siphon the petrol out of the car rather than buying it separately. The tanks held five gallons, more than enough for what was required. The flame-thrower itself had been considerably refined and improved between the time Pearson had left it in Ireland and picked it up

168

again, in parts, in Glasgow. There was a new pump that supplied a steady and reliable stream of fuel, and the actual nozzle had been given a finer mesh filter so that the emerging stream of petrol liquid and vapour was not as coarse as it had been in the first model. The small ignition flame had been moved an extra two inches out to make it six inches from the filter, and that modification coupled with the finer stream of petrol had virtually removed the danger of the flame being swamped and extinguished by the rush of fuel before it had a chance to ignite it. The result was that the flame-thrower had been turned into a giant blowtorch with sufficient control over its flame output to allow Pearson to use it indoors without fear of setting fire to the place. He couldn't, of course, use the flame jet that would be hurled against the train but he could satisfy himself that it would work by operating the equipment at its lowest range so that the yellow and orange flame was barely a foot long. One night Heaney and McCook had lit their cigarettes off it.

Pearson liked to tinker with all his equipment. He often took the cover off the pump and poked around inside it for no good reason. He cleaned the pipes a hundred times. It took his mind off other things, but this time it did not help him blot out the image of his brother's face under a pile of damp leaves.

• When he heard Stone arrive, Pearson decided to go to his bedroom. He did not feel like making polite conversation. He had decided that the halfwit must be dead. There would be no point in phoning to get help for him once they were safe in Ireland. No point at all. Just as there was no point in worrying about him now.

Pearson saw his machine pistol propped against a leg of his bed. It looked to him as if it was made out of plastic but when he touched it he was surprised at how cold the metal was. He picked up one of the grenades and took it over with him to the window. The road outside was deserted. It looked as if there was not another soul left alive in the whole world. He lifted the grenade to his mouth and pretended to take a bite from it, imagining that it tasted of pineapple. Outside it was starting to rain.

169

Commander James Gunn, head of the Metropolitan Police Royalty Protection Squad and known to his colleagues as Bang Bang because of his name, pressed the palm of his hand firmly against the side of the train door and waited. The electronic locking computer took less than two seconds to recognise him. When it did, there was a click and a whirr and the door swung slowly open. He stepped inside and the door closed behind him automatically. Immediately there was total silence. He could still see the people outside the train running up and down but it was like looking at them from inside a goldfish bowl, an effect that was enhanced by the slight distortion caused by the thick, armoured glass. Fat men looked gross and waddled rather than walked when viewed through the train windows. Thin men were like broom handles. All faces were a blur, like characters in unfinished paintings. When people moved there was always a smeared impression of themselves trailing just behind.

The detective took a step forward and his foot sank silently into the deep pile of the fawn carpet which ran throughout all the carriages of the train. He checked each coach thoroughly, whistling softly to himself most of the time to break the intimidating silence. He paid particular attention to the Royal compartments, sliding his hands down the side of the chair cushions and getting down on his knees to check under the beds. He found a chocolate bar wrapper under the Queen's bed and slipped it into his pocket. In the shower cubicle he noticed that one of the rings holding the plastic curtain was broken but there was nothing he could do about it. He checked the narrow wardrobes, hung with dressing gowns and some casual clothes, and used a handkerchief to wipe a fingerprint off the mirror on the back of one of the doors. In the kitchen he ran water into the sinks to ensure that it would run away down the plughole. In the Royal lounge area he peered into the back of the television set to see if there were any obvious signs of tampering. There were none. He even removed the bunch of freshly cut flowers from their crystal vase to see if there was anything hidden among their stalks. There was not. He finished his painstaking examination of the interior of the train in the first carriage, the one allocated to himself and the other bodyguards. He rummaged through his own suitcase until he found the half

170

empty bag of barley sugar sweets and popped one into his mouth.

Commander Gunn was nothing if not meticulous. He always insisted on carrying out a final inspection personally. It did not make him popular but he was long past caring what other people thought about him. He had been doing the job for ten years, and for ten years before that he had been Prince Philip's personal detective. There was not a blemish on his record and he was not prepared to relax for a moment lest one should creep in. Check and double check. That was the way he operated. He liked the people under his command always to be looking over their shoulders. He followed close behind them like a butler checking up on parlourmaids to see that even the most inaccessible places are properly dusted.

The sniffer dogs had gone over everything in the train looking for explosives an hour earlier. There were five uniformed policemen from the local force strung out along the platform, and another two were down on the track at either end of the train. Three plainclothes men from the protection squad monitored every person who came past the barrier. A wino sitting on the concrete of the station concourse with his back against one of the litter bins was also a member of the squad. Aberdeen Station was nicely bottled up. Any unwelcome visitors among the sparse crowds of late night travellers had little or no chance of making their presence felt.

Gunn crunched the barley sugar between his teeth and swallowed the lumps. He opened the door and stepped down on to the platform. The everyday sounds of the station echoed round him with the background beat of the heavy rain on the roof above. A crowd of servants and equerries were waiting in a tight group at the end of the train. He signalled to them and a door whined open and they began loading boxes and cases into the second last carriage.

The Royal Train stood ready. It had been standing at the platform, closely guarded, since the previous evening. The class forty-seven locomotive and the five carriages were freshly washed and the wine-red paint gleamed under the station lights. The locomotive and each separate carriage was emblazoned in gold with the Royal crest of arms. Gunn strolled

171

towards the front and reached out to touch the horn of one of the unicorns. The paint was thick and smooth. He could feel the rounded contours standing out.

Gunn was tall and his body was still muscular, but he was into his fifties and there was a slight stoop about the shoulders. His face was deeply lined and he had to dye his hair to keep it dark. He was a tired man and had virtually made up his mind to take early retirement when he reached the age of fifty-five. He was a natural worrier and the job he did was all worry. It was a wonder he did not have an ulcer the amount of worrying he did. In twenty years he had yet to draw his Smith and Wesson .38 in anger. He had certainly twitched a few times in the early years but calmness came quickly with experience, calmness that was never to be confused with complacency. That was the great danger of any successful security system; complacency. He liked to see himself and the protection squad he headed as a deterrent, ready to spring into action at a moment's notice, but sufficient in itself to preclude the need for that action. It had worked well for him so far.

He looked up and saw the two train drivers having their identity checked at the barrier. He recognised Colin Barker, the regular driver, but not the other man with him. Gunn had had to report Barker after the incident near Peterborough where he had refused to obey an order to move the train past a stop signal. They were there for at least twenty minutes, a sitting target, but Barker would not budge. He had simply refused to ignore the signal despite Gunn's threats which stopped just short of shooting the bastard. The track ahead could be blocked or torn up or anything, Barker kept saying, and we'll be in a lot worse trouble if we hit something or get derailed. Gunn's humiliation was complete at the private disciplinary hearing when the railway bosses backed their man all the way and even gave him an official pat on the back for his conduct in the situation. Looking back on it, Gunn realised that had been one of the reasons why he had decided to take the option of early retirement. He was thankful the Press had never found out.

There were other reasons, of course. He wanted to spend more time at home with his wife in High Wycombe. And now their eldest daughter was about to present them with their first grandchild. She was already three days overdue. He had travelled so much in the course of his career that he had missed his own children growing up to a large extent. He was determined it was not going to happen with his grandchildren.

'Good evening, Commander,' Barker said with a condescending smile. 'Not such a nice night.'

'No,' Gunn replied curtly.

'May I introduce Mr Derek Devonshire. It is his first trip with us tonight. Derek, this is Commander Gunn. The man in charge.'

'Are you sure about that, Mr Barker?'

'You do your job, Commander, and I'll do mine.'

'That's fine by me. Let's not have any stops tonight, then, eh?'

'I'll do my best.' The smile spread more widely across his face.

'Good.'

Gunn watched the two men climb into the high cab of the locomotive. One of his officers, Brian Jarvis, appeared at his side and tugged at his sleeve like a small child trying to attract an adult's attention.

'Message over the radio for you, sir,' he said in a stage whisper. 'Your daughter has gone into labour and been taken into hospital.'

Gunn looked down at the man and felt a surge of happiness as he realised what he had said. 'Looks like you'll be a grandad before you get home, sir,' Jarvis added.

Gunn watched him walk away down the platform. This would be the last family event he would arrive late for, he decided. He thought about the long train journey stretching ahead of him and wished it was over.

The procession of cars driving east from Balmoral was led by an orange and white police Rover. Then came a dark green Range-Rover with semi-circular bands of dried mud above each wheel arch, a highly-polished black Daimler, a black Ford Granada, and another police Rover. The driving rain bounced like hailstones off the cars as they drove at a steady sixty miles per hour through the darkness. They passed through Ballater and went quickly on to Aboyne along the North Deeside Road, the River Dee itself only occasionally visible on their right when the full moon emerged from behind the clouds and its light made the water flash silver. At Banchory, they had to slow down to pass through the narrow main street which was solidly lined on both sides by parked cars. A group of teenagers sheltering in a shop doorway watched them pass.

The rain was forming continuous channels at both sides of the road as the cars reached the outskirts of Aberdeen, slowing to take the long sweeping bend over the bridge into Culter. In five minutes they reached the first set of traffic lights in the city. They were switched off and a policeman in oilskins with white armbands was controlling what little traffic there was while listening carefully to his radio for the announcement of the approach of the procession. When they did arrive, he waved them through and then walked over to the control box to turn the lights back on. The same procedure was followed at every set of lights along Great Western Road. Few people realised what was happening. The cars did not even have to slow as they followed the side streets parallel to Union Street to reach the station.

At exactly ten-twenty-one the small cluster of pigeons strutting about on the central concourse of Aberdeen Station were scattered by the police Rover as it drove in and turned to one side to park in front of the shuttered news stand, its blue light washing silently over the ground and the walls and the handful of curious travellers still in the station at that time of night. The Range-Rover was a few seconds behind. It drove straight between the ranks of uniformed policemen lining either side of the approach to the barrier for the north end of platform six and came to a halt with a tiny screech of brakes. The Daimler stopped directly behind it and the Granada behind that. The other police Rover stopped at the station entrance.

Prince Andrew stepped down from the driving seat of the Range-Rover and adjusted his suit. Prince Philip got out of the passenger side and held the door open for a young golden retriever to follow him. The chauffeur of the Daimler climbed out and opened the rear door and offered a hand of support for

174

the Queen as she emerged with four corgis, their leads tangled round one another. Prince Edward came out after her and squatted down to try and straighten out the leads. A lady-in-waiting followed them out and took charge of two of the dogs. Four bodyguards had got out of the Granada and moved quickly forward to be near their charges. A trio of elderly women clapped loudly when they saw the Queen. She turned to them and raised her free hand in a friendly wave.

A uniformed chauffeur got out of the passenger seat of the Daimler and got behind the wheel of the Range-Rover. All three cars then reversed out of the station leaving only the police Rover with its relentlessly flashing light.

The diesel locomotive of the Royal Train was running with a muted roar. A liveried footman was standing rigidly to attention on the platform beside the open door of the second carriage. The smooth, dark red metal behind him contained his reflection and those of the other people ranged along the platform.

It was an informal occasion. There were no red carpets and the city's Lord Provost was not in attendance. Only four senior British Rail staff led by the area manager in a short black jacket, pin-stripe trousers and bowler hat, formed the welcoming, or the farewell, party. Immediately behind them two of the bodyguards loomed large. Another one was walking slowly down the platform, his eyes darting from side to side, always checking. The fourth bodyguard was standing beside Commander Gunn with his arms folded across his chest. Prince Philip nodded in their direction as he went past the barrier.

A photographer from the local daily paper was the only member of the Press present. He had been at the airport on Thursday for the departure of Princess Anne and Captain Mark Phillips, and again on Friday when Prince Charles and his wife and children had flown out. He had also been among the group of Pressmen allowed into Balmoral Castle the previous weekend for an official family portrait session. The Queen seemed to recognise him as she followed her husband and two sons towards the train. She smiled obligingly into his lens.

The area manager removed his bowler hat as he shook hands

175

with Prince Philip, Prince Andrew and Prince Edward in turn. The two princes boarded the train followed by the lady-in-waiting dragging the two corgis. Prince Philip stood for a moment beside the footman, whistling softly for the retriever which was running loose without a lead. It responded at once.

The Queen went aboard last, one of her corgis going ahead of her, the other coming behind. The trailing one got its front paws into the carriage but stopped there with its hind legs still on the platform, half in and half out, refusing to move. The Queen gently tugged at the lead, trying to coax it in. The footman glanced sideways but did not move. The area manager saw the problem, stepped forward, and with an exaggerated gesture bent down to firmly pat the dog's backside with his hat. That did the trick. It jumped in. The Queen smiled her thanks and disappeared inside. The footman went in after her and the door swung shut.

Commander Gunn was the last person to board the train after signalling to the guard to start the train.

It was exactly ten-twenty-seven when Colin Barker released the brakes and opened the throttle. The pitch of the engine climbed sharply and the train began to roll forward smoothly, picking up speed.

It was a prestige job driving the Royal Train and over the last few days Barker had made sure that his new assistant, Derek Devonshire, co-opted from Western Region, knew just how privileged he was to get this chance. Ben Morgan, the dour Glaswegian who was his normal partner, had had a bad heart attack a few weeks ago and was in hospital. Barker had sent a postcard from the four-star Station Hotel in Aberdeen where they had been staying for the past two nights, telling him the manager was keeping a special steak dinner for him when he returned to work. He had also mentioned Morgan's illness to one of the flunkeys who had come north on the train on Wednesday in the hope that the news would percolate through. A little get-well note from the Queen herself might do wonders for a man's health.

Barker was an experienced driver with more than thirty years service on the southern region commuter trains and inter-city routes. He prided himself on his encyclopaedic knowledge of the British railway network and claimed to have passed through, if not stopped at, every station in the country. Devonshire was a quiet-spoken bloke only a few years younger than Barker. He seemed friendly enough and maybe it was only his newness to the job, but Barker got the impression that he would not have stood by him as Morgan had over the Peterborough incident when that stupid policeman had tried to get them to go past a danger signal. The rule book was absolutely sacrosanct to Colin Barker. He had lived by its dictates every day of his working life. To pass a signal at danger was unthinkable and the powers-that-be had eventually proved him right. But Commander Gunn had been pretty insistent as he shouted up to them from the track. If Ben Morgan had not been of the same opinion as himself, Barker believed he might have weakened. But the rule book was supreme. They did not go past the signal till it changed. The police might be in charge of the safety of the train's occupants but the drivers were responsible for the physical safety of the train itself.

Devonshire looked like the type that might have been intimidated by Gunn's shouting. Then again, that was perhaps doing him an injustice on so short an acquaintance. The rule book was probably his touchstone as well. If you followed it to the letter and things went wrong then no blame could attach to you. Barker intended to do just that and look forward to the OBE or the MBE that a man in his position could reasonably expect when he stepped down. That would make a talking point for the neighbours in the street.

'Open that up now, will you, Derek?' Barker said, pointing to the small clipboard hanging vertically below the instrument panel holding a brown foolscap envelope.

'This. What is it?' asked Devonshire.

'That will be our orders. Not to be opened until we are underway. They will tell us where we are to stop.'

'But that policeman said it was to be a straight run through.'

'He did. He did. But you will soon realise that the police do not fully trust lowly menials such as ourselves. We are not given certain information until we are safely locked into our cab where we cannot pass it on to Russian agents.'

Devonshire tore open the envelope and took out the small

177

piece of paper inside. He leaned closer to the light coming from the instruments which was the only form of illumination, in order to be able to read the telex message.

'It says Special Stop Order at Kingsbank. ETA 00.28.'

'Kingsbank, eh?' Barker mused. 'That's a new one.'

'You know where it is?'

'Yes. It's a small country station north of Edinburgh. You'll see it on the network plan there.'

Devonshire began unfolding the plan. 'Why do we have to stop there?'

'You will have noticed that two of our passengers are strapping young princes,' Barker explained. 'Well, the boys like to conduct their current love affairs out of sight of the newspapers. Hence a brief stop on the way south to allow the course of true love to run smoothly.'

'I see,' said Devonshire, finding Kingsbank on the network plan. 'We'll be stopping to pick up a girlfriend.'

'That's the usual ploy. Sometimes we stop to let off a prince to go to some secret rendezvous. Kingsbank is new though. I've never had to stop there before.' Barker thought about it for a moment and then shrugged. 'Still, it is in the back of beyond. Just the kind of place they need.'

'It'll take us two hours to get there,' Devonshire said.

'One minute over.'

'I wonder which one it is?'

'What do you mean?'

'Andrew or Edward. I wonder which one we're stopping for.'

'I don't know that. It could be both for all I know,' Barker said. 'Whoever it is is a lucky boy. I've only got the wife waiting for me at the end of this trip.'

Devonshire laughed at the joke and both men settled down in the darkness of the cab as the light from the Girdleness lighthouse on the edge of the city passed over them for the last time and the silvery sheen on the North Sea faded to a slate grey as the rain clouds swallowed the moon.

Old Jock Shaw carefully counted the column of figures in his accounts book for the third time and got the same answer.

178

Satisfied, he entered it at the foot of the column and closed the book with a weary sigh. He rubbed his eyes and then stretched his arms wide to ease the cramped muscles. It had been a long day. The single bar of the electric fire on the bare boards of the floor glowed redly, roasting one side of his body while the other side shrank from the chill in the evening air. He took his fob watch from his waistcoat pocket and flicked it open. It showed a quarter to eleven. He replaced the watch and stood up. The shadow cast on the wall and ceiling by the small powerful table lamp grew larger over him. He took a cloth money bag from the table drawer and stuffed the day's takings into it. He sealed it and tossed it up in the air to catch it easily in one hand. There was hardly enough to make it worth stealing. The station was not exactly paying for its upkeep. It could not be much longer now before they decided to close it down for good. Maybe they are only keeping it going to give me a job, he thought. Aye, that will be right, he said out loud with a cynical shake of the head. Never mind though, he told himself, at least it was the first Saturday night of the month and that meant the regular card session would soon be starting. The thought of that cheered him up immensely. He and his two pals, all widowers, had been holding the all night sessions for years now. First Saturday of the month, to accommodate Bill Wardlaw's shifts, regular as clockwork. The little ticket office at the station soon warmed up with three bodies in it. It could become quite cosy and it was always light before they finished. There had been talk of widening the circle of players. Four would be a perfect number, and Frank Souter's wife had died at the start of August. They might ask him in time for the November session.

Jock Shaw stuffed the money bag in the big pocket of his overcoat and pulled it tightly round himself. He shoved his British Rail cap down securely on his head and kicked the old towel away from the foot of the door where it was placed to stop the worst of the draughts. He went out on the platform. The moon was bright but the deep shadows round the station made it look strange and unfamiliar. The old, empty stationmaster's house was only a few yards away but was almost invisible. Behind it, he could hear the trees shifting restlessly in what little wind there was. Fat drops of rain were beginning to fall.

He looked up at the clouds above him and one splashed directly into his eye. He had to wipe the water away.

Grumbling to himself about the weather, he clambered down on to the track and crossed to the opposite platform. He went down the steps to street level and opened the padlock that fixed the iron gate to the wall, locking it again with the gate closed. He went back up the steps, closing the gate at the top. He waited for a moment, gathering his breath, but then had to hurry across the tracks when he saw the lights of the last Dundee train appear in the distance. It was virtually empty when it drew to a halt in the station. Jock Shaw counted two people, a man and a woman, sitting separately. No one got off. He walked over to the driver and handed him the money bag through the window.

'Don't spend it all in one shop,' he joked.

The driver looked at him for a few seconds and then nodded with a half smile in response. 'Yes,' he said meaninglessly. 'You're right.'

When the train had gone, Jock Shaw went back into his office. He cleared everything but the lamp off the table and pulled it round so that it was nearer the centre of the room. There were four straight-backed chairs. He arranged them round the table and put the electric fire on one so that it cast a red glow across the top. He took a pack of cards from one of the drawers and placed them in a neat stack in the middle of the table. Then he took a small bag of ten pence pieces from another drawer and arranged them in piles of ten in front of the chair he would use. He had six piles and nine coins over. That would easily last him all night. They did not play for big money. He got down three glasses from the key cupboard on the wall and took an almost empty bottle of whisky from the space behind the pipes below the little wash-hand basin. One of the glasses was badly chipped round the rim. He made sure it was not at his seat. Finally he took off his overcoat and checked his watch. It was past time. His friends would be arriving any moment.

Sergeant Bill Wardlaw of Fife Police parked his light blue Vauxhall Chevette in the space opposite the Station Inn and switched off the engine. He was the only policeman on duty in Kingsbank and the surrounding area so he had to wear his full uniform in case he was called out. The two-way radio clipped to his lapel would inform him if he was needed. He had only been called out once on a Saturday night in the last three months. That had been for a bad road accident. He had only ever once been called away from the regular card game and that had turned out to be a false alarm. He was glad he worked in an area where the only criminals he was asked to tackle were speeding motorists. It suited him well. He cherished the quiet life and his one ambition was to die of old age in his sleep in his own bed. The visits of his grandchildren every second week were about all the excitement he could handle. Those and the monthly card game in the station ticket office into the early hours of the morning. The doctor had made him give up smoking so the gambling was his only real pleasure in life, and the occasional strong drink. It was a small vice, easily cancelled out by the fact that he was a well-respected member of the local community: an elder of the Kirk, vice-captain of the bowling club, and scout group leader.

The rain was beginning to fall steadily. Wardlaw was a small, portly man. When he trotted across the road to the pub his whole body seemed to wobble around him. The short burst of activity left him out of breath. He realised he had not locked the car door but decided against going back to do it. Then he thought he would be made to look pretty silly if someone stole the car while he was up at the station. He was supposed to be on duty until two in the morning. Cursing to himself, he jogged back across and turned the key in the lock. He was wheezing quite loudly by the time he got back to the pub door.

Condensation was streaming down the inside of the window in the public bar of the Station Inn. Familiar faces turned to him, recognised him and turned away. Digger saw him enter and set up a nip of whisky and a half pint of beer on the counter. Wardlaw took off his hat and dug in his pocket for money to pay. An underage teenager came to the hatch at the side where drinks were served for the pool room, saw the uniform, and jerked back out of sight. A few seconds later an older boy appeared at the hatch with a five pound note in his hand.

181

'You sound like you've just run a mile, Bill,' Digger said.

'Feels like it,' he replied. 'I'm out of condition.'

'Starting to rain is it?'

'It is. Wind's from the north-east. Soon be chucking it down.'

Wardlaw handed over the money for the drink and swallowed the whisky in a single gulp. He up-ended the spirit glass over the half-pint beer tumbler to make sure that not a drop was wasted. Digger turned to serve the boy at the hatch.

'You'll have to hand back some of your glasses in there,' he said loudly for the benefit of the people in the pool room. 'Davie hasn't put in an appearance tonight.'

Pete Guthrie was dozing in his seat by the fire, chin drooping on to his chest, holding his walking stick across his thighs like a rifle. Beside him, Donald Williamson had tipped his chair back on to two legs so that he could talk to other men over his shoulder. Every few minutes a coughing fit made him fall forward onto all four chair legs. He waited until the fit had passed with his head held almost between his knees then he sucked deeply on his ever-present cigarette and tipped his chair back so that he could continue the conversation.

Wardlaw picked up his hat and his half pint and moved across to their corner. He gently shook Pete Guthrie by the arm and he woke with a start, kicking his feet out and scraping his chair a few inches along the floor. His dog yelped and jumped out from where it had been asleep under the chair. It turned round a few times and then curled up at Wardlaw's feet.

'It's you, Bill, is it? Is it that time already?'

'It is. I hope you haven't spent all your money; I want to win it off you.' The cigarette smoke was beginning to make his eyes water. He rubbed them with the back of his hand.

'Funny that,' Guthrie said. 'I was just having a little sleep there to get my strength up to take all your money off you.'

Behind the bar the bottles on the shelves began to rattle quietly. Vibration came up through the floor and through the counter where Wardlaw's elbow was resting. Williamson fell forward, coughing harshly.

'There goes the last train,' Guthrie said, using his walking stick and the table as levers to force himself upright. 'Let's not keep Jock waiting.'

Wardlaw caught Digger's attention and ordered a dozen cans of beer and a half bottle of whisky. He had to use both hands to take the carrier bag that was given to him over the counter.

'That should keep you going for an hour or two,' Digger said. 'If you run out just send down a message for more.'

'But it's gone eleven now. Closing time.'

Digger returned Wardlaw's exaggerated wink. 'Oh, I'd forgotten. You'll close the outside door behind you, won't you.'

Guthrie had stuffed his tobacco tin into the pocket of his coat and walked over to the door. His dog had obediently followed him. They both waited for Wardlaw who came across muttering goodbyes to the other customers. In the recessed doorway outside they hesitated for a few seconds looking out at the rain. Cars were starting up along the street and couples, huddled together, were hurrying past as the pub lounge emptied and people made for home. Guthrie was first to make a move, hobbling across the road with the rubber tip of his stick bouncing soundlessly off the ground. Beside him Wardlaw clutched the bag of beer cans to his stomach with two hands. The dog trotted behind on stiff legs.

Jock Shaw was waiting for them at the top of the steps. Their footsteps echoed loudly as he ushered them through the corridor, out on to the platform, and into the ticket office.

'I hope this place isn't as draughty as it usually is,' Guthrie said as he went in. 'It will be winter soon, you know, Jock.' He went straight to the electric fire balanced on the seat of the chair to warm his hands.

'I've got an old towel at the foot of the door and an old blanket hanging on the nails above the ticket window. We'll be as cosy as toast tonight.'

Wardlaw dumped the carrier bag on the table and began lifting the cans out of it. He put six in the middle and then put the bag on the floor in a corner. He unclipped the radio from his jacket and it crackled slightly as he placed it beside the wash basin. He sat down at the table and picked up the cards, shuffling them expertly from hand to hand.

'Let's see the colour of your money, then,' he said.

The old dog waited until Pete Guthrie sat down. Then it

183

crawled beneath the table, laid its grey-haired muzzle along its front paws and closed its eyes.

At the door, Jock Shaw reached up to throw the power switch situated high up on the wall. Outside the platform lamps died abruptly. The station shadows grew deeper and seemed to inch in closer towards him. He pushed the door shut and kicked the old towel into place.

For fifteen minutes after the station lights went out no one spoke. Eugene Pearson stood half in, half out of the kitchen trying not to look out the window at the shapeless grey mass of the garden, but his gaze was constantly dragged back in that direction. He had the petrol tanks strapped to his back and six grenades hooked to the harness on his chest. His machine pistol hung over his left shoulder and his right hand held the flame-thrower hose. Every so often he lifted the hose to look down the nozzle and then jerked it away, pretending that it was a jet of water aimed straight at his face. He suppressed a giggle by transforming it into a cough and wondered if he was going mad.

McCook was sitting in his usual armchair staring at the blank screen of the television. He had shaved earlier but the stubble was already beginning to shadow his chin. Heaney was pacing to and fro, his head nodding slightly with every step, as if he was counting things passing in front of him. The big handgun bulged in the waistband of his trousers and his tiny hand looked ridiculously small along the top of the short barrel of the machine pistol slung from his shoulder. It was like a child's hand, Pearson thought. And the grenades clipped to his front were like the nipples of a pregnant alsation. He stifled a laugh by biting his lip.

Stone was sitting on the sofa, his hands clasped tightly between his legs as if he was having difficulty in holding something in the palms. His eyes were leaping from object to object round the room. One foot tapped the floor as though he was listening to music. His face was an unhealthy grey colour. It looked as if it had been shaded in with a pencil.

Pearson turned round and the petrol tanks grated against the

184

doorpost. He went to the back door and stared out into the darkness. Nothing moved. He stared until small lights began to flash on and off in front of his eyes. He held his hand out flat. Heavy raindrops slapped into it, bursting and running together into a pool in the centre. He watched in fascination for a few minutes then he went back to the living room.

'The rain is getting heavier,' he said, feeling foolish as a wide grin split his face.

The three other men in the room looked across at him. He held out his hand to show the rain on it by way of explanation.

'Two minutes and then we go,' said Heaney.

All eyes turned to him as he went out into the hall.

Brian Heaney went into his bedroom and pulled a travelling bag from underneath his bed. From it, he took a small square of folded paper and opened it out carefully into a sheet eighteen inches by twelve. The paper was old and yellowing. The marks where it had been folded for so long were like a grid over the surface. Across the top in heavy black type was the single word: Wanted. Below was a face easily recognisable as that of a young Heaney with the scar and the deep-set eyes and the thick, curly hair. It was the picture that had been taken of him when he was interned. Below the face another two lines of slightly smaller type read: for questioning in connection with the murders of five policemen and for armed robbery.

Heaney smoothed the wanted poster out on top of the bed. He took a live bullet from his pocket and placed it squarely in the centre of the poster.

'Just in case they had forgotten about me,' he murmured quietly and turned to leave.

Something woke Jim Anderson up. It was a soft noise, a distant scraping noise, like the lid being lifted off a coffin. He came back to full consciousness in a fraction of a second, expecting a dead face to be staring at him, feeling the non-existent touch of dead flesh against his own skin. He knocked over an empty whisky glass with his hand. It fell to the carpet with a dull thud. He kicked over an empty beer can. It rolled into the pile of empties that had gathered against the wall like tide-borne debris at the

185

edge of the sea. Lights were blazing all around him. The ceiling light had three bulbs and there were two table lamps. Their brilliance hurt his eyes.

He must have had a bad dream, he realised. Cold sweat had stuck his hair to his forehead and his shoulders ached as though they were badly sunburned. He could not remember what the dream was about. He did not want to remember. He knew the memory was there but, like something concealed by the darkness, he could not make out what it was. He relaxed and lay back in the chair and his hand automatically went down to stroke his knee. His head fell to one side on the back of the chair and he was surprised to see that the roll-top desk was open and the internal drawers were pulled out haphazardly as if they had been hastily searched by a burglar. His medal and the photograph of him with Bill Lowrie were lying together on the table.

He did not remember taking them out. He screwed his eyes tightly shut and furrowed his brow in a futile attempt to recall what he had been doing. He could remember nothing. The last thing that was clear in his mind was seeing the big hare along the barrels of the shotgun as it tried to run away from him. After that it was all a blank. He did not know if it was night or day and had no desire to open the curtains to find out. He did not know what day of the week it was and he did not care. He suddenly remembered seeing Brian Heaney and his body stiffened like the hairs rising on the neck of an angry dog. His eyes snapped open and the bright lights stung them sharply but he forced himself to keep them wide open.

He picked the empty glass off the floor and looked round for the whisky bottle. It was also on the floor, standing just out of his reach. He refused to get out of the chair to get it. He stared at it stupidly and the dryness in his throat felt as if it was choking him. He tried to lick his lips but his tongue was thick and swollen in his mouth and would not move.

He thought of Kathy for the first time in days. At once feelings of self-pity began to build up inside him like snow drifting against a wall. He pictured her as he had seen her, standing on the station platform with her dress moulded tightly round her body. The smell of her haunted him, and the softness

186

of her skin touching his made him shiver with pleasure. He closed his eyes to savour the thought and there stood Brian Heaney. With his thumb and first finger he pulled his eyelids open so that the strong light burned into them.

Kathy would have known how to comfort him, how to soothe him. He was punishing himself by letting her stay away. All she really wanted was to be told that she was loved. It was not much to ask of a person, particularly when that person loved her madly. Why did he not simply make the final gesture, tell her that he loved her? Why had he been holding back? What a fool he was, an utter fool.

Anderson sat bolt upright. Again the empty glass that had been balanced on the arm of the chair tumbled to the floor. The back of his neck had suddenly become intensely cold and the strange sensation was spreading down his spine. He had to speak to Kathy at once. It was the most important thing in the world that he should speak to her straight away.

He pushed himself to his feet but swayed dangerously and had to steady himself against the chair. The room spun around him. His ears were buzzing, his eyes ached and watered continually because of the glaring lights. When he was convinced he could control his movements, he let go of the chair and stood with both arms outstretched like a tightrope walker. He took a step forward, and then another one, moving agonisingly slowly despite the feeling of urgency that drove him on. A great wave of happiness swept over him. He was glad he had decided to tell Kathy at last. Now that the decision had been taken there was no going back. He still feared the consequences. But it was like jumping from the roof of a skyscraper; there was no way of changing your mind but it was a long way down to think about what you were doing. He accidentally kicked the whisky bottle and it fell on to its side and rolled against the wall. The whisky gurgled out on to the carpet.

Kathy's phone number was on the writing pad on the table in the hall beside the phone. She had written it there herself. She had not told him she had done it and he had pretended not to notice at the time. It was quite dark in the hallway and he had to turn on the main light before he was able to read the number.

187

He dialled quickly, his clumsy fingers slipping from the holes so that it was his fourth attempt before he got it right. The decision had already been taken, he kept reminding himself. He could not back out now. The phone rang and rang. Anderson felt weak and sick and had to lean against the wall. Please answer, Kathy, he thought. Please answer.

The phone continued to ring; two short, sharp bursts that echoed inside his head relentlessly. It rang and rang. Please answer, Kathy. If you do not answer I'll never be able to tell you I love you. This could be your last chance. Abruptly the phone clicked. He held his breath.

'Hello.' A man's voice. An older man. Her father probably. 'Yes?'

Anderson struggled to make his tongue and throat form the words he wanted to say. It seemed to take an inordinate length of time.

'Hello. Hello. Who is this?' the voice repeated.

'Is Kathy there?' He sounded to himself like a wee boy asking if a friend was coming out to play.

'Hold on. I'll get her for you.'

Anderson was sweating freely. He rubbed his eyes and yawned then massaged the back of his neck. The phone was hot and sticky in his hand, little droplets of moisture were collecting in the mouthpiece as he breathed over it. He heard a noise at the door and thought it must be leaves being blown about by the wind.

'Hello. Who is it?'

Kathy's voice. He would recognise it anywhere. There was only the very slightest trace of a lisp. She was like a little girl whispering to him from afar. He closed his eyes and this time Kathy appeared in front of him.

'It's me,' he said.

'Jim.' She sounded surprised. Pleasantly surprised, he hoped. 'It's you.'

'I just thought I'd phone you.'

'Oh yes. What for?'

'To tell you I love you.'

He had done it at last. It was not difficult. He did not regret doing it. He supposed it had been inevitable. He picked up the phone from the table and sat down on the stairs with it in his lap.

'That's nice,' Kathy said. 'I love you, too.'

An intimate silence grew between them as the phone line crackled gently. They would have been kissing now if they were together, Anderson knew. He imagined her lips against his, her tongue running along his teeth.

'What brought this on?' she asked.

'I was thinking about you.' Another brief silence fell. The house creaked and sighed around him. 'Will you marry me?'

'I will. Yes. I will.' Her voice broke a little. Anderson thought that she must be crying.

'Good. I'll marry you, too.'

'We'll have to wait for my divorce to come through.' She was talking efficiently now, planning for the future.

'I'm good at waiting,' Anderson said.

'So am I,' she replied.

'Sorry that I kept you waiting so long.'

'It was worth it. And I would have waited a lot longer.'

They talked for ages about nothing in particular, two lovers lost in their own private world. Then Kathy was promising to get the first train back north so that they could celebrate properly and Anderson was saying that it was time he took a holiday and he might come south to see her.

'What will you tell your parents?' he asked, wondering what they would say to their daughter bringing home yet another old man.

'Just that I'm getting married again. Look, I'll have to go, they're calling for me. Phone me again in the morning.'

'OK. I love you, Kathy.'

'And I love you.'

Anderson sat on the stairs with the receiver burring in his ear for several minutes after Kathy had gone. He had drained himself of all emotion. He had finally done it then, he realised. Why was it that he felt no better? Maybe he had just imagined it all. Perhaps he should phone Kathy again to check that he was not playing tricks on himself.

A small noise caught his attention. It was a small, scraping noise coming from outside the front door. It was too loud to be leaves. Maybe it was a cat trying to find shelter from the rain that was pounding down even harder now. He ignored it and went through to the living room. Kathy would get back late tomorrow. He had nothing to do till then. He decided that he would be just as well to drink himself insensible. That would make the time pass quickly. The next time he opened his eyes Kathy would be beside him. He stooped down to pick up the almost empty whisky bottle and the glass. He poured himself a large measure and held it up in a toast. 'Here's to us,' he said.

The noise from outside the front door came again, louder this time. It was no longer a scraping, more a feeble knocking as if someone was deliberately tapping out a message. Anderson swallowed without putting the glass to his mouth. He put it down carefully on the table and walked slowly back into the hallway. The sound had stopped. There was nothing, only the sound of the rain outside. He went up close behind the door and listened intently. He was about to turn away when he heard it again, clear and unmistakable though barely audible. If he had not been beside the door he would never have heard it. But now he knew there was something or somebody outside.

Fear made his skin prickle all over. He swallowed repeatedly but still the saliva lay thickly at the back of his mouth. He wanted to slip quietly away from the door. He could take the whisky and go hide under the covers of the bed. He could wait there for Kathy to return. But he was already turning the key in the lock. His fingers were so weak he thought he was not going to be able to turn it. Then it clicked loudly and the pain in his head echoed the noise. He held the handle until the knocking started again and then pulled it wide open. A rush of cold air hit him in the face. He looked down. Daft Davie lay at his feet, twisting his neck awkwardly to try and look up, one hand sticking forward with the fingers twitching where he had been tapping at the door.

'Christ, Davie man. What the fuck have you been playing at?' Anderson said angrily as he bent down to get a grip under Davie's armpits to pull him inside. 'Who's been feeding you drink to get you in a state like this?'

Davie's clothes were sodden and filthy. Anderson tried to drag him inside but the toes of his shoes caught on the lip of the doorstep and held him there. Anderson could not budge him, so he lay him face down on the floor and began to roll the heavy body on to its back.

'Come on, Davie. What a bloody state to get in. You'd think . . . '

Anderson's monologue tailed off into stunned silence as Davie slumped over and he saw the black-bordered wounds in the purple morass of smeared blood all down his front. One of Davie's hands was stuck to his shirt by the dried blood, hanging in an unnatural position. Anderson looked down in horror as Davie stared up at him, the lips drawn back over the massive teeth in a constant agonised snarl. His skin was blue with cold and was trembling and jumping all over him. The dry heat from the hallway radiator made the soaking clothes begin to steam as if the body they contained was about to burst into flames.

Davie seemed to be trying to say something. His tongue appeared between his teeth and his lips closed over it in a ridiculous pout for a few seconds before they were drawn back in a terrible grimace. Anderson knelt beside Davie, cradling his head on his knee. As he looked down into the misty eyes he saw the tiny spark of life flickering in them disappear, just as it had gone from the eyes of the big hare that morning. Anderson knew then that Davie was dead. After a few moments the body lay completely still.

The three tedious weeks of waiting ended when Brian Heaney led the way out into the back garden. McCook went second. Pearson followed him. All the firearms were wrapped in black plastic bags to protect them from the rain. The pockets of the dark anoraks worn by Heaney and McCook bulged with the explosive charges. Black insulating tape had been put over the metal studs to prevent any reflections. Pearson could not wear an anorak because of the tanks on his back.

They crouched together at the fence at the bottom of the garden. When they moved again no commands were needed. Everything had been rehearsed a thousand times. Each knew exactly what to do. One by one they climbed the fence. Pearson was last and he could not resist a final glance towards the bushes on his left although he could not see a thing in the darkness. He caught his foot and stumbled, falling forward on to McCook and almost knocking him over. The petrol sloshed gently in the tanks behind him. Then the pace quickened. They ran quickly along the footpath between the trees and across the corner of the field. The fence separating the railway embankment from the field had two wires missing from the centre. Heaney and McCook were able to duck through the gap. Pearson had to climb over it. McCook waited for him and held out a hand to help him down. Just like a lady being helped down from her carriage, Pearson thought.

They went up the steep embankment in single file. The long, wet grass soaked the legs of their trousers. The brick wall of the old toilet was running with water. The ground surrounding it was soft mud inches deep that made sucking noises as they walked over it. Heaney looked round the corner.

'Jesus Christ,' he said in a hoarse whisper. 'There is somebody over there.'

McCook and Pearson took turns to peer round the corner, faces pressed firmly against the wet bricks. Both saw the outline of a door clearly drawn by thin lines of white light. It stood out starkly from the deep shadows all around it.

'It's the ticket office,' Heaney said as the three of them stood in a huddle beside the wall. 'God knows what is happening in there but we'll have to get rid of whoever it is and quickly.' He drew his finger across his throat.

'Perhaps somebody just forgot to put the light out,' Pearson suggested.

Heaney looked at him and Pearson was surprised to see how old and worried he looked. A multitude of tiny scarlet veins swam in the whites of his eyes. The pupils gaped large in the darkness. This was the first part of the carefully prepared plan to go wrong. What would be next?

'That's possible,' Heaney agreed, assessing the possibility. 'We'll have to check it out anyway. Cookie, you come with me. You stay here.'

Pearson watched them as they went down the track beyond the platform in order to cross over to the other side. He saw them stealthily creeping along past the boarded-up house. They kept tight up against the wall and were almost invisible in the darkness. If Pearson had not know they were there he doubted if he would have noticed them. The lines of light at the ticket office door disappeared momentarily as someone passed in front of them. The only sound was the steady pit-pat of the rain on the hard-packed ash and the concrete flagstones. A faint smell of urine mingled with the smell of the petrol around him and made him feel sick. Pearson was surprised to hear himself laugh out loud, a throaty chuckle that he imagined running off into the darkness like an unseen animal. He unclipped a grenade from the harness on his chest and pressed it to his lips. Now the next noise I make will be a really explosive one, he thought, and tried so hard not to laugh that he almost choked. It's a pineapple, he told himself. I like the taste of pineapples. His body convulsed with silent laughter and huge tears, as big as the bursting raindrops, rolled over his cheeks.

Heaney and McCook could hear voices coming from inside the ticket office but they could not find anywhere to let them see what was going on inside. Heaney crawled through the exit corridor, keeping his head below the level of the ticket window. From the top of the steps he watched the last few customers leaving the pub. Some got into cars, others hunched their shoulders against the rain and walked swiftly out of sight. The doors of the pub were slammed shut and locked. Only one car was left parked in the street. Heaney could only see its roof from where he was.

He went back into the corridor and sat under the ticket window. The voices were little more than a low murmur. It was impossible to make out what was being said. McCook stood waiting just inside the corridor.

Heaney frowned and scratched his head. He had already decided what had to be done. The office was small. There could be no more than five or six people in there at the most. They could take them out quite easily with the advantage of surprise. But what were they doing? That was the question that bothered him. Every night since they had arrived in Kingsbank he had been up at the station after midnight and the place had been deserted. Why was it different tonight of all nights? He did not like it. It was a bad start to the operation.

He lifted his machine pistol to shoulder level as a signal to McCook and then carefully got to his feet without making a noise. They went round and stood on either side of the door. Heaney took a thin-bladed knife from his pocket and slipped it into the crack beside the large keyhole. It moved freely up and down.

'It's not locked,' he whispered and McCook nodded, then he reached down with his left hand and grasped the door handle. A narrow channel of light swept over his face as he moved round to be ready to push it open at Heaney's command.

Jock Shaw was getting nervous and his hands were beginning to shake. There was more than four pounds in the middle of the table and Bill Wardlaw kept tossing in money like it was going out of fashion. But he had to be bluffing. Shaw had three aces, the queen of diamonds and the ten of clubs. Four pounds was a pretty big kitty for their game. They usually won and lost a lot less than one pound at a time. He took a drink from his can of beer and checked his cards again. They were still the same. He picked up two ten pence pieces and threw them on the pile. Wardlaw looked at his hand and smiled smugly. He leaned over and showed what he had to Pete Guthrie who had packed in his cards at the start. Guthrie was in the middle of rolling himself a cigarette. He stopped long enough to study the cards held up in front of him.

'Not bad, not bad,' he said and licked the cigarette paper to make it stick.

Wardlaw nodded and put in twenty pence. 'And twenty,' he said leaning back so that the chair went up on two legs.

Shaw ran his fingers through his untidy hair and plucked at his shirt collar. He took out his pocket watch and looked at it to give himself time to think. Maybe he wasn't bluffing after all, he thought.

Jock Shaw was sitting with his back to the door. Wardlaw was on his right and Pete Guthrie was directly opposite him. The room had grown quite warm but not enough to let them take off their jackets in comfort. The pile of silver coins on the table glinted brightly under the lamp.

'Come on then,' Wardlaw said. 'Let's have some action.'

'I'm coming. I'm coming,' Shaw protested.

'So is Christmas.'

Shaw made up his mind. He would bet another forty pence and if Wardlaw did not see him then, he would see him and put an end to the suspense. He slid the coins across the table.

'And twenty,' he said, laying his cards down in front of him.

'That makes it more than a fiver,' Guthrie said, clicking his false teeth together as he spoke. 'The excitement is killing me.'

The door crashed open and Guthrie was the first to die. Half-a-dozen bullets tore through his chest and sent the chair he was sitting in hurtling back into the wall. He toppled to one side and fell on to the floor ending up on his back, the thin cigarette still balanced at the corner of his lips.

Shaw and Wardlaw were hit simultaneously. Shaw was spreadeagled over the table by the bullets thumping into his back and his head. The coins and the cards were scattered over the floor. Wardlaw was the quickest to react. He was almost on his feet before a bullet caught him right in the centre of the forehead. It spun him round and bounced him off the flimsy partition that held all the train tickets. One flailing hand clawed down the blanket pinned over the window beside it as another two bullets ripped into his stomach and threw him against the glass so that it shattered and he was left with his hand and arm dangling through it into the outside corridor.

It was all over in a matter of seconds. The loudest noise was the breaking glass of the ticket window. Heaney and McCook waited, standing immobile, for a few minutes but nothing happened. No one came to see what had happened and the drumming of the rain on the roof folded itself round the scene in the little room like a shroud. McCook checked each body in turn to see that they were dead. Each time he looked back at Heaney and nodded.

'It was only a card school,' Heaney said, more to himself than to McCook. 'Only a card school. The poor bastards.'

There was no time for any more sympathy. Now that one extraordinary development had been successfully dealt with,

195

the plan was back on course but behind schedule. Heaney was pleased it had turned out to be such a simple thing that had delayed them. There was nothing sinister about a card school. It had just been a tragic coincidence for the three players that they had chosen the ticket office for their game that particular night. Sheer bad luck on their part. He decided to wait another five minutes just to make sure that no one had been attracted by the noise. He sent McCook to the top of the steps to watch if anybody came sniffing around. Nobody did. Heaney smashed the bulb in the lamp with the butt of his pistol and the room was plunged into darkness. He carefully closed the door behind him and they crossed the tracks by the sleeper pathway, calling Pearson in from the edge of the platform and taking up their pre-arranged positions.

In the ticket office Pete Guthrie's old mongrel woke up underneath the table, stood up and stretched its ancient limbs. The dog had slept through everything because it was almost deaf. Its eyes were cloudy too, so the total darkness in the room made no difference to it. It lifted its grey muzzle and smelled the air. Guthrie's scent came from the corner. The dog went over and bumped into its master's hand. It licked the fingers and waited to be patted on the head as a reward. When there was no response it lay down and curled into a ball with its head lying in the palm of the unmoving hand. Within seconds it was asleep again. The slight vibration from the dog's touch overbalanced the column of ash that had built up on Guthrie's cigarette. It fell onto his chin, leaving a weak pink glow that suddenly intensified as the air fed it, but then just as quickly faded to no more than a glimmer before vanishing completely.

Daft Davie's ugly, square-toed shoes were sticking out of the door. Anderson watched raindrops land on them and run over the leather almost with a sense of purpose to sink into the laceholes. He stood quietly in a trance, acutely aware of the calmness that possessed him although he desperately wanted to scream.

Poor Davie was dead, just as Bill Lowrie was dead. They had both died because of him. He had killed them both as surely as he had pulled the trigger to shoot them himself. There was no escape from that fact. He had wanted Brian Heaney to shoot Lowrie so that he, Anderson, might remain alive. And he had condemned Davie to death by refusing to act on first seeing Heaney in Kingsbank. He should have realised that Heaney had deliberately come to the village to torment him, to taunt him just as he had done seven years ago.

But this time he was not tied to a chair and helpless. This time he could fight back. He had been wrong over the last few days to try and pretend to himself that Heaney would go away. He had refused to face up to the truth and the result of that was now lying at his feet. Heaney would never go away of his own accord. He had to be made to go away or more people would die. Anderson could not allow it to continue. Kathy was coming back, coming home soon. She had to be protected from Heaney or she could well be next and Anderson would be powerless to save her. He had to take control of events and he knew precisely what to do. He had to kill Heaney.

There was a gentle singing in his ears as he stepped over Davie's body and went out into the rain. He looked back at the dead face and its huge rows of teeth already resembling a skull. It looked as if it had been carved from stone and it was hard to imagine that it had ever been alive at all. Anderson went to his car and found the shotgun on the back seat. He loaded two cartridges into the barrels and squeezed another half dozen into his trouser pockets. He acted mechanically having surrendered almost totally to his instincts. He did not have to think. He had the impression that he was watching himself from behind, a disinterested spectator in the drama that was unfolding in front of his eyes.

He had to feel around in the dark in the back of the car to find his knife. There was a dull gleam of metal as he pulled it free of its sheath.

Bob Stone sat rigidly to attention on the sofa and did not move. Success depended on him not moving until Heaney and the others got back, he had convinced himself. Everything depended on him remaining completely motionless. There was

197

a terrible itch on the side of his nose but he resisted the temptation to scratch it. All his senses seemed to be working overtime. If he focused on any object in the room it would be magnified till he could make out every last detail of it, as if he was examining it under a microscope. The air was like sandpaper against his skin and tasted as cold as ice in his mouth. He thought he heard somebody walking round the house but it would only be the leaves blowing in the wind.

They would not be much longer. In his flat in Edinburgh, the model train would still be circling the track. Round and round it would be going. Another hundred times and they would be on their way to the airfield. Not long now.

And his wife, Caroline, would be asleep in bed with her boyfriend. Her hair would be fanned out over the pillow and her lips would be slightly parted. She always slept lying on her back. She would still be asleep when they were flying to Ireland. She would not know what had happened to her beloved Royal Family until much later. What a shock that would be for her. And she would have no idea who had caused it. None at all, unless he phoned her up and told her what he had done. Yes, perhaps he would do that. It was only right that she should know that the whole truth. It was only right that she should know she was really to blame for it all.

There was a distinct sound from the kitchen. Stone's head jerked involuntarily to one side to look in its direction. They could not have returned yet. It was too early and he had heard no train up at the station. He quickly moved his head back, but it was too late. He had moved. He had put the whole operation in jeopardy. Panic began to overwhelm him. His legs and arms shook uncontrollably. From the corner of his eye he saw a stranger enter the room pointing a shotgun straight at him.

Anderson barged his way through a narrow gap in the boundary hedge and cautiously approached the front door of the house. The curtains were all drawn but the lights were on in one room. The door was locked. He made his way slowly round to the back of the house. Rain flickered in and out of the light from the kitchen window. The rest of the house was in darkness.

He crawled along below the window and was surprised to find the kitchen door open. It swung inwards with a grating noise from the old hinges. Anderson had to act quickly. Anyone inside would have heard the noise. He went into the kitchen. It was empty. A single internal door led further into the house. He kicked it open. There was one person sitting on the sofa. That person did not look round but it was obviously not Heaney. No one else. Another door to Anderson's left, closed. He kept himself face on to the door as he walked sideways into the room. The man did not appear to be armed and made no attempt to move, though his whole body was trembling as if an electric current was passing through it.

'Where is Heaney?' Anderson said taking up a position in front of the seated man.

There was no reply. The man did not even look up.

'Where is Heaney?' Anderson repeated.

Again there was no reply. Anderson raised the shotgun barrels and clubbed the man in the side of the head. He grunted and fell to the ground, rolling over to lie on his back, looking up at his attacker for the first time. A black stain began to form where he had been struck, but there was no blood.

Anderson placed a foot on the man's chest and held the barrels of the shotgun a few inches from his eyes. 'Where is Heaney?' he demanded again.

The man's mouth was twitching. His lips writhed as he desperately tried to form words, just as Davie's had used to do when he got excited.

'Where is Heaney?' Anderson repeated. 'Is he in this house?'

The man shook his head furiously. His eyes bulged.

'Is there anybody in the house?'

He shook his head even more furiously. Anderson glanced at the closed door. If Heaney had been in the house he would have arrived by now.

'Where is he, then? Where is Heaney?'

Anderson pressed the shotgun into the man's face, squashing his nose. The man arched his back and raised his arms so that he looked as if he was being crucified.

'A. . .a. . .a. . .at the st. . .st. . .station,' he finally managed to stammer.

'The Station. What the fuck's he doing there at this time of night?' Anderson said, thinking he meant the pub.

'The tr. . .train is coming. The train.'

Anderson understood. 'You mean the railway station,' he said.

The man nodded. Anderson believed him. He remembered how Heaney had looked up at the station when he had first seen him from under the bridge. It had been a sign. Anderson had not realised it at the time but it had been a sign. I'll see you up there, Heaney had been saying.

Anderson removed his foot from the man's chest and stood astride him. He kept the shotgun pressed into his face but he could not shoot him. That would make too much noise, alert Heaney up at the station. But he had to die. He could not be given the chance to send a warning.

Anderson used the knife, plunging it between the ribs low down on the chest directly into the heart. The man's hands came inwards as the point broke the flesh to clutch Anderson's wrist, as if he was helping to push it further in. He gave a little gasp, his eyes closed and his head lolled to one side. Anderson withdrew the blade and wiped it clean on the man's shirt.

He did not bother to search the rest of the house. There was no point. Heaney was waiting for him at the station. One way or the other it would be settled between them soon.

There was little or no sensation of motion inside the Royal Train while it was travelling at a steady speed but James Gunn could feel the momentum being lost as it slowed down. They had just passed through Dundee Station and would be going into the long sweeping curve that led on to the Tay Bridge. There was a forty miles per hour speed limit on the bridge. They would not begin to build up speed again until they reached Fife.

From the window, Gunn could see the pattern of indistinct yellow dots that outlined the city streets mingled with the streaks of rain on the glass. The city fell behind and the darkness closed round the train. The mile-wide River Tay was out there but he could not see it. It was impossible to see past the reflection of his own face and that of the interior of the carriage.

'Where are we?' asked Detective Inspector Graham Tindall tapping his pipe on the ashtray on the table beside the chess set. Tindall was the duty officer. Gunn was up simply because he could not sleep.

'Just leaving Dundee. Still a long way to go.'

Tindall had been the latest recruit to the Royalty Protection Squad three months previously when 'he was appointed as Prince Andrew's personal detective after several years of irregular substitute work covering all the family members. He was in his middle to late thirties with powerful broad shoulders and a narrow waist that was very nearly out of proportion. He sat with his shirt sleeves rolled up, studying the chess pieces laid out in front of him. The dark hair smothering his forearms ran down the backs of his hands and on to his fingers. He reached out and moved his bishop, leaving a fingertip on it for a few seconds before withdrawing it.

'Check, I think,' he said and began to fill his pipe with tobacco.

Gunn reluctantly left the window. He was grudging every minute of the train journey. He wanted to be at home with his wife so that they could wait together for news of his daughter and their first grandchild. Perhaps he was already a grandfather. The thought made him feel very old.

He sat down opposite Tindall and tried to concentrate on the game but his mind would not function properly. He was tired as well, too tired to sleep. He pretended to think about the move then pushed his king on to another square.

Tindall immediately moved a knight. 'Checkmate,' he said triumphantly. 'If I didn't know you better, Chief, I would say you let me win that game.'

'I've got things on my mind. My daughter's having a baby.'

'Congratulations. First grandchild is it?'

'That's right. I don't look old enough to be a grandad, do I?'

'What do you want?' Tindall asked. 'A boy or a girl?'

'I hadn't really thought about it. A boy, I suppose. Sisters should always have big brothers to protect them. She can have a girl next.'

201

'I've got three boys myself. We never managed a girl and I've had the operation now so we never will,' Tindall confessed.

'They can always untie the knots.'

Tindall smiled and held up two fingers to make a cutting motion. 'Snip, snip,' he said.

Gunn raised his eyebrows in mock horror. 'Ouch,' he said.

'Oh well, it seemed like a good idea at the time. When is your daughter due?'

'Right now. They took her into hospital just as we left Aberdeen.'

'You could well be a grandfather now. Maybe not. These things take time.'

'I could.' Gunn looked across at his reflection in the window. 'I could indeed.'

Tindall lit a match and sucked the flame down in among the tobacco in the bowl of his pipe. Blue smoke drifted lazily upwards and then suddenly shot into the small space between roof and ceiling where the extractor fan was fitted. Gunn decided to change the subject. He thought he could feel the train gaining speed but he was not sure.

'How does it feel to be with the squad full time then, Graham?'

'It's good. It's good. I like it,' Tindall said seriously, poking at the smouldering tobacco with the end of the spent match.

'Have you ever been on this train before?'

'No. I must say I'm not used to travelling in such luxury. I'm almost up to my ankles in this carpet.'

'This train is like a mobile nuclear bunker. About five years ago it was decided that it was too vulnerable to outside attack so they spent millions on armour plating and stuff.'

Tindall shook his head seriously. 'Another game?' he asked, beginning to rearrange the pieces.

'Before they spent all that money, there wasn't even bulletproof glass in the windows. Any trigger happy terrorist with a bit of gumption could have made a name for himself. Now it is hardly worth their while. They would just bounce off this baby like the rain.'

'That probably won't stop them thinking about it.'

Gunn shrugged. 'That's true. A decent size bomb or a big

202

enough obstruction on the track would derail us but no more than that. We would get thrown around a bit in here but we would easily survive.'

'That could be why the carpets are so thick: padding,' Tindall suggested.

'They're not half as thick as the walls of this train. Even so when the driver decides to stop in the middle of nowhere for half an hour it doesn't do my nerves any good.'

'I heard about that,' Tindall said sympathetically. 'It's unbelievable that the driver can refuse to obey your orders and then get the British Rail top brass to back him up.'

'I know. I know,' Gunn said, holding his arms out to signify exasperation. 'I can stop the train by phoning ahead and getting the signals changed but I can't get the driver to move it on again unless he is in the right mood. It's crazy.' He narrowed his eyes and tilted his head back to look down his nose at Tindall and mimicked Barker's voice. 'We're not in a police state yet, Commander.'

Tindall sniffed and took the pipe out of his mouth to have another poke at the tobacco. 'It's this fashion for walkabouts that really worries me,' he said. 'Your Royal goes wading into these massive crowds and there could be any number of lunatics in there with guns or knives. What are we supposed to do?'

'First principle of your training. Watch and wait and jump on anybody who tries to get at him.'

'And God help you if it is just somebody reaching for their wallet.' The tobacco had gone out. He started the process for relighting it.

'One of the penalties of living in a democratic society is that Royal bodyguards are expected to have ulcers.'

'If this was Russia, our job would be a lot easier,' Tindall said between sucks on his pipe.

'We would get paid a lot more as well.'

Both men laughed. The chess pieces were in their proper order. Gunn turned the board to exchange colours and put black in front of him. He reached behind to adjust the position of his holster so that he could sit more comfortably.

'Your move, Chief,' Tindall said as he put his elbows on the

203

edge of the table and interlocked his fingers to form a base to rest his chin.

Gunn tried hard to concentrate but every second thought was of becoming a grandfather. He willed the train to go faster and moved his queen's pawn two squares forward to start the game. Tindall brought a white knight out from behind the unbroken line of pawns as his opening move.

In the pitch blackness under the railway bridge, Anderson hesitated for no more than a second. He wanted to run but there was nowhere for him to run to. If Heaney could find him in Kingsbank after seven years, he could follow him anywhere. If he was to have Kathy, he could not run away any longer. He had to put all doubts and fears aside, leave them behind in the blackness. Only then would he be a match for Heaney.

The rain was easing off slightly as he emerged on the other side of the bridge. The clouds parted and a flood of pale moonlight softened the harsh edges of the deep shadows. The whitewashed front of the Station Inn appeared in detail as if a curtain had been drawn back. The windows were like empty eye sockets. Anderson saw the police car parked opposite the pub. Then he saw the gate at the bottom of the station steps lying open. It was always locked by eleven-thirty at the latest. Heaney must have arranged to have it left open for him.

The steps were wet and slippery. Anderson crouched low and went up to the point where they curved round to lead directly up to the ticket window corridor. He was not surprised to see that the heavy outside door was open as well and the corridor was clearly defined as a rectangle of grey light in the middle of the black building.

There seemed to be something bulging out from one side. Anderson could not make out what it was without going closer. He approached slowly, the shotgun ready in one hand, the knife in the other. The vague bulge began to take on a recognisable shape, a recognisably human shape. He saw an arm and a head hanging from the ticket window like an empty glove puppet hanging over the edge of a Punch and Judy show box. The arm almost reached down to the floor of the corridor. A thin line stretched the few inches across the gap that separated them. Anderson realised that it was a thread of congealed blood connecting the fingers to a small puddle of blood that shone black in the moonlight.

He knew it was not Brian Heaney but he had to find out who it was. He went down on his hands and knees and crawled forward to come level with the body. Pieces of glass crunched beneath his weight on the bare wooden floorboards. The sound seemed to echo hollowly. He stopped and waited. There was no answering noise, no sudden rush of footsteps. He used the back of his hand to sweep what glass he could see out of his way and moved cautiously forward.

The head was facing the wall underneath the ticket window. Anderson grabbed a handful of hair and pulled it upright to see the face. As he did so, the mouth fell open and the eyes rolled closed like a doll's. He was left staring at the small black hole in the centre of Sergeant Bill Wardlaw's forehead. But he was not seeing Bill Wardlaw, he was seeing his friend Bill Lowrie and feeling his body press hard against him. The white shadows with black holes for eyes swooped down and were behind him, were beside him, were all round him. The constant singing in his ears grew to a crescendo. Anderson snatched his hand away and stuffed his fist into his mouth to stop himself crying out. Wardlaw's head fell back and bumped against the wooden wall with a loud thump.

Anderson held his breath. The fist in his mouth tasted salty from the blood that had been on Wardlaw's hair. Now something was moving inside the ticket office. Soft footsteps hurried across the floor. There was the sound of scratching and an inhuman whining that grew gradually louder and more frantic. Then shadows moved on the platform. Anderson began to back away, scrambling to his feet, finger sweating on the trigger of the shotgun. The pulsing blood in his neck was like the beat of a big bass drum. He stepped backwards out into the rain and each drop that fell on his face was like the stroke of a razor blade.

Pete Guthrie's old dog walked into view at the end of the corridor and stood there sniffing the air. Anderson knew immediately what was going on and relaxed a little. Wardlaw,

Guthrie, and Jock Shaw had been holding their regular monthly poker session in the office and Heaney, for some reason, wanted the station to be empty. So he had killed them. Anderson did not have to look inside to know that Shaw and Guthrie were both dead. Another three people dead because of him. The singing in his ears settled down and he become very calm. Like the dog, he sniffed the air and thought he could smell Heaney's presence.

Without warning, the old mongrel suddenly jumped twelve inches into the air and threw itself against the corner where the ticket corridor met the platform. It staggered back but its front legs collapsed beneath it, then its hind quarters gave way and it lay in a heap with its fat stomach heaving up and down. The dog managed to lift its head and let out a pathetic mournful howl that was cut short by another bullet that thumped into the body and knocked it backwards to the very edge of the wooden floor of the corridor. It did not move again.

Anderson knew straight away that the dog had been shot by Heaney probably from the opposite side of the station judging by the angle of impact of the bullets. It could have been a bad mistake on his part because the body now gave Anderson cover to go forward and get a good view of the other platform. He carefully propped his shotgun against the wall just inside the corridor and flattened himself against the floor, squirming forward on knees and elbows.

The dog's body was still warm. It lay with its eyes closed and its jaw resting on its front paws just as he had seen it sleeping in the pub a thousand times. He put his face against the rough hairs of its coat and slid round till his cheek was against its ear and he could see over to the other side. He thought there were three men standing under the canopy but quickly realised that one of the figures was a pillar and there were only two men. In the dim light and the deep shadow, it was impossible for him to see them clearly, but he could make out that they were carrying guns. One of them had to be Heaney.

The larger of the two men suddenly began running along the platform. Then he was jumping down on to the tracks and crossing over, his head and shoulders bobbing above the platform level like those of a swimmer. Anderson instinctively

206

began to wriggle backwards, freezing momentarily as Bill Wardlaw's stiffening fingers stroked the back of his leg, then he was up and out in the rain. He grabbed the shotgun and ran down the wet stone steps until he was out of sight round the curve. From there he heard the man grunt as he bent to pick up the body of the dog, the crash of the ticket office door as it was kicked open, and the heavy thud on the floor as the dog was thrown inside. Footsteps faded and Anderson imagined the man going back over the tracks. He was not Heaney. The other one must have been Heaney.

Anderson sat with his back against the wall and looked up at the sky. The rain, now reduced to a drizzle, stabbed into his eyes. He opened his mouth wide to catch a few drops. They tasted cool and refreshing. He had to get across to the other side of the station without being seen. Heaney was waiting for him there.

He got up and went to the bottom of the steps and climbed into the overgrown garden of the old stationmaster's house. He waded through the long grass and the bushes and at the other end of the garden the fence was so rotten it gave way underneath him as he tried to climb over it. Crouching low, he ran along the foot of the embankment for two hundred yards then went up the slope and lay flat at the top looking back down towards the station. A red glow was spreading up over the bottom half of the sky. The dark silhouette of the station buildings stood out plainly against it. The gravel of the railway track beds felt rough and sharp as he wormed his way across and let himself roll down the other slope to the foot of the embankment there. He was up in an instant, the shotgun and knife grasped firmly in one hand, and running back the way he had come. Fifty yards from the station he stopped abruptly and dropped to his knees behind a clump of gorse bushes. Ahead, he could see the large man who had been sent to move the dog standing at the corner of the old brick urinal. He was leaning against it with his shoulder and staring into the station. A gun with a long stock and a short barrel was leaning against the wall beside him. He was not Heaney but this man had to be got out of the way. There had been three Irishmen in that rented house. Anderson had already disposed of one. This would be the second. Then only Heaney would be left.

207

Anderson put the shotgun on the ground. He rubbed the palm of his hand dry on his trousers and gripped the handle of the knife firmly. He had to go round the bushes to avoid making any sound, walking with an exaggerated slow motion stride, never taking his eyes off the man ahead of him. He recalled his SAS training in methods of killing. To silence a sentry and prevent him from raising the alarm it was necessary to make death as instantaneous as possible.

When Anderson was six feet away he could hear the man's breathing. Without hesitation he lunged forward. His left hand grabbed mouth and chin and jerked them back. His right hand brought the knife over in a wide arc to sink the blade into the exposed throat, twisting it viciously on entry to sever the vocal cords. At the same time he half turned and pulled the man away from the wall so that he came inwards where he could not be seen from other parts of the station. The knife went in up to the hilt and a rush of warm, sticky blood drenched Anderson's forearm. The man pitched forward on to his face and splashed into the mud with Anderson on his back. Several violent spasms shook his body as he died in perfect silence.

Two dead so far, Anderson thought. One for Bill Lowrie and one for Daft Davie. But it does not work like that. Only Heaney counts.

Colin Barker tapped Derek Devonshire on the elbow and pointed ahead through the rain-spattered windscreen of the train at a cluster of street lights in the distance.

'That's Kingsbank,' he said.

Devonshire looked at his watch. 'Right on schedule,' he announced. 'Let's hope they are ready for us.'

'They will be,' Barker said authoritatively. 'These things are planned like military operations.'

'It's not the way I'd like to do my courting.'

'Oh, I don't know, though. It adds a certain element of romance and mystery to an otherwise humdrum date.'

'A secret meeting at a lonely station in the early hours of the morning. I see what you mean,' Devonshire agreed.

'Mind you when it has to take place in miserable weather like this it will probably dampen the ardour of the young prince and his chosen lady.'

Devonshire laughed as Barker applied the brakes gently and the train began to slow. From his side window he looked out at the horizon and admired the red glow in the sky.

'Red sky at night, shepherd's delight,' he said.

'It's not night, it's morning,' Barker reminded him. 'It's already tomorrow.'

'Red sky in the morning, shepherd's warning.'

'And what is the quote if you have a red sky both sides of midnight?' Barker asked, his tongue poking at the corner of his mouth as he concentrated on braking evenly and smoothly.

'A delightful warning?'

'All shepherds please take note.'

Devonshire turned to look ahead down the track. It neatly cut the lights marking the village of Kingsbank into two halves. He frowned and leaned forward to look more closely. In the cab, the hiss of the brakes being applied became an insistent screech.

'Surely there should be some lights on at the station?' Devonshire said.

'Don't worry. They'll be there, hiding in the darkness just to make sure that we are the right train,' Barker replied.

'But it is silly not to have any lights on,' he insisted.

Barker dismissed his concern with a shrug of his shoulders. 'Ours is not to reason why,' he said as the apparently deserted station grew larger in front of him.

Devonshire suddenly leaned even further forward, his nose only a few inches from the glass of the windscreen. 'I thought I saw a couple of people on the platform there,' he said. 'They disappeared off to the side.'

'What did I tell you?' Barker said. 'They're there waiting for us all right.'

When the dog scratched open the door of the ticket office Brian Heaney at first thought it was one of the card players crawling out on his hands and knees. He wondered where the dog had been hiding to escape their notice when he and McCook had killed the three men. But it was not important, so he did not waste any time thinking about it. The important thing now was that the dog had to be killed before it could run off home and perhaps wake a sleeping wife who would come in search of her husband. It was a pity, because Heaney hated killing animals. It was not the same as killing human beings. There was no malice in a dumb animal. However, it had to be done. The dog just stood there as if waiting for the decision to be made.

He rested his elbows on top of the electricity junction box and took careful aim with the machine pistol. The first bullet knocked the dog over but did not kill it outright. It started to howl in agony. The second bullet put the beast out of its misery.

McCook was coming down the platform to see what was happening, so Heaney went to meet him halfway and get him to go across and move the body. It could not be left lying where it was, in case someone on board the train noticed it and got suspicious. Dead dogs were not a common sight at Royal rendezvous points. McCook went across and threw the carcase back beside its master in the office and then returned to his position at the south end of the station. Heaney looked in on Pearson in the parcels office. He was sitting on the only chair, tossing a grenade slowly from hand to hand. Heaney closed the door and replaced the broken padlock. Everything was in order again. All they could do now was wait.

Heaney crouched beside the junction box, using it as best he could as a shelter from the rain which thankfully, was beginning to slacken off at last. Every few minutes he stood up to relieve his cramped muscles and to walk out to the edge of the platform to check that there was nothing else moving in the station. Nervous energy made him sweat profusely despite the cold and wet. Excitement simmered inside him at the thought of the impending climax of the operation. The hardest part would be over when the train stopped and obligingly opened its doors to invite them in. It would be simple after that, and he was pleased with the way the minor hiccups in the plan had been dealt with so swiftly and so effectively. It was going to work, he kept telling himself. Nothing could stop them now.

The lights of a train appeared in the distance, heading directly towards Kingsbank at twenty-eight minutes past midnight. 'Here she comes,' he said softly to himself and eased himself further back into his hiding place. As he did so, he saw that McCook was walking down the platform towards him. His first reaction was one of anger. The train was in sight. What the hell was McCook playing at? He had his orders. He should be back at the south end. He had to take out the drivers. His part was crucial. What was he playing at?

Heaney swore loudly and then stopped himself, glancing up the track as if he was worried that train might overhear him. They still had a few minutes before the train reached them. He hurriedly scrambled to his feet and stepped out from behind the junction box.

'Get back,' he shouted in a low voice. 'Get back. The train is on its way.'

But McCook took no notice of him. He kept coming, breaking into a run and lowering his head like a charging bull. Heaney noticed that the rain had plastered his thick hair to his scalp, making him look strange and unfamiliar. It was only when he was a few yards away that Heaney realised it was not McCook at all. But by then it was too late.

Jim Anderson thought he could hear Kathy's voice. He lifted his head and looked round but he could not see her. She was whispering to him though, urging him to get up and carry on. I'll be back soon, she was saying over and over again. I'll be back soon and you promised you would be finished before I got back.

He was lying on top of the prone body of the Irishman he had just killed. The man's face was submerged in the black mud that surrounded them. His red hair contrasted sharply with it. The fingers of one hand were spread wide, and the thick mud oozed between and over them leaving only thin strips of white flesh visible like the bones of a skeleton. Anderson got to his knees, still balancing on the man's back, and stepped off him and over towards the brick wall. The body seemed to rise out of the mud slightly as if it was floating.

There was still the singing in his ears, but it was quieter now than it had been. It seemed to him that only seconds ago it had been Daft Davie lying dead at his feet. The events of the last hour were a blur in his mind, like a film being run at a ridiculously fast speed. He could stop the film at will and look at a static picture but he could not create any sequence for what had happened. He had the impression that, despite his conscious attempt to move slowly and deliberately, he was hurtling along at fantastic pace, and was accelerating all the time, getting closer and closer to the moment when it had been decided that he should die.

He looked round the corner of the brick wall and was mildly surprised not to see Heaney standing waiting for him. The station was as quiet as the grave. There was no hint that three men had been brutally murdered earlier in the ticket office, or that another lay dead behind him with the knife still jutting from his neck. A deep hush had descended on the place. The trees opposite shifted in the wind but made no sound. The patter of the rain on the hard-packed ash faded into silence like somebody tip-toeing away. Anderson waited. Heaney was there somewhere, waiting for him. They had both waited a long time for this confrontation.

The figure walked out to the edge of the platform and stood there. Anderson knew immediately that it was Brian Heaney. When he turned and disappeared from sight again Anderson had already decided what to do next.

He had to get close to him. Heaney had to see who he was, had to know why he was dying. A bullet in the brain from a safe distance was no good. He had to get right up to him, face to face, and kill him then. But Heaney was heavily armed. He would not easily allow someone to get near him, unless he thought he knew that someone. Anderson was the same height and build as the dead man lying in the mud. In the darkness he could be mistaken for him long enough to let him get right up to Heaney. After that he wanted to be recognised.

He bent down and rolled the body on to its side to enable him to strip the anorak off it. He brushed off the worst of the mud and pulled it on. It was cold and damp but a good fit. He pulled the collar up around his neck and picked up the machine pistol that was propped against the wall. Kathy's voice whispered in his ear: I'll be back soon. You promised. He walked out from

212

behind the wall and began to move along the platform. The crunch of his footsteps on the ash changed to a hard rapping on the stone. Once again, he had the impression that he was hovering outside his own body. This time he was looking down from above the station. He saw himself moving with agonising slowness below but he felt the air tearing past his face as if he was careering down a steep slope and the singing in his ears mounted to an almost unbearable pitch.

When he was ten yards away, Heaney saw him and got to his feet, shouting at him to go back. Anderson saw the small V-shaped scar on his cheek and his heart suddenly began to hammer violently against his ribs. Then Heaney sensed that something was wrong and reached for his gun, but Anderson was already charging blindly and got to him before he could bring the gun up to shoot. The top of his head crashed into Heaney's chin, sending him spinning backwards against the wooden fence that lined the parapet of the bridge. Heaney yelped like a puppy as he lost his grip on his gun and it flew over the edge to clatter on to the street below. Anderson was on him again in a flash, hammering at the side of his head with the butt of the machine pistol he had taken. Heaney fell to one side, his hands going out to break his fall. Blood flowed from a cut beside the eye. The coarse ash rammed itself under his fingernails.

Anderson could have killed him then. He had him at his mercy just as he had been at Heaney's mercy seven years previously. All he had to do was pull the trigger and Heaney would have been ripped to pieces by the hail of bullets. Or he could have killed him with a single bullet through the forehead. But he did not. Instead he laid the gun on the platform and walked up to Heaney, confident in his total superiority. He felt a smile spread through his lips, just as Heaney had smiled at him when they first met seven years ago.

'Remember me?' Anderson asked quietly.

Heaney stared up blankly. Anderson saw him go for the revolver tucked into the waistband of his trousers in plenty time to kick it out of his hand. It bounced on the ground once and landed on the railway tracks. Heaney began to shuffle backwards, crab-like, never taking his eyes off Anderson who followed him casually, looking down on him with that fixed smile.

213

'Remember me?' he repeated. 'You must remember me?'

Heaney sprang to his feet and tried to turn and run but Anderson tripped him up. He was over the bridge and off the platform. He fell onto the embankment and tried to roll down it to get away. But Anderson kept up with him, never more than a few feet away. Heaney snatched a grenade from the harness on his chest but before he had a chance to pull the pin Anderson had grabbed his wrist and forced him to drop it. Then, with both hands, he took Heaney by the neck and squeezed as tightly as he could, almost lifting him off the ground as above them the train roared past with the brakes squealing in high-pitched bursts.

Heaney tried desperately to beat off the hands fastened so firmly round his throat but his small hands, like a child's, were hopelessly ineffectual. He could not breathe at all. He was completely helpless. Unconsciousness swept over him like a gust of wind. He blacked out and then recovered. The hands were still round his neck, squeezing the life out of him. The strange, smiling face was only a few inches from his own. He could feel hot breath and warm spittle against his raw skin. 'Remember me?' The words boomed inside his skull and he wanted to shout out, 'No. Who are you? Who are you?' but it was impossible to talk. Unconsciousness came flying at him again. If he let himself go under he knew he was dead but there was nothing he could do to prevent it. He was picked up like an autumn leaf and whirled into the black air.

Anderson stared directly into Heaney's bloodshot eyes as he gripped his throat so tightly he thought he must be crushing the bones in his neck. He saw the eyes change as they glazed over and dulled, just as had happened with the hare and with Davie. At that point, all the strength seemed to drain out of Anderson. The dead weight of Heaney's body suddenly became too much for him and he was dragged to his knees by it. He let go and the body rolled untidily on to the level ground at the foot of the embankment. Anderson bowed his head and wondered if Heaney had recognised him.

Commander James Gunn could not afford to lose his queen. He had already lost most of his pawns, both bishops, a knight and a

214

rook and had only managed to take a couple of pawns and a knight from Tindall in return. He was making a hash of the game because he could not concentrate properly. He had his queen only, because Tindall had missed an easy chance to take it earlier on. Now he decided to move it to threaten the white bishop that was guarding the king.

Tindall nodded in approval of the move and removed his pipe from his mouth to speak. 'Attack is the best form of defence, eh, Chief?' he said.

'That's the idea anyway,' Gunn replied.

He put his hands above his head and yawned. If his daughter had given birth his wife would have got through to him on the radio telephone. He could not be a grandfather yet, he decided. He might even make it to London in time for the happy event.

The train began to slow down. Tindall had blocked the threat to his bishop with a pawn. Gunn studied the board and began working out a new strategy.

'We're slowing down again,' he said.

Tindall sucked at his pipe and nodded agreement.

'We're slowing right down,' Gunn went on, looking up and out the window. 'Christ, I think we are going to stop.'

'There are no scheduled stops.' Tindall said.

Gunn was on his feet and at the window, holding a hand over his eyes as he tried to see out into the darkness.

'We are. We're stopping.' The train came to a halt with the very slightest of jerks. 'We've stopped.'

'Where are we?' Tindall asked coming to the window.

'I don't know. It's too dark. I can't make out the signs but we seem to be at a station. I don't see anybody about.'

'I don't like it, Chief.'

'It's that bastard Barker again. I bet he is doing this on purpose just to annoy me. I'm in a hurry to get home.'

Gunn went out of the carriage into the corridor. From that side of the train he could read the station signs.

'Kingsbank, it says. Where is that?'

'Never heard of it,' Tindall said, standing by his shoulder.

Gunn looked up and down the platform and satisfied himself that not a soul was in sight. 'Well, I'll have to go and find out what the hold up is.'

215

He tried to put his hand on the electronic pad which controlled the door but Tindall stopped him. 'Wait a minute, Chief. I don't like this at all,' he said.

Gunn sighed. Normally he would never have been so hasty but he wasn't prepared to back down and have Barker make a fool of him again. Besides, every second wasted meant a longer wait to see his daughter and first grandchild.

'It will be all right, I tell you,' Gunn said, scanning the empty platform outside. 'I haven't worked with the Royals this long to lose one now.'

'Shouldn't we wake up some of the others, Chief?' Tindall suggested, drawing his Smith and Wesson.

Gunn had already placed his palm on the pad. The opening mechanism began to hum. 'They'll know soon enough if anything is wrong,' he said.

Eugene Pearson was wet and uncomfortable. He had got soaked through standing in the rain waiting while the other two had gone to investigate the light in the ticket office. It had been some old blokes playing cards. Jesus Christ, he thought, what a night to pick. They had been wiped out, and then a while later a bloody dog appeared on the scene. Heaney shot it. It appeared that anything found alive in Kingsbank Station was going to be killed. As long as we are doing the killing and not the other way around that will be all right, he decided.

The parcel office was dark and musty. He sat on the chair with its straight back against his chest looking out through the strip of plain glass that ran along the bottom of the window that was otherwise opaque. To pass the time, he tossed a grenade from hand to hand. He did it with his eyes open and then with his eyes closed. Only once did he drop it and the thick cushion of dust on the floor caught it safely for him. He heard a mouse scratching around somewhere at the back of the office and rolled the grenade towards the sound thinking, 'Here is a pineapple Mickey. Bite on that.' The scratching stopped for a while then started up again.

Pearson knew he was not going mad. He was putting on an act for his own benefit because he could not understand what he

216

was doing. He was not a hardened killer like Heaney and McCook. He was not a raving Republican. He was not a smart politician. Then what was he doing here in a deserted country station after midnight, waiting to take part in a Royal assassination? Why had he gone along with everything right from the start? He must have had thousands of opportunities to find some excuse to pull out without loss of face. He never had, though. The only explanation he could give was that he wanted to do it but would not admit it to himself.

He took out the cheap gas cigarette lighter he was to use to prime the flame thrower and began flicking it off and on. The jumping flame had a hypnotic effect on him, reflecting in the pupils of his eyes where he imagined he could feel it burning into his brain.

He had decided that once he got back to Ireland he would phone up about the poor halfwit he had buried in the leaves in the garden after all. Even if he was long dead he was entitled to a proper funeral and it might be long enough before his body was found in the normal course of events. It would be good to get home, Pearson thought. It would be good to be patted on the head by his father for a job well done and it would be good to see his twin brother Eddie again and give him a detailed account of all that had happened. He would not mention to Eddie how much the simpleton under the leaves had reminded him of his brother. It had probably just been his over-stretched imagination at the time that had seen the resemblance anyway.

Pearson must have been lost in thought because he was suddenly aware that the Royal train was sitting in the station in front of him, steam rising up over the lip of the platform. Surprising himself with his composure, he got up and moved the chair out of his way. Then he lit the ignition chamber of the flame-thrower and put the lighter back in his pocket. He turned the valve on his hip to let the petrol from the tanks into the tubes and everything was ready.

He could see two men looking out from the door of the train. Heaney and McCook would be watching them as well. Three to two. They were already outnumbered. He could see the Royal crest, like a stain on the side of the carriage. All these details had to be remembered so that Eddie could be told the full story.

217

The red sky was particularly beautiful. He would have to remember to tell Eddie about the red sky.

The two men behind the train door looked as if they were going to open it any second. Pearson put his shoulder to the parcel office door in readiness to burst out on to the platform. He took a deep breath and held it as if he was about to dive under water.

Jim Anderson was free. Brian Heaney was dead by his hand and the debt was settled. The ghost that had haunted him for so long had been exorcised. Now he could begin to live again after seven wasted years, and Kathy was on her way back to help him do just that. New energy surged through him. He would be able to share his secret with her now that he had proved to himself that he was not a coward.

Anderson climbed up the embankment, pulling himself up on clumps of wet grass, refusing to look down at Heaney who lay on his back staring up into the sky with his eyes wide open. He walked back along the platform and the questions he had been successsfully avoiding since first seeing Heaney began to nag at him insistently. What had Heaney and his friends been doing in Kingsbank with all their weaponry? What was so important that they were prepared to kill at least four people to achieve it?

The train must have something to do with it, he thought nervously. It stood motionless by the platform. Gauze curtains covered the windows. Nothing and nobody moved in the station except him. Anderson went suddenly cold. The singing began in his ears and a sick feeling gripped his stomach. He picked up the gun that he had dropped onto the platform earlier and pointed it ahead of him. The white shadows were closing in on him again. He thought he had rid himself of them for ever, but they were all round him again.

There was a click and an electric whine and he saw that a door was opening towards the front of the train. It was Kathy. She had got the first available train back to him. She was going to come off the train. Heaney had been trying to stop her reaching him. That was the explanation. But Anderson had beaten him. He began to run towards Kathy.

218

The crash of the parcel office doors flying open made Anderson swing round instinctively, levelling the gun from his waist. He saw the strangely dressed figure, immediately classified him as a danger, and pulled the trigger. Five rounds thudded into the man who stumbled backwards and fell as a great yellow and purple fountain of flame shot upwards and flattened itself out along the underside of the canopy. The gun had hardly made any noise at all. Anderson looked down at it, wondering if he had really fired the shots.

He felt two hard thumps on his chest, followed closely by two ear-splitting bangs. He found himself sitting down on the flagstones and when he tried to get up he fell back and hit his head. The ground moved under him. He was lying on the loose stone and was being rocked from side to side. He saw the flames eating hungrily at the dry wood under the platform canopy. Then he saw a man in shirtsleeves on one knee by the open train door holding a gun in both hands and pointing it straight at him. Another man was running and shouting. His words were drowned by the crackling of the flames. He saw them grow bigger and fatter and louder. The train was moving, the door was closing. Kathy was not there. She had not got off. He wanted to shout after them but he could not move except to rock gently from side to side, like a baby being lulled to sleep and the crackling of the fire swelled around him and the heat stroked him softly. The whole sky was on fire, glowing crimson. The whole world was burning. There could be no escape.